continued . . .

"An excellent historical mystery that brings to life the unsavory side of the 1890s in San Francisco."
—*Midwest Book Review*

"King hasn't lost his cutting edge, nor his wry humor. . . . Jack London is surely an inspired choice for a sleuth."
—*Booknews* from The Poisoned Pen

"The hard-living, hard-drinking Jack London makes an excellent detective and Peter King brings him fully to life. . . . Pure entertainment. Not only are we treated to a cunningly deceptive mystery, but the cast of characters reads like a Who's Who of the time." —*Romantic Times* (Top Pick)

Praise for Peter King's previous mysteries

"King's novels are filled with cliff-hanger endings and near-death adventures. . . . A fun read."—*Ventura County Star* (CA)

"An appealing detective series. . . . [King] keeps the well-spiced plot bubbling along."
—*People* (Beach Book of the Week)

"[An] engaging hero." —*Alfred Hitchcock's Mystery Magazine*

"Fast, fun, delightful characters." —*Library Journal*

The Golden Gate Murders

A JACK LONDON MYSTERY

BY
PETER KING

A SIGNET BOOK

Signet
Published by New American Library, a division of
Penguin Putnam Inc., 375 Hudson Street,
New York, New York 10014, U.S.A.
Penguin Books Ltd, 80 Strand,
London WC2R 0RL, England
Penguin Books Australia Ltd, Ringwood,
Victoria, Australia
Penguin Books Canada Ltd, 10 Alcorn Avenue,
Toronto, Ontario, Canada M4V 3B2
Penguin Books (N.Z.) Ltd, 182–190 Wairau Road,
Auckland 10, New Zealand

Penguin Books Ltd, Registered Offices:
Harmondsworth, Middlesex, England

First published by Signet, an imprint of New American Library, a division of Penguin
Putnam Inc.

First Printing, November 2002
10 9 8 7 6 5 4 3 2 1

To my wife, Dorie,
for her support, help,
encouragement, advice and love.

Chapter 1

The four men sat silently around the table, their eyes staring straight ahead of them. One wore Western garb: chaps with a wide, intricately tooled leather belt, a dark blue shirt and calf-high boots. Two others wore city garb: black suits, white shirts with high collars and polished boots. The fourth, older than the others, had a neatly trimmed beard, piercing eyes and a high forehead. His brown trousers, loose leather jacket with fringed pockets and collar and muddied brown boots suggested recent time in mining country.

Two men watched them from a discreet distance. One of them was Tom Tullamore, a big man with a barrel chest and long arms. He had a large head and slick black hair. His white silk shirt was monogrammed and his black trousers were new and neatly creased. His Silver Dollar Saloon was one of the establishments on the Barbary Coast of San Francisco that permitted gambling. Many did not because it led too frequently to the use of a pistol or a knife to settle a quarrel.

The Silver Dollar was on Pacific Street, which ran through the Devil's Acre, the roughest and toughest part of the Barbary Coast, with its five thousand saloons, music halls, nickelodeons, theaters, bars, brothels, parlor houses, deadfalls and opium dens.

At least one murder and a dozen muggings and robberies occurred here every night, where every form of vice and depravity practiced by the human race could be found.

Tullamore nudged the man next to him. "Man in the cowboy clothes is a rancher from Grass Valley. Comes in about twice a month. He's a big loser. The two city men are with the Crocker Bank—though I guess the money they use is their own," he added. "The other is Lucky Baldwin—you probably know him."

The man with Tullamore shook his head. "Heard the name a lot of times. Never met him, though. Never saw him either. He must be a regular winner here with a nickname like Lucky."

"He needs to be," Tullamore said, keeping his voice low. "He's got four wives and twice as many mistresses."

"What is he? A Mormon?"

"No, he just likes the ladies. His divorce suits alone keep one law firm busy and he's always fighting at least half a dozen 'seduction' suits."

"Lucky's Pacific Stock Exchange is still doing well, I take it," said the man with Tullamore. He was in his twenties, six feet tall and strongly built with broad shoulders. One of the features that people noticed first about him was his bright blue eyes. He had a habit of running fingers through his unruly brown hair.

"The nickname's not fair," said Tullamore. "It was hard work and determination that got Lucky established, though maybe he had a bit of luck to get him his nickname."

"How did that happen?"

"He told his brokers to sell off most his mine holdings before he set off on a year's travel. But when he sailed, his stocks were in a locked safe and he had the key in his pocket. So the brokers couldn't sell, and before he realized this, the stock value had shot up and made him five million dollars overnight."

"That was luck."

Tullamore grinned. "Going to use it in one of your stories, London?"

"I might," he said.

Born and raised in the San Francisco Bay Area, Jack London had tried his hand at many jobs. He had worked as a lumberjack, a cowboy and a sailor. He had washed dishes in cafés and sold vacuum cleaners door-to-door. He had been a prizefighter and a law enforcement officer. He had been a hobo and ridden the rails and served time in the Erie State Penitentiary for those transgressions. He had been a gold miner in the Yukon Gold Rush and carried one-hundred-and-fifty-pound packs over the Chilkoot Pass in howling blizzards at temperatures that froze men's hands and feet into solid blocks.

It was writing that was his passion, though, and he was always on the alert for new material. He now studied Lucky Baldwin, who was intent on the cards in his hand. The piles of coins and notes on the table suggested a high-stakes game. Jack glanced at the other tables. There were five of them and all had equally tense games in progress, but none had as much money on the table as the one he and Tulla-more were watching.

At the end of the room farthest from the single door was a window with iron bars. A figure was occasionally visible behind the bars. Jack knew that a scale was there, for many gamblers came directly from the gold mines and, skeptical of banks, brought sacks of gold dust or small gold bars to change directly into gambling money. Jack also knew that somewhere set into the walls was a concealed panel hiding a man with a shotgun. The lawless Barbary Coast saw robberies every day, and the rewards in gambling halls like Tom Tullamore's Silver Dollar Saloon were high enough to tempt many a villain.

Tullamore slowly moved to the next table, staying at a distance. One man looked up at him and nodded recognition. Onlookers were not permitted, as the advantage of an accomplice behind an opponent at the table was too obvious. Jack followed Tullamore, staying close to emphasize his nonparticipation too.

Jack was, in fact, puzzling over why he was here. Tullamore had left messages at two of the places Jack frequented asking him to come to the Silver Dollar. Upon his arrival, Tullamore had ordered him a whisky and a beer chaser at the bar, and they had chatted in the manner of two men who had not seen each other in a while. Then Tullamore had brought him up here to the gambling rooms.

Jack's experience as a law enforcement officer had been with the Fish Patrol, but his wide acquaintance with the Barbary Coast, its people and its places had resulted in his help being enlisted on different occasions by both the mayor's office and the police department. Did Tullamore have some similar assignment in mind? Perhaps he was worried about the possibility of being robbed. Jack was not a gun-carrying guard, though, and it was not likely that Tullamore would want to hire him as such. No, he must have something else in mind.

"Politicians' table here," murmured Tullamore, and Jack saw a couple of men he recognized as city council members. They walked slowly past the iron-barred window and Tullamore exchanged nods with the shadowy figure behind it. For a moment they watched the game. Most card players used the overhand shuffle, but Jack, though not a gambler himself, knew enough about cards to be aware that the riffle shuffle was being employed here to divide melds and sequences. The dealer was mixing cutting in with shuffling, keeping the cards barely an inch above the table so that none of the players could see the bottom card.

"He's a mathematician," Tullamore told Jack. "Teaches at the university at Berkeley."

Jack looked at the dealer, a lean-faced man with an unhealthy, almost gray complexion and thinning hair, despite having the appearance of being little more than forty years old.

"Keeps claiming to have an infallible system for winning," Tullamore went on. "But if he does, he's got an awful lot of patience. Spends a lot of time here."

After a moment, they walked on and Tullamore led the way out. They descended the stairs to the main floor and went to the bar. The orchestra was playing songs from Broadway shows and the place was filling up in anticipation of the show, due to start shortly.

The Silver Dollar didn't draw big names like Lily

Langtry or Lillian Russell or Eddie Foy—who appeared regularly at the Bella Union or the Olympic or the Adelphi a few blocks away—but the prices of seats were lower, the tone of the shows was bawdier and the girls' costumes were flimsier.

"Same again?" Tullamore asked Jack as he beckoned to one of the bartenders.

"Just a beer," said Jack. After an earlier period of over-drinking, Jack was now being careful. The one whisky he had drunk earlier was all he permitted himself in an evening, and mostly he drank only beer.

The bartender brought Tullamore a whisky and Jack a schooner of beer. "Then I want to talk a little business with you," said Tullamore, raising his glass. Jack picked up the schooner in a return toast. They both drank. Jack was going to learn at last why the saloon owner had asked him here, he thought. He took another swallow of beer in anticipation.

"I need your help on a very confidential matter," Tullamore said. "We'll go to my office and talk about it, but first enjoy your drink." He drank half of his whisky. The orchestra had evidently been primed with its first drink of the evening, for its volume had increased and its timing had sharpened as it embarked with enthusiasm on "Daddy Wouldn't Buy Me a Bow-Wow," a popular number of a few years ago.

Tullamore was emptying his glass when one of the bartenders came along behind the bar. "There's a man wants to see you—says it's urgent."

"Who is he?" Tullamore wanted to know.

"Didn't give a name. Never saw him before."

"What's it about?"

"Didn't say—just said it was urgent."

Tullamore muttered something under his breath. To Jack, he said, "Won't keep you a minute. Have another drink on the house." He hurried off.

Fifteen minutes later, one of the bartenders came to Jack. "Show starts in a few minutes. Want another drink?"

"Is Tom still talking to that fellow back there?"

"Don't know. I've been too busy tending bar. Want me to go look?"

Jack nodded, and a few minutes later, just as the orchestra was preparing to launch into its music introducing the chorus girls, the bartender came back with a puzzled look on his face.

"Can't find Tom anywhere. Doesn't seem to be around. He must have gone off with that fellow."

"Tom said he had something important he wanted to talk to me about," Jack said. "Surely he wouldn't have left."

The bartender shrugged. "Not like him. But I can tell you he's nowhere around."

"Could he have gone upstairs?" Jack asked. He was thinking that Tullamore had taken him upstairs for a reason. Maybe that had some connection.

But the bartender was emphatic. "No, he's not up there. He's just nowhere."

Jack turned and watched the show. The girls were pretty and uninhibited, the comedians were smutty and got plenty of laughs, the dance team was acrobatic and a magician received applause for making his dogs disappear, then show up at the back of the auditorium.

By the end of the show, Tom Tullamore had still not come back from his meeting with the mysterious visitor, nor had any word been received from him. The staff was as perplexed as Jack, and he left wondering uneasily what had been important enough to the saloon owner to cause him to vanish so abruptly.

Chapter 2

The big brass alarm clock shattered the early-morning quiet. Jack set it every night to allow himself five hours' sleep; his underlying motive was to give himself the maximum number of hours for writing. After a sparse breakfast, he sat down at his desk, ready to write his thousand words.

This was his daily quota. He wrote for as many hours as it took to achieve that number. If, for any reason, he failed to reach it, he forced himself to make up the difference the next day and still write that day's quota too. Jack did not consider it a chore. He loved to write. He loved words and treasured the satisfaction of finding exactly the right one.

Time was his archenemy—he needed time to master his craft before lack of food and money overcame him. The nineteen hours a day he so often spent writing were not enough. He begrudged the need to take on special assignments to make ends meet, but he did not begrudge the time they took away from his writing. He loved the city with a passion, and there was always the added advantage that each of his investigational escapades yielded fresh ideas and new characters that he could weave into his stories.

His thoughts went back to the previous night. He believed he had been about to undertake a mission for Tom Tullamore. But what had happened to Tullamore that was so important it dragged him away from the Silver Dollar Saloon without a word of explanation or apology?

After he wrote his quota for the day—which he expected to complete quickly—he would go to the Silver Dollar and satisfy his curiosity. The reason he was confident of writing his thousand words swiftly was that he had been on an exhilarating streak of success lately. He had sold "To the Man on Trail" and then "The White Silence" to the *Overland Monthly,* and the magazine's editor, a man named Umbstaetter, had written glowing words of praise for Jack's work.

He had also sold "A Thousand Deaths" to *The Black Cat,* and the prestigious *Atlantic Monthly* had bought "An Odyssey of the North." These achievements had bolstered his self-esteem enormously, although only the previous week Jack had written to his friend Cloudesley Johns, the postmaster in the small town of Harold, California, that he was prepared to write children's stories for Frank A. Munsey if that was the only way he could keep writing.

But Jack was not one to rest on his laurels and he took out his notes for the story he was assembling now and concentrated on them. The thrust of the plot was not clear to him yet, even though he had some shadowy characters that he would flesh out into real people. Plots were the bane of his writing, and he sometimes despaired of ever improving. What he enjoyed most at this stage in his career was depicting the struggle between the individual and the wilderness—and the wilderness he described was the harsh and unrelenting northland of the Yukon with its snow, its blizzards and its killing cold.

He began to write. The words came slowly at first, but his determined routine had helped him to learn the lesson that, once started, a story became easier. Problems and difficulties were forgotten and the flow of words increased like the melting of an ice floe in spring.

He had written about six hundred words and was pounding the keys of his old Underwood in a frantic burst to describe the frozen terrors of the Klondike when there came a heavy pounding on the door. It was time for the mailman, but Jack knew his gentle knock. He was tempted to ignore this thumping and keep writing but it came again, loud and imperative. Jack finished the sentence and put down the first words of the next one so as to maintain continuity, then went to the door.

A uniformed policeman was there. Jack knew many of the men on the force but not this one. He had a big mustache and a voice as loud as his pounding on the door.

"Mr. Jack London? You're wanted at the station."

Was it something to do with Tom Tullamore? That was the first thought that flashed through Jack's mind, but experience had taught him not to ask questions like that—at least not until the name had already been brought up.

"Why?" Jack asked. "Who wants to see me?"

The policeman did not answer the first question, but to the second he said, "Captain Krasner, at the Madison Street station."

Behind the man, Jack saw a police cab waiting, the horse snorting impatiently. "Just a minute," Jack said. He went back to his work, sorted his notes into neat piles, put on his seaman's jacket and cap, locked the door and climbed into the cab.

They sat in a tiny room with damp walls and air that was chill and penetrating.

"You visited Mr. Tom Tullamore yesterday evening, I believe," were the captain's opening words, and Jack's heart sank.

"Yes, I did."

"Tell me exactly what happened."

Jack did so and the other man listened without interruption. Krasner was about Jack's height, black haired and grim faced. He spoke with a very faint German accent. He looked athletic and competent.

When Jack finished, Krasner asked, "So you don't know who it was that Tullamore went to see when he left you at the bar?"

"No, I have no idea. None of the bartenders knew?"

Jack wasn't sure that he would get an answer to his question, but the captain said, civilly enough, "No, none of them knew who he was."

Krasner had a direct gaze that Jack liked. He said, "I hear you helped us out in that business of the saloon girls being murdered. They say you're a straight shooter."

"Has Tom been found?" Jack asked.

"Yes," said the captain, "he's been found. Down the alley at the back of the Silver Dollar. He had a knife in his back. The doc says he was killed around midnight, give or take a couple of hours. Where were you at that time?"

Jack groaned in dismay. Death was never far away on the Barbary Coast. He tried to concentrate on the captain's question. "I left when the first show ended," he said. "That was between twelve and one. The bartenders will probably remember that I was at the bar the whole evening, from the time I was talking to Tom and he was called away until I left after the show."

The captain's stony expression suggested that he had already heard that from the bartenders. Another question followed quickly. "Why did Tullamore ask you to go to the Silver Dollar?"

"I don't know. I was curious myself. He was just about to tell me when the call came for him to see this mysterious visitor."

"You must have some idea!" The captain's voice was getting more accusatory.

"When I arrived, he took me upstairs—"

"Into the gambling rooms?"

"Yes. We walked around, watched some of the games."

"I thought the players didn't like that."

"They don't," Jack said. "We only stayed a minute or two near each table. It did make me wonder if Tom was going to tell me he had some kind of problem connected with the games."

"But he didn't?"

"Nothing to suggest why he had asked me there."

"Did you see anyone you knew?"

"I recognized a couple of members of the city council. Tom pointed out two men from the Crocker Bank and—oh, Lucky Baldwin was there."

It was impossible to tell from the captain's face whether he knew all this or not, but Jack went on. "Also, Tom showed me a professor from the university at Berkeley, said he was a mathematician with a system."

"Anyone else?"

"No one I recognized."

"And still he didn't tell you why he wanted to talk to you?"

Jack was getting a little angry at this persistence but he controlled himself. "No. He said he wanted to talk business with me and said it was confidential, but he gave me no clue as to what it was about."

Krasner grunted, perhaps out of dissatisfaction because he was making no progress.

Jack waited, cooling down. He asked, "No clues at all as to who killed him and why?"

"His pockets were emptied," said the captain.

"You think he was mugged?"

"If his killer wanted us to think that, it would be an obvious move to rob him."

Jack nodded. "I wish I could tell you more, Captain, but I can't."

Krasner asked him a few more questions, but the answers that Jack readily provided added little. The captain leaned back. "You can go. If you think of anything, let me know at once."

Jack agreed, glad to be allowed to leave the depressing room, unhappy that nothing indicated the identity of the killer or his motive. The journey back home was spent in contemplation that was no more fruitful.

Chapter 3

When Jack walked into the Midway Plaisance, it was in its afternoon doldrum period, with only a few dedicated drinkers at the bar. One of the most popular music halls on the Barbary Coast, it offered something for everybody—from bawdy sketches that usually ended with girls losing their clothing, to less risqué shows with singers, dancers, acrobats and jugglers, all the way to operatic performances by stars such as Enrico Caruso, Luisa Tetrazzini and Nellie Melba.

Jack recalled seeing oddities such as Doctor Cook, who told of his experiences at the North Pole, and Bessie de Voie, who read purple passages from the love letters she had received from millionaires such as Frank Gould and John "Bet-a-Million" Gates.

Jack's attention was focused on the stage now, where Flo was rehearsing the chorus girls in a Hawaiian number. Flo had been known by another name just a few years ago, when at the World's Fair in Chicago she had danced under the sobriquet of Little Egypt. The hoochy coochy dance she demonstrated there had made her famous all over the world and every performance had been a sellout. When the fair ended, Flo had received job offers by the dozen, but she was an unusually levelheaded girl and knew how fleeting fame could be. She turned down all offers to dance and instead became a dance teacher.

After engagements in New York, she accepted a highly lucrative contract at the Midway Plaisance, where she was responsible for hiring and training the chorus girls and selecting musical numbers and costumes.

When Jack had first met her, there was an instant mutual attraction. Flo was not only an efficient businesswoman but was sensual as well. Jack found the combination rare and exciting. On her side, Flo found the young adventurer an unusual mix of the intellectual and the physical.

The Hawaiian number concluded with a wild Polynesian version of the hoochy coochy and Jack went up onto the stage. "Take five minutes, girls!" Flo called out as she turned to greet him with a smile. He kissed her passionately, his arms wrapped around her warm, shapely body.

"The number needs more work," said Flo, "but it's coming along."

"You're a perfectionist, Flo. Will you ever be satisfied?"

"Come opening night, I'll have to be." Her heart-shaped face enthralled him as it always did and he kissed her again. They stepped down from the stage and sat at one of the front tables.

"So are you keeping out of trouble? Or is that a foolish question?"

Jack grinned. It was an engaging grin that made him look no more than eighteen years old. "I may get into trouble once in a while but I always get out of it."

"That last job you did almost got you killed in Chinatown."

"It did get a little risky at one time," Jack admitted.

Flo sighed. "This is a dangerous town. Did you hear about Tom Tullamore over at the Silver Dollar being found dead?"

"Er, yes, I did." Jack knew better than to try to conceal anything from Flo. She had a sixth sense that was unerringly accurate. "As a matter of fact, I was talking to him the night it happened."

Flo's large dark eyes widened. "He was mugged, wasn't he? In the alley behind the Silver Dollar?"

"That's what it looked like."

The shrewd glance was typical of Flo as she promptly

seized on Jack's choice of words. "Looked like? You mean it might not have been a mugging? Why? Did he tell you something?"

"It was more what he didn't tell me. He said he wanted to talk to me but he was called away before he could tell me what it was about. I never saw him again."

Flo frowned. "He didn't give you any hint of what was bothering him?"

"Nothing. Not even a hint."

"The police will be talking to you, won't they? I mean, if you talked to Tom Tullamore the same night . . ."

"They already have talked to me. I told them what I just told you."

Flo leaned back, pensive. "So you won't be going off on another of your adventures?"

"Doesn't look like it. That means I'll be here every day."

"You never come here every day."

Jack reached across the table and clasped her hand. "Maybe I will now."

Flo returned the squeeze. She asked, "Did you ever meet his wife?"

"Tullamore's? I didn't know he had one."

"I met her once at a birthday party at the Silver Dollar." Flo put on a scowl that was inappropriate for her lovely face. "Maybe you'd better not meet her—she's a good-looking woman."

Jack squeezed again. "I wouldn't even notice. You're the only woman for me."

"Ha!" Flo's tone was skeptical but she smiled with a charm that was totally natural.

"How long are you going to be tied up with these rehearsals?" Jack asked. "I thought we might go on a picnic to Point Reyes one of these days."

"The girls are coming along well. We should have this Hawaiian number pinned down soon. But then," Flo went on, "we have a sailor number to rehearse."

"Men sailors?"

"Of course not. Men are the audience. They like to see

girls on the stage. And girls in sailors suits have a certain appeal, don't you think?"

"They do when they're wearing suits that you design," Jack said. "I must be sure and see those rehearsals."

Flo released his hand and gave him a mock rap on the wrist. "You don't need any stimulating. I think I'll have you barred from rehearsals." She rose and kissed him quickly. "Onstage, girls!" she called out.

Andy, one of the bartenders, knew Jack well and he gave the young writer a wave as he walked back across the floor. Andy had dreams of going to the Klondike and making enough money from gold mining to be able to open his own saloon. He never missed an opportunity to talk to Jack about his experiences there and refused to believe that Jack had not come back with a fortune.

The wave seemed to be more than just a greeting; he seemed to be calling Jack over. Jack supposed that the bartender wanted to ask yet more questions about prospecting in the Yukon. He walked over to the bar.

"Flo's really driving those girls," Andy told him, "and they love every minute of it."

"True," Jack agreed.

"Time for a beer?"

"Think I'll wait a while," said Jack.

Andy gave him a look of surprise. "Not on the water wagon are you?"

"No," Jack said, "just easing up."

Andy nodded. "Man over there looking for you," he said. "Want to talk to him?"

Jack followed the direction of Andy's glance. Pale and thin, the stranger wore a shabby jacket with gray pants.

"Sure," Jack said, and Andy waved the man over.

"You Jack London?" the other asked in a piping voice.

"Yes, I am."

"Mr. Hanrahan at the Green Bottle asks if you could come and have a drink with him this evening. About six o'clock, he says."

"Yes, tell him I'll be there," Jack said.

The man nodded and hurried off.

Jack looked at Andy. "Know any more about 'Shanghai' Hanrahan than I do, Andy?"

"Rough-and-tumble Irishman—or was in his crimping days," was the prompt answer. Jack knew about crimping—the shanghaiing of unwary drinkers in disreputable bars and pressing them into service aboard the merchantmen that came into San Francisco, one of the world's busiest ports. The extraordinarily low prices of drinks were irresistible to many and the chloral hydrate or the laudanum with which they were laced quickly resulted in a mental darkness. Unlucky drinkers awoke on the deck of a ship already out at sea on the way to some foreign destination.

"A few dollars a sailor," Andy said, grinning, "and a lot of sailors. That's how Hanrahan bought the Green Bottle."

Jack knew the place. On Turk Street at the edge of the Devil's Acre, the Green Bottle had a semirespectability that displayed Hanrahan's ambitions.

"He runs it pretty straight," Andy went on. "No watering of drinks and he don't allow muggings of drunk customers."

Jack knew Hanrahan to be a determined and resourceful man, clearly set on raising his status in the shifting sands of San Francisco society. "Owns a construction company too, doesn't he?" Jack asked.

"Right," said Andy, "and he's reformed enough that he's been elected the head of the Saloon Owners Association."

To Jack's knowledge, this was an uneasy alliance to say the least, for the association members demanded that their leader be hardheaded, ruthless and individualistic.

"He's tough and knows how to handle men and situations—that's what got him the job," Andy added.

The inevitable thought flashed through Jack's mind: Did this have anything to do with Tom Tullamore? It was highly likely, it seemed.

He turned to Andy. "Give me a beer. It might help me think."

Chapter 4

It was three beers later when Jack left the Midway Plaisance and walked over to the Green Bottle. Six o'clock was much too early for pleasure-loving San Franciscans, and as at the Midway Plaisance, only a few drinkers were at the bar and the tables were still empty.

The Green Bottle was not as large as most of its competitors but its layout was the same—a bar stretched the full length of one side and bottles behind the bar filled three shelves against the wall mirror. The small stage was curtained and two colored waiters were putting the tables and chairs in a semblance of order.

Opposite the bar, the wall was covered with banners of Civil War regiments, with both sides represented. A map hung there too, alleged to have been the one that General George Washington had used to plan the Battle of Princeton; apparently there were those who doubted its authenticity, though, because the corner containing the date had been ripped away. Uniforms worn by both armies were nailed to the wall, and the extensive staining on them was maintained to be blood.

As soon as Jack mentioned his name to a bartender, the man said, "Mr. Hanrahan's waiting for you." He took Jack past the stage to a room equipped as a surprisingly efficient office.

Shanghai Hanrahan was separating a pile of bills. He set them aside and offered his hand to Jack. "Have a seat," he said, waving to a comfortable-looking basket-weave chair.

Hanrahan was a stocky, thick-necked man with a pudgy

face and cold eyes. He managed a smile but it appeared out of place, though his voice was pleasant enough. "We have a few things to talk about, you and me."

Jack returned the smile but said nothing, preferring to let the other show his cards first.

"I'm a man who believes in coming right to the point," Hanrahan said. "You were talking to Tom Tullamore the night he was killed."

"Yes, I was. He'd asked me to see him."

Hanrahan shook his head sadly. "Poor Tom—he'll be missed."

Jack did not get the feeling that this sympathy was all that sincere but he waited for Hanrahan to continue. "In a way, though, it may have been his own doing," Hanrahan said.

"How do you mean?" Jack asked.

"Tom was a renegade, a maverick."

"In what way?"

"He wouldn't join the Saloon Owners Association."

"I didn't know that," Jack said.

"A few owners of smaller places, bars mostly, didn't feel that they could afford to join, but Tullamore was the only owner of a bigger place who stayed out. We tried to persuade him, me and some of the others, that it was in his own interest, but he wouldn't listen. He was a loner, Tom was, and said an association was not for him."

Jack listened to this with some surprise and wondered why Hanrahan was telling him these things.

"What did he want to talk to you about that night?"

Hanrahan's question was typical of his head-on approach and Jack answered in a similarly forthright manner. "He didn't get the chance to tell me. He was just going to when he was called away to speak to someone. I never saw him again."

Hanrahan digested that for a second. A hint of disbelief came into his voice as he said, "He didn't tell you anything, anything at all?"

"Nothing. Nothing at all."

A box of Cuban cigars was on the desk alongside the pile of bills. Hanrahan opened it, took one and offered the box to Jack, who shook his head. "They blend these just for me," Hanrahan said as he opened a large box of matches and struck one. It flared sulfurously and Hanrahan sucked at the flame. He threw away the match and looked at Jack through the smoke cloud.

"You must have had some idea what he wanted to talk to you about."

"Not the least," Jack said. "He merely said he wanted to talk some business with me. He said it was important but he gave me no hint as to what it was."

"So you had no idea?" Hanrahan was clearly reluctant to let go of his conviction. He puffed on the cigar. It was a distinctive aroma, almost enough to persuade Jack to take up cigar smoking.

"When I first arrived," said Jack, "Tom took me upstairs. We walked past the gambling tables. He didn't tell me if he was looking for something, but we stopped only briefly."

"Was there anything unusual?"

"Not that I noticed."

Hanrahan generated another smoke cloud. "You know any of the gamblers?"

"A couple of bankers from the Crocker, a couple of city councilmen—that was all. Tom pointed out Lucky Baldwin."

That name brought a reaction. Hanrahan took the cigar out of his mouth. "Baldwin was there?"

"Yes."

"You know him?"

"No," Jack said. "I've heard of him, of course. Everybody in San Francisco has heard of him, but I'd never seen him before."

"Was he winning or losing?"

"I don't know. A lot of money was on the table, though."

"Anybody else?"

"A professor of mathematics at the university at Berkeley.

Tom said he was in often, trying to win with some system of his own."

"O'Sullivan."

"Tom didn't mention his name," Jack said.

"Well, that's it," Hanrahan said sharply. "O'Sullivan." Hanrahan contemplated the glowing tip of his cigar. "You are probably wondering why I'm asking you these questions."

"I don't have the least notion what this is all about."

Hanrahan's tone softened, not much but enough to show that he was a good choice for the leadership of the Saloon Owners Association. "As I said, Tullamore was a maverick. He liked to go it alone. He wasn't a joiner." He leaned forward, pointing with his cigar. "He was going to ask you to make some inquiries for him."

"How do you know that?" Jack asked.

Hanrahan shrugged. "One of the advantages of being the boss man of the association is I get to hear a lot."

"What does this have to do with Tom's death?"

"Like I said, he was going to have you do some investigating for him and we—the Saloon Owners Association— we want you to make the same investigations for us." Hanrahan put the cigar back in his mouth and talked around it. "You did a fine job helping the police on that business a while ago after the Pinks backed out. You saved Chinatown from a real bad fire, they say."

"Sounds like you know a lot about me."

"Enough to know that you're the right man for this."

"It got Tullamore killed," Jack said.

"I'm not saying it's a job without risk," Hanrahan said, his tone a little unctuous. "But you're used to that. You like a few risks. You took plenty at sea, you took plenty in the Yukon and you've taken a lot of them on the Barbary Coast."

Jack managed a smile. "I have to admit that you're right there."

"Sure I am. Now here's our proposition. We'll pay you

ten dollars a day, seven days a week. Out-of-pocket expenses will be paid, of course."

That was a higher rate than Jack had ever been paid before. As an oyster pirate, he had sometimes made two hundred dollars in a night, but that endeavor had meant the chance of being shot by the police or by other oyster pirates jealous of his catch. He had several stories out, but acceptance was unpredictable, and even if he had a streak of luck, writing for magazines brought an erratic income at best.

"What do I have to do for this?" Jack asked.

"Keep your eyes and ears open."

Jack shook his head. "Nothing doing."

Hanrahan took the cigar from his mouth in disbelief. "Nothing doing? That's good money and you know it is! How much do you want?"

"It's not the money. I want to know what you want me to do. Telling me to keep my eyes and ears open means nothing. What am I looking and listening for?"

Hanrahan put the cigar back in his mouth and puffed. "Every saloon and music hall on the Barbary Coast is threatened," he said slowly, and Jack felt his blood chill at the words. Hanrahan was a bluff, often-crude, always-blunt character who was unlikely to be intimidated by anything less than the most dire threat.

"What is threatening them?" Jack asked.

"We're trying to find out. As soon as this position gets clearer, we'll tell you. But we decided at our last meeting not to wait till the threat got stronger. We wanted to get you with us right now."

Jack shook his head. "It all sounds too vague to me."

"We're pretty sure that it sounded vague to Tom Tullamore. He stumbled onto something that made it clearer. It got him killed."

"He was mugged."

"Bah! Nobody believes that. Whoever killed him wanted it to look that way."

"The police say he was mugged."

"They say it," Hanrahan said contemptuously. "They don't believe it. But I happen to know they are calling in an expert lawman to help them."

"A Pinkerton?"

"The Pinks are losing their reputation. Nobody has that much faith in them anymore."

"I'm only one individual," Jack explained. "I don't have the organization that the Pinks or the police have."

"The police!" Hanrahan sucked at the cigar and looked for somewhere to spit. He hooked a brass spittoon closer and aimed accurately into it. "That's what I think of the police. Half of them in this town are on the take."

Jack had read that same statistic in Ambrose Bierce's column in the *San Francisco Examiner.* He knew from personal experience that any investigation that had their participation was severely compromised from the start.

"You're a smart young fellow," Hanrahan said. "You know everybody on the Coast and everybody knows you. If there's something to be learned, you're the man to learn it. None of us knows yet just what this threat is, but if you stumble onto anything relating to it, you'll know it."

Hanrahan was shrewd. He could see that Jack was wavering, tempted by the offer, lured by the challenge. "What have you got to lose? Give it a try for a couple of weeks. Before that time is up, we'll have something more solid to bite on, I can almost guarantee."

"You say the police are calling in an expert lawman to help them. Do they know what they're looking for, any more than I do?"

Hanrahan barked a laugh. "I doubt it."

"Then how do they know they need to call in an expert?"

"They've heard rumors, whispers of serious trouble. Not enough for them to know what they should do or how to do it but enough to worry them."

Jack watched him puff on the cigar. "It's the craziest thing I've ever heard," he said finally, "and maybe I'm crazy to go along with it—but all right."

"Good man." Hanrahan examined the final inch of his cigar. "No need to tell you that this is confidential. So just a few details on how to get in touch with me when you learn anything. And remember, you're watching for any signs that might threaten the saloons and the music halls. Now, I'm here most of the time, but if I'm not, here's what you do. . . ."

Chapter 5

A short train ride and an even shorter ferry trip brought Jack to Tiburon. A mere handful of the small community turned out for Tom Tullamore's funeral, and Jack recognized only two saloon owners. The preacher had obviously not known Tullamore well and his words were few, the ceremony brief.

A gusty breeze blew in from the bay, chilly and somehow appropriate. The mourners scattered as they emerged from the graveyard and Jack was left alone with the black-clad figure of the widow. She was tall, with glistening black hair, and her figure was striking even in funeral garb. She was just as good-looking as Flo had suggested. She was handsome rather than pretty, and probably in her mid-forties. She was quite composed despite the occasion, pale and dry-eyed.

Jack turned to her. "I thought the funeral was severe, didn't you?" he asked.

"Yes, I did," she agreed. "Still, I suppose ministers don't have a very high opinion of saloon keepers. They associate them with the worst aspects of the Barbary Coast." Her voice was low and controlled.

"Some ministers have not taken note of their own sermons on humility," Jack observed.

"I fear that ours today is one of those," she said. "You're Jack London, aren't you?"

"Yes. I was hoping I'd have a chance to talk to you. Do you have a few minutes before I go back? There isn't another train for an hour and a half."

"Of course, let's go to the house. There's no one there. A few people are coming over later." She led the way to a horse and carriage that was waiting.

The Tullamore home was large and situated on two or three acres of land with a view eastward. It was a sprawling ranch-style house, and Jack wondered if the widow would continue to live there.

She led the way into the house. It had several rooms, many of them sizable, but she took Jack into a snug sitting room with deep sofas and comfortable armchairs. Indian rugs covered the floor and an Indian tapestry covered much of one wall. The furniture was in a dark tropical wood, and the ceiling beams were of the same material. A bowl and an urn glistened, both with the same bronze sheen. A stone fireplace with a cord of wood beside it added to the cozy feeling.

When they were seated, Jack said, "Did you work with Tom in the Silver Dollar? I wasn't a regular but I don't recall seeing you there."

"No," she said. "Oh, I would have liked to be more active there but Tom didn't like the idea. I think I would have been good at it, don't you?"

Jack agreed. He had just been thinking of the similarity in appearance between Tess Tullamore and French Kitty, the owner of the popular music hall on California Street. Males dominated the entertainment scene on the Coast, but that made the few women who owned establishments all the more prominent.

"But Tom did talk to me about the Silver Dollar," she went on, "his problems and his successes, and as a matter of fact, your name came up last week."

Jack nodded encouragingly.

"Tom knew that you had done some investigating since you came back from the Yukon. You worked for the mayor, didn't you?"

Jack nodded again. That task had been confidential at the time, but now he was beginning to realize how many people knew about it.

"When I was with Tom the night he died," he said, "I felt that he was going to ask for my help with something. Do you have any idea what that was? Someone came to see him. He went out to meet them and I never saw him again."

She sat erect, a proud figure. "Tom learned that a very serious threat was hanging over the Barbary Coast—a threat that could involve every establishment there—but especially places like the Silver Dollar."

Why especially the Silver Dollar? Jack wondered, but he did not want to interrupt the widow now that she might be about to answer some of the questions that had been plaguing him ever since that evening with Tom Tullamore.

"I wish I could tell you exactly what the threat is," she continued, "but I don't know. Tom might have known but I think he wasn't fully sure and didn't want to say any more until he had more information—information that he hoped you would help him to get."

That was disappointing but Jack felt she might know more. "Do you have any notion of what started him on this? Someone he talked to, something that happened?"

"I am not certain but this may be of help. . . ." Her eyes glowed with a slight but distinct radiance that contrasted with her pale face. "There was a gold miner called Sam Hooper. He and Tom had known each other for a long time. Sam used to bring his gold in every few months and Tom would buy it from him. Sam knew that he got a fair price and wouldn't take his gold anywhere else."

Tess Tullamore leaned back in the armchair and rested her hands on the padded arms. Jack was listening intently.

"A couple of weeks ago," Tess went on, "Sam came into town. He had Tom exchange his gold for cash and then the two talked for a long time. Not that they weren't always friendly, but when Tom told me about it, he seemed reticent. He could have told me more but I knew he was holding back."

"He didn't tell you anything further?" Jack asked.

"A day or two later, he was unusually quiet. When I

asked him what was wrong, that was when he said that a threat was hanging over San Francisco and that all the establishments on the Barbary Coast could be in danger."

"And this was connected with what he and this Sam Hooper had talked about?"

Tess was normally composed and in full self-control, but at the question she looked ready to burst into tears. Instead, she made a great effort and nodded calmly. "Yes, I have to think that."

"Do you know where Sam Hooper can be found?"

"I don't know where he lived when he came into town."

"Did he drink in the Silver Dollar?"

"Only when he came in with gold to sell."

"Did he drink anywhere else?"

"Yes, he used to go to Every Man Welcome." It was one of the wildest bagnios on the Barbary Coast. Its name was known from Dawson to San Diego. "I couldn't go there," said Tess. "Oh, there are some places where women go for for other women, but that's not one of them."

"So I believe," Jack agreed. He was frustrated with this news. If Sam Hooper had frequented a bar, there would be a chance that he talked when drunk—to bartenders, other customers, waiter girls. That would mean that nothing remained secret. Yet it would be hard to extract any information from anyone at Every Man Welcome, where the very nature of the bagnio business made all concerned less communicative. He didn't want to let any hint of his disappointment be obvious to Tess, however.

"I'll make a visit to Every Man Welcome," Jack said, "and see what I can find out."

"Will you promise to keep me informed?" she asked as she rose.

"Of course."

"And, Jack, please be careful."

Her eyes pleaded the sentiment as sincerely as her words.

Chapter 6

Back in his room, Jack took care of his correspondence first. His letters to postmaster Cloudesley Johns were on a near-weekly basis and he had now begun a weekly exchange of letters with Anna Strunsky, whom he had met at a socialist lecture in Oakland. In a recent letter, Jack had told Anna of his passion for the work of Rudyard Kipling. He had not expected her to reciprocate, for he viewed Kipling as primarily appealing to male readers, but to his delight she replied by quoting passages from "Mandalay." He penned an enthusiastic response.

Next was an invitation to a literary event hosted by the Bohemian Club. He scribbled an acceptance and turned to writing a letter to the Houghton Mifflin Company, who had requested biographical details from him. Then he settled down to rewrite "Dutch Courage," a story he had submitted to the magazine *Youth's Companion*. The editor had said he liked it and would buy it if Jack would make a few changes, which he listed. Payment was not mentioned and would probably be small, but Jack's desire to write was so consuming that it overrode any mere commercial thoughts.

He wrote on until the evening. He reread what he had written and was satisfied, so he placed the typed pages in a large envelope, added his covering letter and set the envelope out for mailing.

A hammering came on the front door.

"Captain Krasner!" Jack's mind was still in the world of writing, and seeing the captain at the door caught him by surprise. He had been expecting further investigation by the police, so the presence of the captain was not completely unexpected.

Krasner nodded toward the desk covered with papers. "How's the writing going?"

Jack had not mentioned his writing in their previous conversation but Krasner obviously knew about it. Jack told him of the offer from *Youth's Companion* and Krasner congratulated him. They sat, Jack at his desk and Krasner in an uncomfortable spindly chair.

"I've talked with Hanrahan," the police officer said briskly. "This is all such a vague business that it's understandable everybody who might be able to help should be called in. It's like trying to catch smoke in a bottle, nothing to put your finger on, don't even know which direction to head."

"An expert lawman is being called in, I hear," said Jack. "Know who he is?"

"Yes, but I can't give you his name until it's confirmed that he's willing to work with us on this. That should be in the next day or two," Krasner said, "and I'll try to keep you notified. The trouble with this business is that it's so cloudy and uncertain and everyone involved is so spooked, that other investigators may be brought in and we may not be told."

"The Pinks? Are they in it yet?"

"We haven't been told of any involvement by the Pinkerton Agency, no." Krasner leaned back in the spindly chair. It creaked. "Tell me what you know of Tom Tullamore."

Jack told him, keeping it brief. Krasner listened, then said, "I am authorized to ask you to help us in this matter. You were a friend of Tullamore, so from what I have heard about you, you'd probably keep poking your nose into it anyway—am I right?"

Jack grinned. "I probably would."

"What action do you propose?"

"I'm going to take a close look at some of the gambling places. Tom took me on a tour of his tables, so it's obvious that it's something to do with them. Some of them probably have adequate protection, some don't, so robberies on a large scale are a possibility."

"You think that's likely?"

"Could be," Jack said. "Perhaps someone has figured out a foolproof plan for robbing them."

"You say 'them,' meaning several?"

"Well, we wouldn't be seeing so many people all stirred up if it was just one place threatened, would we?"

Krasner said nothing.

"There's an awful lot of money out on those tables," Jack went on. "The haul from half a dozen of them would be enormous."

"There's more to it than that," Krasner rapped. His voice was hard and brittle. "Trouble is, I know no more than you what it is."

"Like you said—smoke."

"All right." Krasner stood, clearly glad to get up from the uncomfortable chair. "You still patronize the Midway Plaisance, I take it."

"Yes, I do."

"Any of the bartenders you can trust, know you well?"

"Andy."

"Good. I'll communicate with you through him."

"How do I get in touch with you if I need to?" Jack asked.

"Leave a message at any police station. Most of them have a telephone now—they can get through to me at once. Those that don't soon will."

With a curt nod and a "Good luck," Captain Krasner was gone. Jack was too aware of the corruption that was rife in the police department to have complete trust in him until he knew him better. For now, he would have to go it alone against this unseen and shadowy menace.

Chapter 7

Every Man Welcome was in one of the toughest parts of the Barbary Coast. Along Kearny Street were cribs and deadfalls, the two lowest levels in the hierarchy of the brothels. The littered sidewalks were full of people, mostly men. Sailors, miners, gawking tourists and wide-eyed college boys rubbed shoulders with men carrying advertising boards or handing out dodgers.

Raucous music blasted out from a street-corner speaker and nearby a bald man with a trumpet voice was reading passages from the Bible sprinkled with references to Sodom and Gomorrah. A small cart sold slices of bread with hot meat, and Jack wondered how many of the customers paused to ask the origin of the meat. The aroma was tempting but the risk was considerable.

The *San Francisco Call* had recently reported that Kearny Street was not safe for respectable citizens and condemned "the utter shamelessness of its denizens." It had gone on to say, "The women of the locality are of the lowest class and there is not an hour of the day or night when the vulgarity of these females is not unveiled to anybody who happens to be going past."

The line of dens that Jack was walking by was known as Battle Row, and it was a very rare day that did not see half a dozen brawls and at least one robbery. Most of these ended in a murder. Half a dozen well-dressed men who looked like visitors were entering the Morgue, a particularly unsavory dive that had previously been called the Slaughterhouse, a name that was equally appropriate.

Jack wondered how many of the men would survive the night. A drunk almost staggered into him but Jack turned quickly to avoid him. That was a standard tactic of muggers, some of whom could rob and kill a man and escape before the knifed body hit the sidewalk. A little farther along was Every Man Welcome.

It was a cellar deadfall and dance hall. It consisted of one large rectangular room, half of which was taken up with rough tables and chairs and the other half cleared for dancing. Against one wall was a row of hard benches and along the other was a bar that extended the length of the room. On a platform in one corner a pianist and a fiddler were playing furiously.

About twenty pretty waiter girls, as they were called, were serving drinks, exchanging badinage and dancing with customers. Behind the platform were several curtained booths, which the girls could use whenever their partner could afford the rental fee.

When Every Man Welcome opened, the girls wore short black skirts and black silk stockings but nothing above the waist. The police, under heavy pressure from the Committee on Morals, ordered them to don blouses. They obliged, but the blouses were thin and diaphanous as well as being worn unbuttoned, and the customers preferred these to the earlier nudity.

The previous owner had maintained a standing offer of free drinks for the evening to any customer who found any of the girls wearing undergarments, but Marty Gallagher, the current owner, had discontinued that practice once it was established that the offer never resulted in the house having to pay up.

Jack had been there a few times in his younger, more reckless days, but it had been some time since his last visit, and as he looked around he saw no one he knew. That was a rarity for him but he consoled himself with the thought that the evening was young, ordered a beer at the bar and waited for one of the waiter girls to bring it.

When it came, the girl smiled invitingly at him. She was

a pretty blonde, but though she was still young, her face was already taking on a hard expression. "The end booth's empty," she said boldly. "Shall we take it?"

"Maybe later," Jack said. He paid for the beer and gave her a generous tip. "Thought I might see Sam Hooper in here," he said, casually looking around.

"Sam? Haven't seen him this week. When he does come in, he always looks for Rosie."

"Rosie? Is she here?"

"What's wrong with me?" She put a hand on her hip and posed provocatively.

"Not a thing that I can see," Jack assured her. "But I've got a matter to settle with Sam Hooper and I need to find him."

"That's Rosie over there." She pointed to a tall dark-haired girl serving a nearby table.

"Send her over," said Jack. "Maybe after I've asked her about Sam Hooper, you and I can see if that booth's still empty."

The girl nodded and strolled off. Jack watched the two of them talking and saw the blonde motion toward the bar where he stood. After a few moments, Rosie came up to him.

"You a friend of Sam Hooper?" she asked, suspicion in her tone. She was thin and her face was pale under makeup but her eyes were lively.

"Sam makes it hard on his friends," Jack said with a smile. "Particularly those of us who live in San Francisco. He doesn't spend enough time here for us to get together often enough. Where is he now? Off digging for gold again?"

The answer softened her suspicion and she found Jack's boyish charm appealing. "Most men who come in here looking for somebody want money from them," she said.

"Not me," Jack said. "Anyway, Sam's not the type to owe anybody."

He waited for the answer. He was taking a chance, but it was based on Tess Tullamore's description of Sam.

"I guess so," said Rosie, and Jack eased out his breath.

"Heard he's back in town. Can't figure out why he hasn't looked me up. Has he been in here?"

"A week ago or so," Rosie said.

"Not since?"

"No."

"How can he stay away from you that long?"

Jack's tone was joking but Rosie answered seriously, "He's usually in more often."

"Maybe I should go see him," Jack said. "Make sure he's all right."

"Know where he lives?"

"Never really been over there," Jack admitted truthfully. "He's more often in a bar."

She paused, uncertain. "He doesn't like me to tell people. They think he's brought back gold. They don't know he likes to cash it in right away. He's afraid they'll think he has some stashed away."

"I won't say that I'm exactly worried about Sam—he can take care of himself," Jack said. "But any man who is known to have gold is at risk in this town, like you say. I just need to be sure he's all right."

That satisfied Rosie, who seemed to have a genuine concern for the miner. "When he's in town, he stays in a rooming house on Portland Street, corner of West."

"Mother Kelly's?"

"Yes, that's it."

"When you saw him a week ago, had he just come into town?"

"Yes."

"Did he say where he had been?" He caught the flare starting in her eyes and added, "Had he been at his usual prospecting site?"

"No, he hadn't," said Rosie, the recurrent suspicion quelled. "Running into a dry spot, he said." Jack knew that that meant Sam Hooper had followed a vein that had run out. "He had been shanking," Rosie said. "He didn't want to come back empty-handed."

Shanking was mining slang meaning Hooper had worked for a mining company that paid by the hour plus a small percentage of the gold value mined. Miners occasionally did that when their own claims had temporarily dried up.

"Who was he shanking for?" asked Jack. "Did Sam say?"

"No," Rosie replied. Jack was deciding this was a dead end when she said, "Wait a minute—he did say something. . . . He was complaining about the heat. He mentioned a place—let me think. . . ."

Jack waited. She frowned. "It was a nice name," she murmured, then brightened. "Sunset Valley—that was it!"

Jack's gold-mining experiences had all been in the Klondike, but he had talked to many miners who had prospected in California. He knew all the names—Grass Valley, Coloma, Nevada City, Hangtown—but Sunset Valley was not a name he had heard. "Are you sure?" he asked her.

"Yes, Sunset Valley, he said."

Jack nodded, gave Rosie a tip and on the way out gave a similar amount to the blond girl. "Maybe next time," he said and winked.

He was about to push the door open when a man came in. He was gray faced and lean with thinning hair. He had a preoccupied air and didn't see Jack, who stood aside. Jack recognized him immediately. He was the mathematician he had seen playing cards in the Silver Dollar the night Tom Tullamore had been murdered. His name was O'Sullivan.

Jack stood inside the door for a moment, watching. O'Sullivan walked up to the bar and exchanged some words with one of the bartenders. Then one of the waiter girls came to him and spoke. O'Sullivan answered and there followed some discussion. He went to a table and sat, alone.

Jack watched but nothing happened. O'Sullivan shifted in his chair. If he moved farther, he would see Jack watching him.

Jack pushed the door open and went out into the street. It was even more crowded than before. More advertising boards were out there now, touting all manner of wares from fortune-tellers to clothes, from a newly opened cable car line to a scotch whisky. The noise level had increased too. A brewery wagon clattered by, then a lumber cart with huge logs from Muir Park.

He walked to Portland Street. He knew Mother Kelly's rooming house. It was a massive four-story place with a variety of accommodations from just above poverty level to tolerably acceptable. Mother Kelly ran as tight an operation as could be found in San Francisco. Prices were reasonable and Mother Kelly did her best to keep out drugs, drunks and crooks. Rooms were small but habitable and clean.

The hostess herself weighed three hundred pounds and looked more than capable of throwing out any man who broke her rules. She had lost three front teeth doing just that and her grin looked evil, but it was no more than a weapon she used as part of her arsenal. Jack knew her slightly and he dropped a few names that instantly secured him entrance.

Sam Hooper stayed here for a week at a time, sometimes two, Mother Kelly told him. He was usually flush with money when he arrived but he always left before he had spent it all. Much of it went to Every Man Welcome, but Mother Kelly confided to Jack her soft spot for him was based on the fact that he put part of every haul in a bank account in the name of a young niece in St. Louis.

His room was on the fourth floor and at the back. Mother Kelly had not seen him for a few days but said he must still be here. Jack climbed the wooden stairs and found the number she had given him. He pounded on the door but there was no reply. He could see nothing through the tiny window. Perhaps Sam Hooper had left after all, Jack thought, gone off on another prospecting expedition. Perhaps it wasn't his usual practice to depart without telling Mother Kelly, but it was possible that had happened.

It was quiet up on the top floor. There was no one for Jack to ask if Hooper had been seen and he didn't expect further questioning of Mother Kelly to produce any useful information. He hesitated then took out his large jackknife. He had used it for this purpose on a couple of earlier occasions; his acquaintance with burglars and thieves had taught him a lot. He inserted the blade at the side of the door handle and probed for the tang of the lock.

After a couple of minutes, he paused and looked cautiously up and down the corridor. No one was in sight. He returned to his task and at last came the click of success—he pushed the door open.

Jack went in, feeling in his pocket for the box of sulfur matches that he always carried. Their light was feeble but adequate and revealed a boxlike room, sparsely furnished, with few items of a personal nature. There was an unpleasant odor and Jack decided against lighting the lantern on the wall. He advanced carefully toward a second room, the bedroom. He tripped over an impediment on the floor and held out the match to see what it was.

The flaring yellow light showed a man sprawled on his back with a gaping bloody wound at the side of his throat.

Chapter 8

The body was cold. The blood in the wound had congealed but was still red, so Jack guessed that death had probably occurred one to two days earlier.

He had no doubt that this was Sam Hooper. He looked to be about fifty years old, with a weather-beaten face and scarred and gnarled hands from years of scraping in sand, mud and soil.

The wound had been caused by a large knife. A single powerful thrust had penetrated the side of the throat and severed the windpipe. The knife had probably been twisted to enlarge the cut and the main artery had been slashed open in the process. A great deal of blood had flowed but Sam Hooper had already been dead by then.

Jack had seen dead men on many occasions, had watched them die on some of those occasions, but he was never able to face death without a profound sadness. He was not a praying man but he said a quick and silent prayer for Sam Hooper, who might have been.

He completed a rapid search of the two rooms in case some trace remained that might yield a useful clue either to who had killed Sam Hooper or what his role might have been in all this. He found nothing of any help, and when his last match sputtered out, he stood in the dark, pondering what he should do.

There was only one thing he could do. By asking questions at the Every Man Welcome and talking to Mother Kelly, he had left a trail a yard wide, so it was pointless not to tell the police. He went downstairs, found Mother Kelly and told her to send someone to the nearest station.

Jack stayed downstairs talking to Mother Kelly until Captain Krasner arrived. Krasner glared at Jack. "Another body?"

Jack declined to be provoked. He gave him a bare outline of finding the body, leaving the captain with the impression that he had known Sam Hooper and was looking him up before Hooper went off on another of his prospecting trips.

"How did you get in?" the captain demanded.

"I pushed hard at the door."

Krasner walked over and examined the lock carefully. "Turn out your pockets," he ordered. Jack did so and the captain picked up the clasp knife and opened the big blade. He looked at it carefully, then went to study the tang of the lock. Jack wondered if scratches were visible on it. The captain straightened up but said nothing. A policeman appeared at the door. "Excuse me, Captain, but a man's here asking for you."

The man who pushed his way into the room was an inch or two taller than Jack's own six feet. He wore Western garb and moved like a man more used to sitting in a saddle than walking. His yellowish-brown hair was luxuriant though stranded with white, and he had a large mustache. He was dressed in a neat, tailor-made pearl-gray suit and a lighter gray linen shirt. When he spoke, his voice was soft and had a pronounced Western drawl.

"Don't mind me, Captain. I was told I should come along. You just carry on like I wasn't here."

Krasner hesitated, then nodded and resumed his interrogation of Jack, concerned mainly about his acquaintanceship with Sam Hooper. Jack evaded direct questions adroitly and maintained the position that he was not a close friend of Hooper. He said he had been in Every Man Welcome and one of the girls, Rosie, had said that, though she knew Sam was in town, she had not seen him for a week. Jack made it sound as if it had been at her request that he had come to see why Sam had not been around.

The Westerner listened intently but said not a word. He had keen, wide-set eyes under heavy brows and a strong, firm nose. His gaze roamed through the room. When Krasner had finished questioning Jack, he glanced to the Westerner to see if he wanted to comment, but he did not respond to the silent invitation.

"You can go," Krasner said curtly to Jack, who left, puzzling over the role of the Western stranger.

Although Sacramento, as the state capital, carried the mining records for the California counties, these were mostly claim forms and details of renewals. The latter were important because if a property was not worked within three years, then the claim was no longer valid and another prospector could stake his claim on it. The town hall in San Francisco also had a department containing files relating to mining operations, but it was less comprehensive. Jack had a friend from his days at Berkeley who worked in the records office there. Paul Carpenter was an ardent fan of Jack's writing, the two of them having been in the same class.

Paul had red hair and big ears and was excited at being able to help. He led the way toward a bank of narrow drawers, each with a brass handle. He selected one and pulled it open. "These are the twenty-seven original counties of California," said Paul. "Sunset Valley, you said? Any idea which county it's in?"

"I'm afraid not," Jack said.

"No matter," Paul said, "we'll just go through them all." After a few minutes, he stopped. "Here it is—just east of Lodi." He pronounced it in the local manner as "load eye."

"Do you have a map of that area?" Jack asked. Paul turned to another drawer.

The corps of engineers map showed the valley clearly and Jack scrutinized it. It was at least thirty miles long but it was narrow, and on either side the altitude lines squeezed nearer and nearer together. Paul followed his finger. "Over four thousand feet high, those mountains."

"Any towns there?" Jack asked.

"San Lorenzo seems to be the only one."

"Does the fact that this map was prepared by the corps of engineers mean that this is a mining area?"

"Over a dozen mines in Sunset Valley," Paul said.

"What do they mine?" Jack asked, disappointed.

"Mining law in California does not require that you state a particular mineral. You stake a claim on the land and then you can mine anything you find there."

Jack thanked him and they chatted for a few minutes about the other members of their class, few of whom were left in San Francisco.

Outside the town hall, a news vendor was shouting, "Read all about the big fight!" and Jack stopped to look at the headline of the *Examiner*. In his new affluence, he could afford a luxury that he often missed—he was able to buy a newspaper. He did so and stood for a few moments reading the story splashed across the front page.

San Francisco was a strong claimant as the boxing capital of America. It was a claim disputed by New York, which had long enjoyed that prominence, but many of the greatest boxers of the day lived in the Bay Area. Best known of these was Gentleman Jim Corbett, who had won the world heavyweight title in 1892 under the newly introduced Marquis of Queensberry rules.

The boxing world revolved around Corbett, and his residence in San Francisco kept interest there in boxing at a fever pitch. After Corbett had won the world heavyweight title, he had gone on to the vaudeville stage, which was much more lucrative and much less dangerous. The *Examiner* described all this, finally getting to the climax of its front-page story.

A match had been arranged between "Sailor" Tom Sharkey, a short, stocky Irishman, and Bob Fitzsimmons, a native of Cornwall in England but now a resident of Australia. The latter weighed only 170 pounds, which put him at a great disadvantage with opponents, who often outweighed him by thirty pounds or more. He had long, spindly legs but tremendous upper body strength and seemingly endless vitality.

The fight was to be for the world heavyweight title, considered to be vacant, and would be held in the Mechanics' Pavilion in San Francisco, which could easily hold more than ten thousand people. The *Examiner* omitted any mention of the illegality of the contest, and Jack had no doubt that the city police had already been paid off. The rest of the article went on to say that a major problem was being addressed—the choice of a referee.

In rough-and-ready San Francisco, few referees could be found who had any acquaintance with the Marquis of Queensberry rules. The National Athletic Club was considering several national figures, the *Examiner* reported. Jack grinned as he read the final part of the article, which stated that the better seats would be priced at ten dollars each—an astonishingly high figure. Even the "cheap" seats would be two dollars, an unprecedented amount but one that Jack could afford for once. He was an avid fan of most sports, and as a former prizefighter himself who had boxed an exhibition bout with John L. Sullivan, he was determined to attend this match. The *Examiner* was already heralding it as the fight of the decade, the most important sporting event of the century on the West Coast and a star-spangled day in the history of the city.

He glanced through the dramatic story again, noting the fine hand of the *Examiner* editor, Ambrose Bierce, behind it. Bierce considered himself Jack's mentor and Jack acknowledged a debt to Bierce, whose lucid prose style had been an influence on him. He would have to pay him a visit at Luna's, where Bierce could usually be found. The editor had his finger on every pulse that beat throughout the city and might be able to cast some light on the mysterious threat that both Hanrahan and Tom Tullamore viewed with fear.

Putting the newspaper under his arm, he went back to his room. The mailman had been by in his absence and one letter immediately caught Jack's eye. He could hardly wait to open it.

Chapter 9

The letter was from Houghton Mifflin, one of the more prestigious publishers, and it was signed by the editor. Jack could scarcely control his excitement as he read it. They wanted to publish a book of short stories containing his Alaskan experiences. A whole book just of his short stories!

He sat down to read the letter again. It was true. The thrill of knowing that one of the top publishing houses in the country wanted to produce a book of his stories was a tremendous satisfaction in itself. Reading the letter for a third time confirmed that, but now he could add another thought—these were stories already in existence, he did not have to write them.

He made himself a cup of strong coffee. The occasion demanded something more convivial but he was following a rule of not having any alcoholic drink in his room. It was too tempting and he was determined not to slip back into what he termed his John Barleycorn days.

Instead, he drank the coffee and read the letter yet again. The offer still held good. He pulled his chair up to the old Underwood and promptly wrote an answer accepting the arrangement. Then, still glowing with the thrill of achievement, he reread the story he had just started. He intended to call it "The Law of Life." It described an old man, an Indian, abandoned in the snow by his tribe because he was blind and thus an inconvenience. He sits by his fire and his pitifully small stack of wood.

He listens to the sounds of the tribe breaking camp, loading supplies, harnessing dogs, calling to one another.

The sounds reach a crescendo, then dwindle slowly as the tribe moves off, and the old man sits alone in his painful solitude. His mind wanders into the past. He recalls memory after memory. The only contact with the present is the howling of a wolf pack as it moves closer and surrounds him.

Jack had the whole story clearly in his head and he was now in the middle section of it, vividly experiencing the numbing cold and the terror of the encompassing wolf pack. He reached the final part of the memory sequence. All that remained now was the inevitable ending. He decided to leave that for his next writing session, because he had several letters he wanted to write.

First, he wrote to Anna Strunsky. He considered her a genius and had the highest regard for her intellect, although he was aware that their shared passion for socialism was also a factor. He wrote until evening, sharing the news of his latest good fortune, then dressed for an evening on the Barbary Coast and headed out.

He stopped at the Cobweb Palace, one of the most popular and certainly one of the more eccentric establishments in the whole state of California. It had opened in 1856. Abe Warner, who had operated it for forty years, loved spiders and would not allow any of his staff to kill one. Consequently they proliferated, as if aware of their protected status. The place originally had another name, but no one remembered what it was; it was widely known simply as the Cobweb Palace.

Every inch of the walls and ceiling was festooned with cobwebs. They draped over the light fixtures, dangled from bottle to bottle and hung low over the doors and windows. Spiders were not the only form of nonhuman life in the Cobweb Palace. Sea captains who had been regular customers had given Abe Warner monkeys, parakeets and macaws, and these sat in the dozens of cages stacked against the walls. One large parrot, said to be over eighty years old, had the freedom of the place and flew out of his ever-open cage door without warning, terrifying newcomers. He was able to swear fluently in four languages and did so whenever he was inebriated, which was much of the time.

The museumlike atmosphere was perpetuated by walrus tusks, whales' teeth and stuffed sharks mounted on the walls. The eccentricity of this eclectic collection was amplified by Abe Warner's personal collection of over a thousand drawings of nude women. Complaints about these were exceedingly rare, but when they did occur it was hard to force any action, as the location of the cobwebs seemed to cleverly bestow a modesty on the women.

As Jack approached the bar, he was greeted by the present owner, Hap Harrison. Almost as colorful a character as his predecessor, Hap was not a collector, but he had the good business sense not to cut down a single cobweb. As usual, he wore a clean white shirt with pearl buttons and baggy black trousers known as auctioneer's pants. These were held up by gaudy red suspenders with brass clasps.

Hap was a loose-limbed, awkward-moving man with a smile that was a permanent feature due to a knife slash, now healed over. It had earned him the nickname Happy, since contracted to Hap. He had become aware, sometime earlier, of an article of Jack's that had appeared in *Overland Monthly* magazine. One of the characters in this had been an irascible but kindhearted saloon owner, and Hap had immediately concluded that this character was modeled on himself. Jack had achieved the status of a preferred customer by not pointing out that, in truth, the saloon owner described was Tommy Tree at the Eureka.

Tippy, the invariably drunk piano player, was playing over the chatter of the audience already gathering for the first show of the evening. Hap was leaning against the bar with a half-full glass of whisky in front of him. He sipped at it, and a stranger would have formed the erroneous opinion that Hap would be drunk long before the evening was over. In fact, he was never seen to be drunk, which was just as well for he had a hair-trigger temper. The ten-inch razor-sharp bowie knife that Jack knew was concealed somewhere on him was always within reach and Hap was never reluctant to use it.

"Jack, my boy, haven't seen you in a coon's age!"

"Busy writing, Hap. Good news today, though—kinda made it all worthwhile. A big publisher wants to bring out a book of stories about my time in Alaska."

"Great news, Jack! Great news! Here, have a whisky on that." He gestured to one of the several bartenders, who though desperately busy always managed to see Hap's wave.

A glass of whisky appeared in front of Jack before he could protest. He decided to drink the one but no more. Hap raised his own glass and they both drank. Hap's gaze was on Jack. He was not cross-eyed but his eyes did not operate in unison. One eye would seem to be focused while the other roved around. What baffled strangers was that sometimes one eye roved and sometimes the other did. So far, no stranger had been reckless enough to ask about it.

Jack took a look up and down the bar. He lowered his head and Hap, always willing to chat, leaned toward him. "What's on your mind, son? I can see something's bothering you."

"That's what I came to talk to you about, Hap. Is anything bothering you?"

Hap thrived on conspiracies and suspected plots. He focused one eye on Jack and let the other trace rings around him. "You're up to it again, aren't you?" he said in a low voice.

"Yes, I am," Jack told him. "The trouble is, I don't know what I'm up to. There's trouble brewing here on the Coast and I don't know what it is. I can't find anybody who'll tell me. What do you know, Hap?"

Hap turned slowly and rested his back against the bar. His swiveling gaze crisscrossed the room, making sure that there was not a human ear within range. "I'm one of the founding members of the Saloon Owners Association," he said in that same low voice. "I know that Hanrahan approached you on our behalf. Whatever he told you, I know it wasn't much because we don't know much. That's what we want you to find out. I was the one who proposed you because I thought you were the right man for the job."

Jack digested this while he took another sip of whisky. He could think of no reason why Harrison would be keeping anything back. He tried a different angle. "Your gambling tables, Hap. If there's a plot brewing, that's where it seems to be centered. Have you noticed any changes there? New customers, strange behavior, unusual bets?"

The shows at the Cobweb Palace presented some high-level entertainment, but gambling remained a big source of income. The lower costs and the minimum of upkeep made it an important part of a saloon or music hall operation. The Cobweb Palace was not in the very top echelon of gambling locations, but it was high in the next ranking and Hap Harrison kept a close, if roving, eye on this aspect of his business.

He didn't answer immediately. He continued to watch the customers, their numbers swelling by the minute. Then he said, "Not much there, Jack. Tell you this, though—when we were talking about this at the association, one name came up more than once. A professor at Berkeley thinks he can break the banks—"

"O'Sullivan. I know him by sight. Is there any truth to his claims?"

"Not that any of us could figure out."

"But if he really has a system," said Jack, "why isn't he rich? Why hasn't he already broken you?"

"We've argued that out among us," said Hap. "Called in a few experts, even a couple of other mathematicians. Of course, none of us is going to admit to big losses, but I know I haven't had any and I'm pretty sure none of the other owners has."

"You must all watch this Sullivan closely when he comes in."

"Sure we do." Hap winked. "I've slipped a man into one of his games more than once, unknown to the professor.

Not one of 'em could spot what he was doing different. The other owners say the same."

"I still have a few friends out at Berkeley," said Jack. "I think I'll make some inquiries up there and see what they tell me about him."

Hap shrugged. "Try it, sure."

"Lucky Baldwin play here?" Jack asked.

"Haven't seen him in months."

"I hear he's still trying his luck."

"He can afford it," Hap grunted.

"One of the richest men in the state, they say."

"And still opening stock exchanges."

"Still?" Jack asked.

"He opens an exchange in any town that's in or near a gold strike. Owns dozens of them."

"So he's really involved with gold mining?"

"He sure is," Hap said. "Up to his eyebrows."

"What about robberies in the gambling saloons?"

"Only what you read about in the *Chronicle*," said Hap.

"It's the ones I don't read about there," Jack replied. "Come on, Hap, we both know they don't all get reported."

"Hasn't been any of those for a while."

"What's wrong with our thieves?" Jack wanted to know. "They used to be the best in the country."

Hap chuckled. "Maybe they got so rich they don't need to rob saloons anymore."

"Then they'd come in here to spend it and you'd get it all back."

Hap turned back to the bar. "Another whisky, Jack?"

"No, thanks, Hap. Got a few more calls to make."

The Best Idea on Stockton Street was Jack's next stop. He knew that the owner, Mike Manston, spent little time there, relying on his younger brother to run it. Al Manston was not too bright but he was loyal to his brother and managed to see that the staff did not pocket more than a limited portion of the money that changed hands. The Best Idea had a lively show and Jack watched the last part of it. Afterward, he found Al Manston and talked to him briefly.

Al was bristly haired, slack mouthed and not particularly friendly. Mike had introduced Jack to him, but Jack's being a writer had immediately established a barrier that Jack did not even hope to break. The world of books was foreign to Al. He did not read them and was suspicious of any word that appeared in them. He listened now to Jack's carefully stated queries then shook his head. "Never trouble with gambling, not here. Sure, we have tables in the back, but they don't give us no trouble."

Jack doubted the veracity of that but wanted to keep the conversation on an amicable basis. "That's good to know," he said. "What I hear is that there's a fellow on the Coast with a system he says is going to break all the banks in the city."

"The professor? He comes in here now and then. He hasn't broken us yet." Al tittered. "We have some rough characters in here. I don't think they'd take too kindly to the professor using a system on them."

Further careful questioning brought no additional information, and Jack moved on to the Imperial, where it was known that big-time gamblers often went. But he was no more fortunate there. Again, the professor had gambled there on occasion but had neither won nor lost any significant amount of money, despite the well-known story about his system.

It was the early hours of the morning and Jack had learned little. The pattern was consistent and he decided that tomorrow he would have to employ a different technique.

He went out of the Imperial onto the busy sidewalk, and when the attack came, it was completely unexpected.

Chapter 10

A quartet of businessmen were walking by, trying not to look conspicuous to the point where they would be espied as easy marks. A man and a woman were talking loudly in Midwestern accents, comparing San Francisco unfavorably to Chicago. A lone man, who looked like a newspaper reporter from back East, was examining the saloon fronts intently. Half a dozen college boys were disagreeing over which saloon to go into and two drunks were in a loud argument that consisted mostly of calling each other disparaging names.

The other pedestrians were avoiding the two drunks, and Jack had the same intention until one of the drunks pushed the other. He staggered into Jack, who tried to fend him off, but the man's hands were on him. The two of them tottered in the direction of the second drunk, and it was the firm grip of the man's hands that caused Jack to realize their drunkenness was an act.

The three of them stumbled against the wall. One man held Jack while the other pummeled him. The blows were not aimed at critical targets, the intent simply to cause pain. One jab below the belt sent an agonizing wave through Jack's stomach, and a blow to the throat almost cut off his breathing. He struggled to pull away but the grip on him was strong. Jack tried to call for help even as the comprehension came that they must look like three drunks in a fight and no help could be expected.

Jack almost got his right arm free but the hold tightened. In desperation, he kicked out with one heavy seaman's boot and an anguished gasp was his reward. But the man holding him renewed his grip and more blows rained on Jack's body. Both men shouted imprecations, maintaining the picture of three drunks tussling. A well-dressed man gave them a contemptuous look and sidestepped them.

A piercing lance of fire seemed to penetrate Jack's ribs, and as he caught sight of a metallic gleam streaking toward him, he knew that the man doing the punching wore a set of brass knuckles.

Jack was less concerned with being able to study his attackers than with evading the hail of blows, but he had a fleeting yet clear glimpse of the man holding him. He had a bullet-shaped head and hair cropped very short. He was not tall but he had arms long enough to be out of proportion to his body. These made him ideally suited to his task of restraining Jack. He yelled another curse and Jack thought he detected a German accent.

The man punching was stocky and muscled. Eyes glared out of a dark face. He looked to have Latin origins and had probably been a bare-knuckle prizefighter.

The brass knuckles came at Jack again. They would have hit him on the side of the face but he was able to parry with his forearm. The impact left the muscle temporarily numb. Another blow came, a kidney punch, but Jack twisted away despite the hands holding him, and the power of the punch was lost.

The long-armed man moved in for a tighter, closer grip and Jack punished him with an unexpected elbow jab that made him grunt loudly. The stocky Latino shifted his position, shouted a curse and came boring in at Jack. He raised the brass knuckles to shoulder height but his intentions were too obvious, and Jack drove home a long straight left deep into the other's midriff.

The man gasped and doubled over, and Jack took advantage of now being man to man with the holder. He turned on the man and, in spite of his grip, drove his knee low and hard into the other's groin. The man moaned and his grip weakened. Jack tore one arm loose and threw jabbing punches at his face just as hands closed around his neck from behind.

The long-armed man staggered back from him, blood streaming from his nose, and Jack bent forward, pulling the Latin man behind him close. Jack relaxed completely and fell backward, his body weight full on the man beneath him.

It was the second time the attacker had had all the air forced out of his lungs, but he recovered remarkably quickly. The two rolled away from one another, both determined to gain a brief respite. To Jack's amazement, the long-armed man, trying to stem the blood flow from his nose, did not resume the attack, but muttered something to the other that Jack did not catch. The Latino snarled as he climbed to his feet. "This was just a warning! Mind your own business!" he hissed.

The two of them melted into the flow of pedestrians while Jack regained his breath from the fall and rubbed his still-aching ribs. He received one or two glances from passersby but the sight of men fighting or drunk or both was common enough. He stood for a few minutes, feeling his pulse return to normal, massaging his sore neck.

He must have been followed as he had gone from music hall to music hall. Someone resented his investigation, obviously. Well, Jack thought ruefully, they must think I know more than I do. Or perhaps it was more likely that someone was afraid of what he might find out. That must mean he was close. Heartened by the thought, he headed back home, tempted to stop for a couple of medicinal whiskies but determinedly resisting. He needed all of his wits about him—both to figure out the danger threatening the saloons and to avoid a more lethal attack the next time.

Jack woke at five o'clock the next morning and groaned as he turned over and pain surged through his chest. The bruised ribs protested as he climbed out of bed and his neck was sore as he tried to turn his head. Both pains subsided as he ate a light breakfast and were mere discomfort by the time he settled down in front of the typewriter.

He concentrated on finishing his tale of the old blind Indian. Not satisfied with the way he had ended the story, he wrote it over again. Then he spent some time reading through his Alaskan stories, for he wanted to make sure that those he sent to Houghton Mifflin for inclusion in the book were as good as they could be. Early in the afternoon, he completed the work and headed north out of Oakland.

The University of California at Berkeley was only a short bicycle ride away, and as he reached the stately buildings, Jack could see new structures rising. Large signs indicated the departments of agriculture and engineering, the first in an ambitious enlargement scheme.

He was not sure who to talk to for information. His closest friends were both gone. Fred Jacobs had died the previous year on board a transport ship bound for Manila, where the Spanish-American War was being fought. James Wright had just graduated, and Jack knew only that he had left the city.

David Starr Jordan was still a prominent member of the staff, but Jack felt that he would be reluctant to say anything about a fellow faculty member. Frederick Ward Putnam was becoming renowned in the field of anthropology and Jacques Loeb was surely rising to a similar eminence in biology. Jack had a temporary pang of regret that he had not spent more time in the classes conducted by Thorstein Veblen, who was now becoming acknowledged as a prominent economist. Still, Jack realized that he had not at that time become so passionately interested in socialism and Veblen's classes had held little attraction for him.

Jack parked his bicycle and went into the administration building. He did not see a single face he recognized, but a board showing schedules of classes caught his eye. He walked over and studied it. He found the name of Andrew O'Sullivan, but to his surprise, the classes he was listed to teach were in geology. He approached a young girl behind one of the desks.

"I thought Professor O'Sullivan taught mathematics," he said. "The board shows he's giving classes in geology."

"He teaches both," said the girl with a smile. "Geology is his principal subject, though."

Jack looked the board over and stopped at the name of Ezra James. He said to the girl, "Ezra James was a trainee teacher when I was here. I see he's teaching English lit now."

"Oh yes." The girl smiled. "He's one of our most popular teachers. He has a class starting in about an hour. Would you like to sit in on it?"

"I'm a former student here," Jack said. "I knew Ezra. Perhaps I can have a few words with him before his class starts."

"I'm sure you can. Do you know where room twenty-seven is?"

Jack did, and when he reached it, a man only a few years older than he sat alone, poring over papers. He had curly golden hair and looked like an actor, but Jack knew he had aspirations toward becoming a writer. He frowned as he saw Jack approaching him.

"We were in classes together," he said. "You wrote a story that I really admired. . . . Jack London! Now I remember! I've seen your name in the magazines, haven't I? *McClures, Overland Monthly*—you're beginning to get a reputation."

Jack was pleased, not only at the recognition, but he felt that this might make his task easier. They talked about classes they had shared and Ezra confided that he was still having trouble getting stories accepted. "But you're doing great. Those stories of yours set in the wilderness are really gripping."

"Houghton Mifflin wants to publish a book of my Alaskan stories," Jack told him.

"That's wonderful, Jack! I'm truly glad for you."

Ezra had always been full of praise for Jack's work and was genuinely pleased at the success of others in the class, Jack recalled. They discussed their classmates, and Ezra mentioned two or three who he thought had promise but had not yet been able to break into print.

"It's a hard business," Ezra admitted. "Magazine editors are a tough breed and it's not easy to figure out what they want. I don't think you've done that, though. You haven't sent them what they want—you've sent them what you want to write. You've found a way to communicate the harsh, bitter reality of the North and the rough-hewn characters who have learned to survive there. You have shown how man can be puny, cowardly, insignificant, but also how he can still become great."

Jack did not conceal his pleasure at Ezra's analysis of his writing. He was surprised and pleased that his fellow student, now a teacher, understood as clearly as he did just what Jack was trying for. But he had not forgotten why he had come here to the campus and he pushed the praise aside.

"You have a lot of new teachers here since my day," Jack said.

"Yes, we do," said Ezra, "and the campus is growing rapidly."

"I saw the new buildings," Jack said. "Engineering must be a popular subject."

"It is," Ezra agreed. "Mr. Herbert Hoover has made it an exciting field of endeavor."

"Geology must be growing along with it," Jack said. "I hear you have a great teacher, fellow called O'Sullivan."

Ezra nodded less than enthusiastically.

"There's another fellow by the name of O'Sullivan," Jack added. "A mathematician, ran into him the other day."

"It's the same man," said Ezra.

"It is?" asked Jack. "But this mathematician says he has a system for winning at the gambling tables. Can't be the same man."

"It is. The authorities here don't like the gambling association, of course, but he still teaches some math classes. He is a good teacher of geology, though."

"Two dissimilar subjects, surely."

"Yes. Geology is O'Sullivan's first subject though. He

worked in a mine for some time and has a first-rate knowledge of the practical side of mining as well as the theory."

"I did some mining myself," admitted Jack. "Up in the Klondike. I wasn't very successful, though. Still," he added, "that was different. That was gold mining."

"The mine O'Sullivan worked was a gold mine," Ezra told him.

"Really? Where was it?"

"Somewhere here in California—don't know just where."

Jack kept the conversation going, but Ezra had nothing further to contribute except that Professor O'Sullivan was not popular with his colleagues and had no friends on campus.

On his ride back to Oakland, Jack was able to think over what he had learned. O'Sullivan had not only worked in a mine, but it had been a gold mine. Did that have some connection with the gold mine where the unfortunate Sam Hooper had worked? Hooper had known too much and had been murdered. How much did O'Sullivan know?

So many questions . . . Fortunately, Jack knew one reliable source of answers. It was time to visit Ambrose Bierce.

Chapter 11

The renowned editor saw Jack's reflection in the long mirror behind the polished mahogany bar with its brass foot rail. Luna's was located on the boundary of the notorious Devil's Acre, but was unique in having no actual address. It thrived on its racy location but managed to retain its relatively sedate atmosphere and resembled a fashionable men's club more than anything else.

Jack walked past the potted palms and the dark wood-paneled walls with their photographs of the famous. He took a bar stool alongside Bierce, who was nearly sixty years old but looked much younger. Bierce's thick hair, ample mustache and bushy eyebrows were fair and added to his youthful appearance.

One of Luna's more renowned clients, Bierce was editor of the Hearst-owned *San Francisco Examiner.* His sarcastic, bitter and often-cruel command of language was a delight to his regular readers and a terror to those whom he pilloried in his daily column. Among the latter were the Big Three—Collis P. Huntington, Fred Crocker and Leland Stanford—whose malevolent influence he saw behind every scheme and plot in California.

"Ah, my young friend!" Bierce greeted him. "You have managed to spare some time from those violent and anguished stories of the frozen North to visit the sybaritic haunts of us scribes who prefer the softer, more comfortable venues of civilized society. How about a Sazerac?" He raised his own nearly empty glass and the attentive bartender came near.

"Another, Mr. Bierce? And the same for your friend?"

"A schooner of beer for me," Jack said.

"Yes, I'll have another Sazerac," said Bierce. "Let me see now, a schooner of beer . . . You must have sold one of those brutal scribblings of yours. You're not getting a lot of money for it or you'd be drinking scotch, but you're ardent in your desire to write about the snow and the mountains, the suffering and the passion, so you're not ordering a small beer, you're having a schooner. Tell me, am I right?"

The relationship between Jack and "the unspeakable Ambrose," as his enemies called him, was a strange one. Bierce was not averse to claiming credit for Jack's progress as a writer, though Jack was not aware of receiving much help or encouragement from Bierce, who was always more critical than complimentary.

Jack respected the editor's opinions and was ever willing to take advantage of the other's comprehensive knowledge and extensive contacts. He now proposed to do just that. He grinned. "I never could fool you, Ambrose. Yes, you're close. Houghton Mifflin wants to publish a book containing my Alaskan stories."

Bierce nodded, satisfied. Jack couldn't tell if the satisfaction was because of Jack's success or his own shrewdness. "You know, Jack," Bierce went on, "American fiction is going through a weak and fluffy period. It may well be due for some of your anger and red-blooded realism. Your timing for making the break from magazines into books is probably right."

The bartender brought Bierce's Sazerac and Jack's beer. On the bar were large bowls of frogs' legs, pickled squid and oysters, and fried shrimp. Jack took a handful of shrimp. They were heavily salted and caused Jack to take a large swallow of beer, as they were supposed to do.

Jack said, "I know the soft and fluffy writers you're referring to. Stanley Weyman and George Barr McCutcheon are the two who come to mind most immediately. They prettify. They evade. They throw a spurious veil of romance over their characters. They avoid anything that cuts deep.

They are literary pygmies." Emboldened by his theme, he spoke more vehemently. "They have no originality, no writing philosophy, no true knowledge—"

"They must have something," Bierce said craftily. "They sell more words than you do."

"But the stuff they write is dead, Ambrose! No light, no life, no color shot through it. All they have is a formula for saccharine romanticism."

"Whereas you want to give readers truth?"

"That's a dangerous word to use in relation to writing, I know. But life is so strange and wonderful, filled with problems and dreams, to depict it accurately demands fevers and sweats, forlorn hopes, terrors, tragedies."

"Your friend Richard Harding Davis writes the same kind of fluff," Bierce said, never missing an opportunity of turning the screw. " 'Soldiers of Fortune,' 'Princess Aline.' "

"I don't know why you call him my friend," Jack said. "You introduced me to him."

"A better war correspondent than a writer of fiction," said Bierce, accompanying the words with another sip of Sazerac. "So you're still a fan of Kipling, I suppose."

"He touches the soul of things. He has opened new frontiers of the mind in literature." Jack took another mouthful of beer and swiveled his stool to face Bierce. "I shall always be grateful to you for introducing me to him."

"Poor Ruddy. I'm afraid we may not see him out here on the Coast again." Jack knew that Kipling had inflammation of the lungs. "He's very ill. He has periods of being well and apparently healthy; then the sickness will sweep over him and he has great difficulty in breathing. As you say, he has opened new vistas of writing fiction."

"I've also developed a fondness for John William Draper," Jack said. "For a professor of chemistry, he writes uncommonly well on history and philosophy."

"He's on a lecture circuit right now," Bierce said. "He may come out this way. If he does, I intend to invite him here and wheedle a column out of him. You may get the chance to meet him too." He eyed the younger man in the mirror. "On a more parochial level, what is that insatiable mind of yours probing now? Never mind McCutcheon's Graustark and Davis's Paris. Have you got your long nose into any matters involving San Francisco?"

Jack acknowledged that he could not hope to evade Bierce's incisive reasoning for long. Sooner or later, the editor would worm out of him the details of his latest investigation. Better to give him a little now . . .

"There's a rumor going around the Barbary Coast of some severe threat hanging over us," Jack said ruminatively. "Have you heard anything?"

"What kind of threat?"

"Nobody seems to know."

"So you've come to me."

"Who else?" said Jack. "You know more than any other person in San Francisco what's going on here."

Bierce gave him a wolfish grin. "Flattery is like cologne water—it's better smelt than swallowed."

"Is that one of your sayings?" Jack asked.

"It is now. So we're under a mysterious threat, are we?"

"Yes, and it's a very serious one. It may be responsible for two murders already."

Bierce straightened on his bar stool. He drained his glass and called for two more drinks. The bantering tone had gone from his voice when he replied, "It is a very serious threat in that case. Who are the victims? I must have reported them."

"Tom Tullamore at the Silver Dollar was the first one."

"He was mugged, wasn't he?"

"There was probably more behind it. That may have been a cover."

"And the second?"

"A miner called Sam Hooper."

"Killed for his gold?"

"Probably not."

Bierce viewed the full glass that the bartender put in front of him. Jack had not said he wanted another beer but one appeared on the bar.

"Hmm," Bierce said, and Jack waited for him to go on. "It's true that there are insubstantial rumors drifting about. Vague as smoke up to now. Seem to have some connection with the music halls." He glanced sideways at Jack. "I suppose that's why you're involved?"

Jack wanted to keep him going. "More specifically, their gambling operations."

Bierce nodded slowly. "That has been one of the associated notions."

"What's behind it, Ambrose?"

"I don't know—yet. But I've got my reporters going on their way with their ears wide open. Oh, one other thing. A famous lawman is here, probably to deal with this threat. He's about to take up his duties in the next day or so."

"Who is it?" Jack asked.

"I've heard whispers," Bierce said cautiously.

"It isn't Jim McParland, is it?"

"The head of the Pinks? I doubt it. He left San Francisco a while ago when his men didn't have any success with the dock strike." Bierce regarded Jack with one of his piercing looks, knowing that the young man had been deeply involved in that affair.

Jack knew that the Pinkerton failure made it unlikely that they had been recalled to deal with something as unclear as this. "So who else?"

"I believe we'll know tomorrow," said Bierce.

"I have to wait and read it in the *Examiner*?"

"Only because there's another involvement, one that's connected with it, and it will be made public tomorrow too."

Jack shook his head, mystified. "You're not much help, Ambrose."

"I'm right then? You're helping to investigate this threat?"

"Yes," Jack said.

Bierce nodded. "I can guess who hired you so you don't have to break any confidences."

"You're usually a good guesser," Jack said drily. "Tell me,

Ambrose, after tomorrow's revelation, will you be able to tell me more about this threat?"

Bierce shook his head decisively. "No, I won't, Jack. But the secrecy over this business is not of my making. Maybe if the lid comes off soon, we can exchange confidences over this threat—which I can assure you I'm taking seriously, little as I know about it."

"I suppose a few well-known people are behind it," Jack suggested. Both of them knew Jack was referring to Bierce's antagonism for the Big Three.

To Jack's surprise, Bierce shook his head. "I haven't heard of them being mixed up in this matter. Although," he added darkly, "it wouldn't surprise me if they were."

"Tell me, Ambrose, is gold mining still a lucrative enterprise? The sensational finds that we heard about in the Klondike overshadowed mining here in California. Is it still big here?"

"We don't hear as much about it but it's still big."

"I heard that Lucky Baldwin is still opening up exchanges in every town in or near a gold find."

"He's well named," growled Bierce. "He doesn't need to dig in the ground or even hire anybody who does. He makes a fortune from those exchanges."

"Then loses it at the gambling tables?"

Bierce nodded. "They say he does that. He keeps his wins and losses at the tables to himself, though."

"One other thing," Jack said. "I read your piece on the big fight coming up."

Bierce looked pleased with himself. "Yes, that really was a promotion. Did you hear the fight was sold out already?"

Jack groaned. "So soon? I was just going to ask you how I can get a ticket."

"Completely sold out," said Bierce. "However . . . I can use my influence and get you a good seat. I'll have the ticket sent to you."

"Thanks, Ambrose. You're a gem."

"I expect nothing in return—other than the full story on this mysterious threat and your undying gratitude."

"You'll be the first to know," Jack promised.

"There is one minor matter in which you might be of help, however. . . ."

"If I can."

"Someone is buying up newspapers. Have you heard anything that might shed some light?"

"No," Jack said. "You've taken a sharp look at your competitors, of course?"

"Naturally. It's not the *Call* or the *Chronicle*. The *Herald* doesn't have the money, and neither does the *Post*."

"The *Star*?" suggested Jack.

"Out of the question. They're a weekly and only interested in scandal and politics."

"Your two favorite topics."

Bierce chuckled. "I have ways—no, it's not the *Star*."

"Not *Our Mazeppa* or the *Sentinel*?"

Bierce grunted his disdain. *Our Mazeppa* printed only social gossip and the *Sentinel* was the official organ of the Christian Science movement.

"An out-of-town operation?" Jack offered.

"I've considered New York and Chicago. Both negative."

"How many have they bought so far?"

"None as yet, but several offers have been made. All to papers within a hundred miles of our fair city. All to small papers too."

"Don't the recipients of the offers tell you anything?"

"They have no clue as to the identity of the prospective buyer."

"Strange," Jack said.

"Very," Bierce agreed. "I didn't think it was the kind of knowledge likely to fall your way but you might stay alert. You can understand why I'm worried: I don't want the people of San Francisco believing anything unless it's what I tell them."

Jack laughed. "Not likely, Ambrose. You have them in the palm of your hand."

Chapter 12

Jack read the story from the morning edition, right through to the end, standing there near the newsstand. Then he read it again. The perfect candidate had refused—he had refereed all the fights he wanted, he said. Groom and Gibbs then told him what a great honor it would be for him to officiate in such a major event; whereupon he thought about it for a while, then said, "I don't know but what it will be a little tony to referee a fight of this kind. I think the two best men in the world are coming together right now." Then he accepted.

His name was Wyatt Earp.

The *Examiner* strove to support Earp's credentials by listing most of the thirty-five fights that he had refereed in the San Diego–Tijuana area. Naturally, no newspaper could present such an extraordinary story without reminding its readers who might have forgotten the details of who Wyatt Earp was.

Several lengthy paragraphs described how Deputy Marshal Wyatt Earp strode down the dusty streets of Tombstone, Arizona, at three o'clock on the afternoon of October 26, 1881, bent on arresting the Clanton brothers, Johnny Ringo and other members of a cattle-rustling gang.

The tale of the gunfight at the OK Corral followed, but Jack skimmed through that after he had studied the photograph of the stern-faced, mustached Wyatt Earp in the third column.

It was a face he recognized. It was the face of the Westerner who had been present when Captain Krasner had interrogated Jack after he had found the body of Sam Hooper.

Jack headed to the ferry, his mind whirling. The famous Western marshal, Wyatt Earp, might be refereeing the big fight, but that was not his only purpose here in San Francisco. Before he had accepted the refereeing assignment, he had been permitted by the police to attend the scene of a murder investigation.

Was it just a courtesy, allowing a visiting lawman such a liberty? It did not seem likely, nor did Earp seem the kind of marshal who would enjoy seeing a dead body. He had seen dozens, many of them the victims of his own Colt revolver.

What had Earp said when he had entered Hooper's room? Jack reached into his memory—"I was told I should come along." That sounded like a direct connection with the police. True, he had not asked any questions, but he had looked over the room as thoroughly as human eyes could. Then there were the words of Shanghai Hanrahan, who had said that an expert lawman had been called in to help the police. Finally, Bierce's admissions had been confirmation.

Jack mulled over the implications of all this as he rode the ferry to the Barbary Coast. A light drizzle was falling, encouraged by damp air drifting in from the bay. The weather seldom affected the crowds and tonight was no different. The bright-colored lights of the bazaar fronts glowed more brilliantly in the moist air, the Italian balloon sellers were out waving their clusters of balloons and a sidewalk organist performed with a monkey in a red and gold vest. Men with wing collars and big mustaches were passing out dodgers advertising music halls and restaurants, while drummers were hawking stomach remedies and barkers yelled invitations to palm reading and tarot card predictions.

This was the city Jack loved and he turned onto Pacific Street and made his way through the crowds to the Silver Dollar. His intention was to have another look at the gambling tables and see if he spotted something he might have missed on that fateful night he had accompanied Tom Tullamore.

To his amazement, there behind the bar was Tess Tullamore. Her lustrous dark hair was piled high on top of her head and she wore a tight black gown of some shiny material. Black was an appropriate widow's color, Jack thought, but the cut, low over the breasts and raising them noticeably, was more suited to the Silver Dollar. The rouge on her cheeks, the bright red lips and the eye makeup were also befitting a saloon.

The red lips smiled at Jack. Was it a mocking smile? He wasn't sure; perhaps it was just amusement at his obvious surprise. He went up to the bar. "How about a whisky on the house?" she asked. Her voice sounded huskier than it had in Tiburon.

He nodded and she poured him a large sour mash. Replacing the bottle, she said in a voice nearer to the one he remembered, "Not what you expected, I suppose. Well, after going through Tom's papers, I decided that if I didn't take control this place was going to be a liability. I came in and right away found I really enjoyed it. Besides, it's better than staying home and brooding."

She was an extraordinary woman, Jack thought. "You look great," he told her, wanting to compliment and encourage her but not wanting to sound too personal. He looked around the room, which was noisy, bustling and almost full. "And you seem to be doing fine."

She nodded, pleased. "A lot of people have come in just out of pity. I don't want that, I want to build the place up again, make it a real success."

"All the staff have stayed on, have they?"

"Yes. They've been wonderful."

"I remember you said you would have liked to be more active here," Jack reminded her, tasting the sour mash.

"And now I am." She smiled but it faded quickly. "Poor Sam Hooper, though. The police came and asked me about him, told me he was dead."

"I found him," Jack said, and her face clouded.

"How awful for you!"

"What did the police ask?"

"What I knew about him. I told them I knew nothing. Tom had mentioned his name but I had never met him."

"What else did they ask?"

"Not very much. They could see I couldn't help them. But there is something I haven't told them."

"Go on," urged Jack.

"A man came in this morning. Said he'd heard about Tom and that I was here running the place now. Said he was a friend of Sam's and wanted to know if I had found something of his or Sam's among Tom's belongings. I told him I hadn't as far as I knew. He asked me to look again and I asked him what I was looking for. He didn't seem to want to tell me."

"And what's his name?"

"Magnus Swenson. He has a Swedish accent but speaks English well. He's about forty years old and has fair hair. Said he was a miner and worked with Sam."

"Have you found anything?"

"I haven't looked yet. I've been so busy here. This man Swenson said he would be in tomorrow night about ten. I'll have a look through the house and see what I can find."

"Are you going to tell the police?"

"If they come again, yes. I have the feeling they're not trying very hard."

It was not an uncommon complaint on the Barbary Coast, with its sky-high crime rate.

"Can you be here tomorrow night?" Tess asked.

"At ten, yes, all right."

Her eyes searched Jack's face. "Have you been able to learn anything?"

"A number of people in the city are concerned about this threat," Jack said, choosing his words carefully. "But no one knows much about it. I'm still looking for leads."

"I hope you'll tell me if you find out what it's all about."

"I will," Jack promised.

"You'll be able to find me here," she told him and her voice took on that husky quality again. "You won't have to come out to Tiburon—although you will be very welcome if you should come."

Jack nodded acceptance of the invitation as he sipped the whisky. He was aware even more than he had been the first time he'd met her that she was a very attractive woman.

"I asked you to help me when you came to Tiburon before, now I am going to ask you to help me again." Her eyes sought and held his.

"If I can."

She leaned forward against the bar. Her voice was low. "I was talking to Martin Beck yesterday. He is going to bring Lillian Russell here."

"Martin Beck, the Broadway impresario? Bringing Lillian Russell here to San Francisco?"

"Here to San Francisco, yes, but also here to the Silver Dollar."

Jack absorbed this remarkable news as he emptied his glass. The widow promptly refilled it.

"She—she must be expensive," Jack said, then regretted the naivete of the remark as soon as it left his mouth.

"She is, but she could be the saving of this place. The Silver Dollar could be right up there among the top entertainment spots on the Barbary Coast once a celebrity like her appears here."

"She's a strong proponent of women's rights," Jack said, "so she would be very sympathetic to your cause. That might help persuade her to come here."

"That's what Martin said."

So it was Martin already. Jack had to admire the courage and spirit of the widow. She knew how to make use of her attributes to get what she wanted.

"But you said you wanted my help," he said. "What can I do?"

"I understand that you are a friend of Little Egypt, as she used to be known."

"That's true."

"Martin says that Lillian Russell is very choosy when it comes to her chorus support. He also says that Little Egypt is the best teacher of chorus girls in the country. Now if you could persuade her to help me. . . ."

"I see," said Jack.

"Another whisky?"

"No, thanks. I have a few more visits to make tonight. Well, I'll speak to Flo, see if she can do it. She has a busy schedule at the Midway, but she might be willing to help you out."

The widow leaned closer. It might have been because the noise level in the Silver Dollar was rising. "I would be very grateful to you if she would."

"Before I go," Jack said, "I'd like to look around upstairs. When I saw Tom that night, he took me up there. I'm sure he was going to tell me something relating to gambling. I'd like to wander around and see if I spot any connection."

"Of course," Tess said. "You'll be unobtrusive, I know."

Jack left and went upstairs, wondering if he had gotten himself into a situation that might require very careful handling.

The faces were all different at the gambling tables. Neither Lucky Baldwin nor Professor O'Sullivan was there, and the city council and Crocker Bank were without representation. Jack recognized one of the leaders of the longshoremen's union and a ship's captain who was well known as a gambler.

He watched the games from a distance, not standing in any one place very long. A lot of money was changing hands on all of the tables, but none of the games was overheated and the atmosphere at each was reasonably genial. That was a factor that could change without warning, as Jack well knew, but right now an occasional smile and an exchanged word kept the proceedings cordial.

Jack found it difficult to assess the security precautions. There was little visual evidence of any, but Jack knew that they were well concealed. He could ask the widow for details but decided against doing that tonight. It was an aspect worth evaluating at the other gambling places, though.

He went on to the Alcazar and the Haymarket. Activity was not any greater at these. Plenty of money was moving from pocket to pocket but no one was getting steamed up about it. Security was not obvious at either of these but Jack had no doubt it was there. He studied exits, stairways, hidden locations for observers and weapons, and he was obliged to conclude that these places were well protected and discreet about it.

He realized he'd need to be discreet himself to get anywhere in this investigation.

Chapter 13

At the Midway later that night, many of the crowd were leaving as Jack entered. Flo listened with her customary equanimity to Jack's account of the widow Tullamore's ambitions for reviving the fortunes of the Silver Dollar, until Jack told her the name of the Broadway star who was to commence this revival. Her eyes widened.

"Lillian Russell! She's aiming high, isn't she?"

"I suppose she wants to start off with as big a name as she can get," Jack said.

"I'm surprised Martin Beck has agreed to bring Lillian Russell here. Still," said Flo, "she comes once or twice a year, and the last visit was January, so that's almost a year. Maybe she was due and Beck hadn't booked her yet."

They sat at a table in the emptying Midway. The last show had concluded and many patrons were leaving, but the late drinkers were still there and some gamblers continued, oblivious to the clock.

"She's expensive too," Flo said. "If the Silver Dollar is in such a bad way, where is she getting the money to pay for Lillian Russell? She probably gets a thousand dollars a week."

Jack whistled. "That much?"

Flo gave Jack a pitying look. "Star of Broadway? Beautiful, good actress and singer? One of the leaders of the rights for women movement, which keeps her in the headlines? Yes, she can demand that much. Mind you, that's usually for a run of ten weeks. It will be a shorter run here."

"Still, she'll bring in big crowds, won't she?" Jack approached his point gingerly.

"She packs the place wherever she goes."

"She, er, mentioned one other thing. She'd like to have you train a chorus for her."

Flo flashed him a look. "She would, would she? And this is the way she does it, using you to ask me because—"

"No, no," said Jack, extemporizing quickly. "She said she had heard from Martin Beck that you were the best trainer of choruses in the States. She hoped you would be available and I said I'd mention it."

Flo looked at him sternly. His candid blue eyes were round and ingenuous. Jack produced his clincher. "You're probably familiar with Lillian Russell's act anyway, so it would be easy for you."

"I've never done a show with her," Flo said.

"No?" Jack put on a look of surprise.

"No."

"Then it would be a real feather in your cap to do this one?"

"Yes," said Flo. She examined Jack's face; then she smiled. "I'll talk to her. I can get enough time off here to do it. Fritz is very understanding."

"Good," Jack said, releasing his breath slowly. That had gone more smoothly than he had expected.

"She's a very good-looking woman, isn't she?"

"Yes, I suppose she is. Still showing signs of the stress of Tom's death, though."

"So she's running the Silver Dollar now?"

"Yes."

"She'll make a good job of it," said Flo.

"With your help, she should do very well," Jack said, congratulating himself. He felt that he had improved in his ability to handle Flo.

The next day was a productive one. Still fired with enthusiasm at the prospects of the book to be published by Houghton Mifflin, Jack went through each of his stories of the Yukon that had already been published. He made revisions and improvements, some of which allowed him opportunities to expand on a theme. This was a luxury he could not indulge in when submitting to magazines, which always had word-count limitations.

Then he went through his files and selected stories that he felt were of publishable quality but had been rejected by one or more magazines. With the knowledge that a major publishing house thought his stories good enough to put into a book, he was going through the rejections and preparing to send them out again.

Some needed rewrites, some did not. He prepared several of the latter for immediate submission and made notes on the work necessary to improve the others. It was a task that he would normally have shunned or at least delayed, but filled with the conviction of beckoning success, he tackled it energetically.

In the evening, he headed first for Molly's Melodeon. The gambling tables were active already, piled with coins and notes. Players wore tense expressions on their faces amid dense clouds of tobacco smoke. Jack watched from a judicious distance but nobody paid him any attention. The players were mostly out-of-towners, though he recognized the assistant to the head of the city planning commission and the son of a prominent shipping line owner. Once again, he could see no security measures.

Jack's second stop, the El Dorado, was not a familiar haunt. He did not go there often, as gambling was the main business and he was not a gambler. The El Dorado had started as a canvas tent, catering to the forty-niners coming back from the California gold dust or nuggets. At first, the tent had been the point of exchange; then, within a year, a large square hall of rough-cut wood had sprung up.

The exterior was still primitive but inside the place was a forty-niner's dream castle. The furniture was baroquely elegant. A dozen large chandeliers hung from the ceiling and the mirrors behind the bar were of the finest cut glass. Curtained booths were available for gentlemen to take the pretty waiter girls to between games of faro and roulette, and the walls were covered with oil paintings of nudes.

The El Dorado had a wheezy melodeon as well as occasional live performers, but the gambling upstairs was the attraction here. On the bar was a scale for weighing the gold, and one man had the responsibility of overseeing it. Its use had declined with the drop in gold output from the California mines, but the miners returning from the Klondike had revived its use a little.

The owner of the El Dorado, Josh Klein, said he kept the scale for sentimental reasons, but Jack knew he had a more commercially based motive. A pinch of gold dust, the amount that could be raised between forefinger and thumb, had been the price of a shot of whisky, a practice that originated the expression "How much can you raise in a pinch?" The scale sat on a square of carpet, and Jack knew that the material had a thick pile. The few grains spilled in each weighing operation mounted to a considerable total by the end of each night's gambling.

The scale looked forlorn for lack of use, for on the tables were mainly silver dollars, five-dollar coins and ten-dollar gold eagles, as well as paper money. The coins gleamed and glittered on the green baize tabletops. Here, security was evident, perhaps out of a belief that it might act as a deterrent. There were two tough-looking guards, each of them lounging inside one of the two doors. Pistols hung close to their right hands and both men looked capable of using them without compunction. Other measures were surely in force too, but Jack could not see what they might be.

Most miners played faro, most cowboys played poker. Both games were in progress tonight. Faro (the name derived from the image of a pharaoh that was on the back of most packs of cards) was believed to be foolproof against manipulation and give the player an even chance, but Jack knew better. He watched one table where a faro game was being played. After shuffling and cutting a deck, the dealer placed the cards in a box. Such boxes traditionally had a tiger painted on the lid, giving rise to the term "bucking the tiger," meaning betting against the faro bank.

The players were drawing cards from a slit in the box, in pairs, faceup. Every pair drawn was a turn. Every card from ace to king was painted on the table on a wax cloth called a layout. Players had placed their bets in the form of gold or coins on the card of their choice. If the card a man bet on was drawn first, he lost. If it came up second, he won. If neither, he could bet again. The dealer was raking in the bets and Jack was watching as he became aware that a man had entered the room and was standing near him. He turned to look at the man.

Tall and lean, he was dressed in Western clothes. Jack recognized Wyatt Earp.

Earp took a couple of steps forward to stand beside Jack. The players paid them no attention, intent on their game. The dealer threw them a look but continued his duties. One of the guards by the nearest door was watching them but without any change in expression.

"Howdy," said Earp, his voice low. "Last time we met was over a dead body."

"That's right. Since then, I hear you got a new job," Jack said. "Referee, isn't it?"

Earp grinned faintly. The grin did not look as if it appeared very often on the usually stern face.

"Kinda talked me into it." He nodded toward the faro table they had both been watching. "Used to be a faro dealer myself. Glad I gave it up."

He was soft-spoken, but Jack noted that Earp's steely-blue eyes were steady and alert. His Western garb had not seen much recent riding across the range, though it was no doubt authentic enough. The boots and the belt were shiny and new.

"Maybe you and I should have a talk," Earp said conversationally. "I have a feeling we might both be looking for the same path, and it would be a shame if we collided with each other looking for it."

"Fine with me," Jack agreed.

"Let's go downstairs."

The guard gave them an impassive look as they left, probably registering their nonparticipation in any of the games.

Earp found a table near one wall. It was empty because of its location, which gave it a poor view of the stage, but it was ideal for a quiet conversation. The melodeon, wheezing out tunes from *The Belle of New York*, could be relied upon to drown out any words before they reached another table.

A pretty waiter girl approached them. Earp ordered a whisky and Jack a schooner of beer. "Bring us a pack of cards too," Earp ordered. Neither spoke until the drinks and the cards came. Earp tore open the wrapper and spread cards on the table. "Make it look like we're playing a nice friendly game," he explained to Jack.

Jack nodded. "I'm looking forward to the fight tomorrow night," he said. "Managed to get a ticket." He hadn't, but Bierce was always as good as his word and Jack had no doubt that a ticket would arrive in time.

"Not sure I am," said Earp. "But I said I'd do it and I will. Be quite an event anyhow. You folks here in San Francisco never cease to amaze me—you know that?"

"In what way?" Jack asked.

"Allowing women in to a fight like this. Never heard of that, not anywhere," Earp grumbled.

"Think it'll make your job tougher?"

Earp shrugged. "Guess not. I'll be too busy watching the two in the ring. Job's tough enough already. Martin Julian, Fitzsimmons's manager, is dead against me for a start."

"Why is that?"

"Because Sharkey's people okayed me. Don't know any other reason."

"Nothing they can do about it now, is there?"

"Not hardly. Athletic Club's sticking with me, so I'm stuck with the job."

"The *Examiner*'s behind you. That's a help," Jack said.

"Guess so. Anyhow, about this other business . . ."

"Which other business is that?" Jack asked innocently.

"The business that caused you and me to be in the same room as a dead body—a recently dead body."

"I agree that it's a good idea for us to figure out how to keep out of each other's way," Jack said, determined not to let Earp's reputation overawe him. "But first, I'd like to know just what your position is."

"Me too, regarding yours," Earp said amiably.

They exchanged grins. There was a pause as each waited for the other. Earp broke the deadlock as, in his deceptively lazy voice, he said, "Captain Morley spoke well of you, so that explains why you were hired."

Jack had worked with Captain Morley when a scheme to break the strike paralyzing San Francisco Harbor had spread to where it endangered all Chinatown. "You know who hired me?"

"Didn't know anybody did, but I guess you just told me somebody done so. And as you were talking to Tullamore just before he disappeared, he probably wanted to. Then you were seen talking to Shanghai Hanrahan the next day, and everybody knows he's boss of the Saloon Owners Association. So, you see, it's not hard to jump to a conclusion, is it?"

"Pity Morley isn't on this case," Jack said idly.

"Find Krasner sharp at the edges? Yeah, me too." Earp absently swept up the cards and shuffled them again.

Meanwhile Jack was reassessing the famous lawman. He had a reputation as a United States marshal, a gunfighter and a frontier legend. Now there seemed to be a lot more to his character than that. He had a brain too. Jack made his decision quickly. "Whatever job I may be doing, I've been told to keep it confidential. But I'm not going to argue with anything you've said."

Earp pushed cards in front of Jack from those in his hand, then more in front of himself and laid down the deck. It was a purely routine action by a man who was renowned as a gambler too. He nodded as if satisfied.

"Now it's your turn," Jack invited.

Earp glanced casually around them. No one was in

earshot and the melodeon gasped its way into a selection of tunes by Gilbert and Sullivan. Earp said nothing as the strains of "I'm the Lord High Executioner" echoed through the room. His head moved minutely with the beat.

"Always did like that song," he said and Jack tried unsuccessfully to erase an image from his mind of the OK Corral and bodies falling to the dusty ground while gunfire resonated through the main street of Tombstone.

"Reason I came here to San Francisco," Earp went on as the melodeon moved on to "Three Little Girls from School," "was on account of Butch Cassidy and the Sundance Kid."

His face, weathered by sun and wind, was nut brown. Jack stared at it, puzzled. Earp continued. "The Denver stage was robbed and two witnesses aboard it swore that they recognized Butch and Sundance. Wells Fargo lost a lot of money that day and set out to get it back. Among the reports that came in—helped by promises of reward money—was one from Salt Lake and another from Nevada. These suggested that Butch and Sundance were heading for San Francisco."

"Outlaws on the run often come here," Jack said. "The Barbary Coast is an easy place to hide."

Earp nodded. "Yup. But I guess Butch and Sundance didn't come here after all. So while I was kicking my heels, a man I knew, an ex-marshal now in the state government, heard I was here and asked me to get involved in this threat to San Francisco. I guess you know as much as I do from here on—except to say that when I was approached to do this refereeing, it seemed like a good excuse to be still in town."

"I know very little about that threat, I'm afraid," Jack said. "But it's good we understand each other. I'm often in the Midway Plaisance. A message there will always reach me."

"I'm at the Regency Hotel. It's a little more pricey than I like, but some property I had in San Diego just sold, so I'm feeling a little flush."

They finished their drinks. "I may go back upstairs and see how much action there is," said Earp.

"I'm going to the Silver Dollar," said Jack. "Have to meet a man."

They parted with a handshake.

Chapter 14

The Silver Dollar was having a fairly profitable night, even though the fabled Lillian Russell had not yet arrived. Perhaps the word of her coming had spread already.

It was still a few minutes before ten o'clock. Jack could see the lustrous dark hair of Tess Tullamore behind the bar as he moved through the crowd, and Tess gave him a smile as he approached. "Whisky?" she asked.

"A beer," Jack said.

"Schooner?"

"No, just a glass."

By ten-thirty, Tess was bringing Jack another beer. She looked up and down the bar and shook her head. By eleven o'clock, she was still shaking her head, and Jack accepted another beer. As the time neared midnight, Tess came down the bar.

"Looks like he's found a better place," she said.

"Swedes are usually pretty reliable," Jack said. "He wanted you to see if there wasn't some possession of Sam Hooper's among Tom's things. Did you find anything that might be his?"

"I had a small box brought in. It's in the office. It has a few things in it that I didn't recognize. Could have been Tom's, could have been Sam's or this fellow's—I don't know. Want to see it?"

She took Jack behind the bar and they went into a small office. Jack had not been in there before but he doubted if Tom Tullamore had kept it as neat as this.

"Did you have to do a lot of work in here?" he asked.

She nodded. From a shelf she took a cardboard box and put it on the newly cleared desk. Jack looked through the items in it. Tess reached in and took out what looked like a cylinder of thin, pliable rubber with an elastic string attached to it. "What the deuce is this?"

Jack took it and smiled. "Cardsharps use these. It fits up the sleeve of a jacket. The string is rigged so that it shoots a card into the hand."

He picked up some ivory dice, four of them. He examined them carefully. Two were very slightly more yellowed than the others. He weighed them in his hand for a moment. He pushed the box aside and rolled the two yellowed dice on the desktop. They came up a five and a two. He rolled them again. Five and two.

Tess was watching with puzzled surprise. Jack set them aside and took the other two dice. He shook and rolled them. A four and a three. He rolled them again and once more they came up a four and a three.

"They're loaded," Tess said in disapproval.

"They sure are."

"Tom wouldn't use loaded dice."

"My guess is that he took them from someone who had no such scruples," Jack said.

"There's some money," Tess said, picking up a few coins.

A pack of playing cards had a design showing endlessly twisting green vines. "Manufactured by E. M. Grandine of Liberty Street in New York City," Jack said. "Never play in a game where that company made the cards."

Tess picked up several cards and examined the faces. "They look all right to me." She turned them over and studied the backs. "What's wrong with them?"

"They're marked."

She looked closer at the backs. "How? They're all the same."

"They're supposed to look that way. Look very closely. You'll see minor differences."

She frowned. "They still look the same to me."

"It takes a little time. Professional gamblers can tell you

every card in a deck by looking at the backs in a marked deck."

"But what was Tom doing with them?"

"He probably came across one of his less desirable customers using them at one time or another."

Tess looked disappointed. "Then none of these belonged to Magnus Swenson?"

"Probably not." Jack picked up a small buckskin sack. "Some gamblers would hang a sack under the table in front of them with an ace or two in it that they could sneak out and into the game." He turned the sack over in his hands. "Funny, though, there's no hook or hole to hang it by."

Tess took it and kneaded the material between her fingers. "It's very soft. Buckskin, isn't it?"

"Most Swedes are not gamblers," said Jack thoughtfully. "So probably none of this is Swenson's property."

They put everything back and Jack replaced the box on the shelf. "I'd better get back to the bar," Tess said, and Jack followed her.

A couple of men were coming in the door while another, hurrying out, shouted, "Is it over?"

"What's happening?" Tess asked.

"Fight outside," one man at the bar said. His lack of interest was a measure of the frequency of that type of occurrence.

"Another beer?" Tess asked Jack as another man at the bar said, "Some drunks."

Jack was considering if he should have one more beer when that last comment struck a chord of familiarity. Some drunks fighting on the sidewalk . . . He himself had been regarded as a drunk fighting on the sidewalk. . . .

He pushed through the crowd and out into the street where three men were struggling. One had fair hair, a Norse type, and he was getting the worst of the fight. Jack's attention focused on the other two. Yes, they were the same men who had attacked him.

Passersby were walking around them. A few gave them

disdainful looks but most just ignored them. Jack plunged
into the melee.

The Swede was bleeding from the nose and mouth. He
could hardly stand. The holder was shifting his grip from
behind as Jack swung a roundhouse punch that crashed into
his ear. He didn't stop to assess the result because the other
man was rushing at him, as he had expected. Jack drove a
straight left into the Latino's midriff and followed up with a
hook to his face. It sank into his cheek and the man's mouth
opened in pain as a tooth flew out.

Jack saw the glint of metal as one arm threshed in the
air, brass knuckles flailing. More metal shone in the other
hand—a knife. It was obvious now that these two were
killers, but killers who were sadists, enjoying the infliction of
pain and suffering before the final blows. Lucky for him
they were sadists, Jack thought. Had they been true profes-
sionals—like the *boo how doy* that the Chinese tongs employed—he would probably be dead already.

These thoughts flashed like arrows through Jack's mind
without distracting him from the present combat. He did
not give the Latino time to recover but hurled a flurry of
blows at him. Some failed in their intent but many hit a target.

The Swede, heartened at the sight of help, had pulled an
arm loose and was punching his captor. His jabs lacked
vigor but the long-armed holder was taken by surprise. The
two must have thought he was ready to finish off. Jack
leaped to the holder's side and drilled a power-laden one-
two combination. The second hit the collarbone and rico-
cheted into the throat. The man gurgled, choking for
breath.

Out of the corner of his eye, Jack saw the stocky Latino
melting into the crowd, and he gathered his strength for a
final punch at the man struggling to hold on to the Swede.

It was almost a fatal mistake. The knife that he had seen
in the puncher's hand came sizzling through the air. It
plucked at Jack's cheek as it went by and buried itself in the
chest of the long-armed man.

A few cries of revulsion came from passersby, forced to pay attention to the fight at the sight of a figure with a knife in his chest. Jack ignored the crumpling body as it sagged to the ground and grabbed the Swede. Blood still ran from his mouth and Jack knew that he had severe internal injuries.

He eased him into a sitting position in front of the Silver Dollar. The Swede's breath was coming in rasping coughs and he was trying to talk. "My name's Jack London," Jack told him. "I was coming here to meet you. Tess Tullamore asked me to come."

The light blue eyes showed that he understood and he managed a faint nod. He was making a supreme effort to speak. "Sack . . . I gave Tom. Sack of . . ." His voice failed. Blood trickled from his mouth again; the knife had obviously found its mark at least once.

"Don't try to talk," said Jack. "We'll get you help."

The Swede feebly grasped his arm. "Have to tell you . . . reason Tom was killed . . . Sam Hooper and me, we worked together at the mine. That sack . . . gave it to Tom . . ."

"Buckskin?" Jack asked.

"Yes!" The eyes showed a fleeting animation. "You have it?"

"It's empty." Jack expected a protest at this but Swenson showed no surprise.

"Tom was taking it to . . . to . . ." His voice trailed away and his eyelids drooped.

A couple of men who looked like miners had stopped and Jack called to them. "Help me get him inside! He's badly hurt."

In the Silver Dollar, Tess saw them come in and promptly had a bartender show them into an empty booth. One of the men who had helped took off his kerchief and used it to stanch the flow of blood from Swenson's mouth and nose. His eyes remained closed but he was still breathing lightly, though irregularly.

Tess joined them in the booth. "There's a doctor upstairs. I broke up his game. He's coming down."

Swenson stirred, muttered unintelligible words and ap

peared to drift off, but then his eyelids fluttered and he suddenly became alert, tried to sit erect.

Eyes wide open, he looked at Jack and the two miners in turn; then his gaze went back to Jack. He appeared to recognize him from their previous brief conversation. He swallowed and said clearly, "Maria Elena . . ." He gulped and then his voice failed. As he tried to gasp out more words, blood gushed from his mouth. His eyes closed and he slumped in the booth.

A short man in a black suit pushed his way through. "I'm a doctor," he said loudly. He was already opening his black bag, but when he saw Swenson, he immediately concentrated on trying to revive him. Jack, Tess and the two miners watched helplessly, but Jack had seen enough men die that he had little hope. The doctor shook his head as he stopped trying to find a pulse.

"Too much internal bleeding, I'm afraid. He must have been stabbed a number of times."

"He was," Jack confirmed.

The doctor shook his head again. "Have to get him to the morgue," he said as a uniformed policeman came in demanding to know what the disturbance was.

Chapter 15

The next day was a complete loss as far as San Francisco was concerned. The city seethed with excitement and anticipation, and the only topic of discussion was the fight that was to take place that night. Even those with no interest in boxing had their own ideas on which of the contestants would win.

All of the newspapers had analyzed the previous fights of both men in agonizing detail and their private lives were bared for all to read. The *Examiner*, the *Post*, the *Gazette*, the *Bulletin* and the *Call* saw sales go soaring and battle lines were drawn in the newspaper world in unconscious imitation of the boxing match to follow. The *Examiner*, owned by William Randolph Hearst and under Ambrose Bierce's canny direction, and the *Call*, a smaller-circulation paper owned by the fabulously wealthy Spreckels family and operated by Charles Shortridge, conducted their own feud.

The animosity between them had simmered for some time. It had led to a lawsuit being brought against the *Call* by the *Examiner*, whose claim of libel had been upheld. After that, Bierce never missed an opportunity to embarrass their opponent in cartoon caricatures and with his blistering prose. The verbal combat applied not only to the two boxers but also to the referee. The *Examiner* had published a long and laudatory account of Wyatt Earp's near-legendary activities, and the *Call* had responded with equal and opposite criticism of the Athletic Club's choice.

Ambrose Bierce had spared no compliments in his editorial describing Earp:

As a boy, he crossed the plains in a caravan and learned to use a rifle on the Indians who infested the trail. Later, he drove the Wyoming stage through territories devastated by the Sioux. He lived in every mining camp of importance and trailed every desperado of prominence in the country. He was a shotgun messenger, a deputy marshal, a miner, a man hunter and knew every gambler, bandit, gunfighter and badman in the United States. He has the reputation of being the bravest fighter, the squarest gambler, the best friend and the worst enemy ever known on the frontier.

Jack was one of the ten thousand people who packed the Mechanics' Pavilion that evening. Comment was rife on the presence of women and another first was the presence of Chinese. Jack spotted the mayor and the chief of police, and a few seats away from them was Professor O'Sullivan. Evidently, thought Jack, he's gambling on one or the other.

Several saloon owners were spotted among the front rows. Jack could see Hap Harrison, Fritz Danner, Shanghai Hanrahan and Josh Klein of the El Dorado. Doubtless others were here too. Just beyond them was Lucky Baldwin, another man who almost certainly had money on the outcome.

The bleachers rose, framing the ring. In the first dozen rows were those who had paid ten dollars a seat. These included millionaires, politicians, Supreme Court justices, company directors and several heavily veiled women. The seats squeezed closer together as they went higher, all the way up to the two-dollar seats. The narrow aisles were crammed with vendors selling candy, soda and popcorn, and there were even a few helmeted and uniformed police, despite the illegality of the event.

The crowd was treated to five preliminary bouts, which they endured with barely concealed impatience. Then into the ring came Bob Fitzsimmons and Tom Sharkey, the contestants, along with Billy Jordan, the master of ceremonies,

Martin Julian and Danny Lynch, the two managers, and referee Wyatt Earp.

Jack was close enough in the fine seat that Bierce had obtained for him that he was able to see what happened next—for it was not obvious to the vast majority of the crowd.

Another man was climbing through the ropes and Jack recognized him as Charles Wittman, a senior captain of police. He asked Wyatt Earp a question, and the lawman nodded an affirmative answer then drew from his belt a huge six-shooter and handed it over. Someone in the row in front of Jack commented, "That must be the first time in the history of prizefighting that it was necessary to disarm the referee."

The fight began.

Fitzsimmons dominated the early rounds. Sharkey fouled him frequently but the Cornishman kept his temper. Twice the bell saved Sharkey from defeat. In the seventh and eighth rounds, Fitzsimmons seemed about to end the fight, and in the latter part of the eighth he launched a furious attack. This terminated with a powerful blow to Sharkey's middle.

Sharkey fell, grimacing, both hands at his groin. Sharkey's trainer rushed into the ring, shouting that the sailor had been fouled. Fitzsimmons just laughed at Sharkey, who was writhing on the deck. Then to the astonishment of Jack and all those in the closer seats, Wyatt Earp walked over to Sharkey's corner and told his seconds that Sharkey was the winner.

It took a little while for the astounding decision to trickle through the massive crowd, but when it did, pandemonium broke out. Many leaped out of the bleachers and jammed into the ring in protest. The few police who had been enjoying the fight found themselves trying to control a crowd that outnumbered them by hundreds to one.

*   *   *

Later, in the Midway Plaisance, everybody wanted to discuss the fight. Those who had not been able to get tickets were incredulous at the stories they were hearing from those who had attended the big event.

A referee going into the ring with a pistol in his belt? Unprecedented! The great Fitzsimmons the loser? Unbelievable! Sharkey being carried out on a stretcher while he was being hailed as the winner? Absurd!

Jack found himself surrounded by some who knew him and a few who didn't. All wanted to know what he saw and what he thought. I hope my stories will get this much attention, he mused.

Everyone wanted to buy him a drink and the night wore on. Eventually he stood at the bar talking to a fellow only a few years older than himself. Luke Felson was a fisherman and a pal from Jack's oyster pirating days. There was a bond between them that resulted from a shared knowledge of lawbreaking, though Jack had not seen Luke for some months.

"Figured you must have taken off looking for better waters," Jack said.

"How about a whisky?" asked Luke. He had had a lot to drink but was still on the uncertain edge of sobriety.

"No, think I'll stick with beer," Jack said.

Luke ordered another whisky for himself.

"Fishing must be good, Luke," Jack told him.

Luke winked. "Not exactly. I am in the chips, though."

"You've had some good luck at the tables?" Jack knew that Luke liked roulette, though he was usually a loser.

"No. Sold my boats."

Jack whistled in surprise. "Bit young to retire, aren't you?"

Luke shrugged. "Probably won't last long. I'll get the urge to go back to fishing one day."

"When you've spent all your money."

"Be a while," Luke said with a hint of a giggle.

"Who'd you sell to? Shem Bolam?" Bolam had the

biggest fleet of fishing boats in the San Francisco area at the time.

Luke shook his head. "New man here, name's Guilfoyle."

"Don't know him. From out of town?"

"Guess so. I didn't know him either. All I knew was he'd got the money." Luke winked again.

"You must have got a good price," Jack said.

"Sure did. Matt and Greg all did too."

Jack's surprise increased. "This Guilfoyle bought boats from all of you?"

"Sure did."

"Is he starting a fleet?"

"Guess so."

"Hope he knows a lot about fishing. Most fellows start with one boat and build up a fleet. This fellow's taking a risk."

Luke finished his whisky and ordered another. "Didn't seem to know much at all. Real tenderfoot when it comes to the sea. Still, that's his problem."

"Maybe you can buy 'em back from him when he finds out fishing isn't as profitable as he expects."

"Maybe," Luke agreed. "Sure you don't want a whisky?"

The excitement of the fight and its extraordinary conclusion was still being argued over and the show, as good as it was, had to take second place. Jack watched it, and as it ended, he rose to go backstage to see if Flo was still there. He was stopped by a familiar figure.

"Upton! Upton Sinclair!"

"Hello, Jack. It's nice to see you again."

The two had met at a literary evening staged at the mayor's mansion. At that time, Sinclair had told Jack of his urge to be a writer. He had heard of Jack's rising reputation and was eager to learn all he could from him.

Both young men shared an enthusiasm for socialism and they discussed this, Jack noting that it was the first time this evening anyone had opened a conversation on any other topic than the big fight.

"How's the novel going?" Jack asked.

"Oh, I told you about it when we talked a while back, didn't I?"

"Yes, you did."

"It's slow." Upton Sinclair was a slim man, about Jack's age but with a diffident air that contrasted with Jack's breezy self-assurance. "I've got the basic idea but I'm having trouble settling on characters who can portray the story for me."

"As I recall, you're going to tell of the terrible conditions in the meatpacking business."

"Yes, in the Chicago stockyards."

"You plan to go there, I take it."

"Certainly," said Sinclair.

"Better be careful," Jack warned.

"In writing it?"

"No, in being there. You won't be very popular if you let it be known just what you're writing about. I worked in the tuna canneries here on the Pacific Coast. One man who was rash enough to tell a fellow worker that he was writing an exposé of the awful conditions there got pushed into a fish-slicing machine."

"So far I haven't told anyone but you."

"Your secret's safe with me," Jack said.

"It may be a while before I go," Sinclair confessed. "I need to accumulate some more money first. I'm still writing dime novels to do that." He waved a hand in Jack's direction. "What about you? Are you making enough money from writing yet?"

"Not yet, but I have an offer from Houghton Mifflin—they want to publish a book of my short stories."

"Hey, that's great," Sinclair said in sincere admiration. "That's a top name. Once you've sold something to them, you're in solid."

"I hope it works out that way," Jack said, "but in the meantime, I'm doing some odd jobs." And none could be odder than this one, he thought. I'm looking for something and I've no idea what it is. He asked, "Still writing for the socialist papers?"

"Oh, absolutely," Sinclair said. "*Appeal to Reason* published one of my articles in September, and they have a circulation over half a million."

"I think I missed that issue," Jack said. He did not add that at that time he was low on money and had to hoard what little he had.

"My theme was that you don't have to be satisfied with America as you find it today. You can change it."

"A powerful message," Jack agreed. "One that needs more emphasis. There are so many people in the country who *can* change it but they need to be reminded of their opportunity. Are you coming to the literary evening at Berkeley tomorrow night?"

"I hate to miss it but I'm leaving in the morning. Is it going to be a big affair?"

"Not really big." Jack could not tell his friend that he was going only to see if he could learn more about the enigmatic Professor O'Sullivan.

"I'd better go," Sinclair said. "Have to be up early in the morning."

He left and Jack went to seek out the former exotic dancer he knew as Flo.

Chapter 16

It was difficult for Jack to concentrate his thoughts on writing the next morning. His mind was buzzing with unanswered questions. Were they unanswerable too? he wondered.

First was this mysterious threat that hung over his beloved San Francisco. Tom Tullamore had sadly not had the opportunity to tell him either what he knew or what he suspected. Police captain Krasner sounded as if he wanted to cooperate with Jack but he appeared to know nothing of substance. Shanghai Hanrahan, representing the Saloon Owners Association, wanted Jack to investigate but could not tell him what he was to be seeking. Sam Hooper and Magnus Swenson had known something but had been killed before they could tell him what that was.

He was not the only one with problems and questions, Jack thought ruefully. Ambrose Bierce was worried about newspapers being bought up and Luke Felson was puzzled over a man called Guilfoyle, who, knowing nothing about fishing, had bought a fleet of fishing boats.

But Jack had a systematic and logical mind and he was able to put these riddles into compartments in his brain where they might gestate. In the meantime, he read his mail. The most notable item was an announcement that Eugene V. Debs, a longtime member of the Socialist Labor Party, was breaking away and forming his own party, the Socialist Democratic Party.

Jack saw this as both good news and bad news. It was good because Jack had admired Debs for some years and was inclined to support his ideas rather than those of any other member of the Socialist Party. At the same time, it could be construed as bad news because one of the weaknesses of the party was its factionalism. It did not consist of one cohesive organization but instead was splintered into too many smaller groups. To Jack's way of thinking, this diluted the party's effectiveness. Until it could become more united, it could not be more constructive. But then, he reasoned, perhaps Debs was the man to unite it.

The only other item in his mail was a letter from his indefatigable correspondent, Cloudesley Johns. Johns was an ardent fan of Jack's writing and an aspiring writer himself with, so far, modest success in some smaller magazines. In this letter, Jack found Johns bemoaning the same treatment from *Overland Monthly* that Jack had received, and still did — a failure to pay for material printed.

Jack promptly wrote an answer, encouraging Johns to keep writing despite such shabby practice. He added that he had heard it was the custom of the magazine to pay only for the best two or three articles each month and to leave the writers of the other dozen or more works to complain. Charles Green, librarian of the Oakland Free Library, had told him personally that *Overland* owed him more than two thousand dollars for articles and stories printed.

Those enjoyable chores completed, Jack settled down to plan his future writing. He was aware that he had a wealth of material available in his own experiences and adventures over the past ten years. Which should he tackle first? His year with the California Fish Patrol was certainly full of potential. So were the years of riding the rails on the transcontinental trains. Hunting for gold in the Klondike was clearly another rich period, but then so was that exciting time with his first boat, the *Razzle-Dazzle*.

All of these had been used already as background for his short stories, though he had selected episodes at random and much material was still there. But with his recent success with Houghton Mifflin, maybe he should think ahead.

It might be time to move on from short stories and to start considering novels. It was an exhilarating thought.

Jack again bemoaned his great difficulty with plots. He felt comfortable describing the ocean, the snows, the mountains. He was able to construct characters out of the many people he had known. Some he could recall and describe accurately; others he could assemble with characteristics from several persons.

But could he put together a plot that would hold together through a hundred thousand words? It was a daunting thought, but he was a man who loved a challenge. Here was a challenge that was really worthwhile and might shape his entire career.

He set out to list ideas, situations, settings, people and conflicts, and the hours flew by.

On the ferry from the Oakland terminal, he was able to turn these thoughts in the direction of his current investigation. The literary event at the University of California at Berkeley was to be held this evening. Sponsored by the Bohemian Club, it promised to bring together a number of prominent figures in San Francisco's world of letters.

During his time at the university, Jack had been a member of the Ruskin Club, which filled a similar though more limited role for students and alumni. The Bohemian Club was a more comprehensive assembly and Jack knew that many outstanding names would be on the list of invitations.

This alone was a strong enough reason for Jack to attend, but it would also be an opportunity to talk to Professor O'Sullivan. Jack was uncertain whether the professor really figured into the mystery. He was a frequenter of the places that seemed to be in the spotlight. Was he involved or a mere bystander? Jack hoped that he would be able to deduce the answer tonight. It might be no more than a hunch, but with so little to go on, even hunches might bring some progress.

He had time before the literary event to drop by a few of the saloons. As he watched the waters of San Francisco Bay,

Jack considered the role the gambling saloons might play in the conundrum. He pondered the idea that one of the saloon owners was behind the plot and felt this demanded further attention. Each of the saloon owners saw thousands of dollars pouring through every day. If some scheme were to be concocted that could reap that income from several saloons, it could become a vast amount of money.

Had one of the saloon owners seen some flaw in his own operation, some gap that resulted in cash flowing out? Had he then seen a way to gather that outflow from his competitors too? Jack had an uneasy feeling that the answer was closer than he had thought. A chilling consideration followed: Someone was willing to commit murder in order to prevent the scheme from being exposed.

It was early enough when he entered the Silver Dollar that only a few dedicated drinkers and a smaller number of drunks were there. One of the bartenders went to find Tess, and when she saw Jack, her eyes lit up.

"A beer?" she invited. "Not a schooner, just a glass?"

"You remembered," said Jack.

"Of course," she said as she located a glass and pulled the pump handle.

He studied for a moment her lustrous black hair and ample figure. Her attractive face held a touch of haughtiness, suggesting an unassailability that a man might find himself determined to break down. She had an alluring intelligence that was unusual on the Barbary Coast, where it was common to desire women in one way only.

"Have the police bothered you any more?" he asked.

"No. Oh, it's no bother. I'll answer their questions all day if it will help find Tom's killer."

"I'd like to take another look at that buckskin sack you showed me," Jack said. "Magnus Swenson said he gave it to Tom and there must have been something in it. But he wasn't able to say any more."

"What do you think it was?"

"Swenson and Sam Hooper were both gold miners.

Swenson said they worked together at the mine. The obvious guess would be that the sack contained gold."

"It was empty when I came across it," Tess said.

"That means that Tom took out the contents. Can I have another look at it?"

"Of course. Come on back."

Only one bartender was on duty, as it was still early, and Tess told him she would be back in a moment. She led Jack through and indicated the box on the shelf. Jack lifted it down and took out the sack. He examined it much more carefully this time, then turned it inside out. Here and there were tiny snags in the buckskin. They would not have been noticeable from a casual inspection.

Tess saw him pause and study them. "What is it, Jack?"

Jack smoothed out the sack and Tess came close to look. Her perfume was strong as she leaned near him. Jack pointed. "See these small tears?"

"No."

"Look closer."

"Oh, yes," she said excitedly. "Now I see them." She frowned. "What do they mean?"

"These sacks are usually used for gold dust," Jack told her. "But they are sometimes used for nuggets or coins. In this case, it was nuggets. They are chunky lumps with sharp edges and corners that would make little tears in the buckskin. If the sack had held coins, we wouldn't see these."

"But what does it mean?" Tess demanded impatiently.

"Swenson said that either he or Sam Hooper gave the sack to Tom. Swenson was having trouble talking and I couldn't tell which of them it was. Then he said, 'Tom was taking it to . . .' He never finished the sentence but it seems clear that it must have contained gold nuggets when Tom received it. You haven't found any nuggets, have you?"

"No," Tess said, "I haven't."

"Then Tom took it to someone. Now where would he be likely to take it? Some places, the El Dorado, for instance, still have a scale for weighing gold dust. It's going out of style, though, and many have gotten rid of them."

"Tom stopped taking gold, except for coins, a few months ago."

"So Tom probably took it to be assayed." He handed the sack to Tess.

She replaced it in the box and faced him. "There must be a lot of places in this town where he could have taken it."

Jack nodded. "That's true. Well, all I can do is start with the most likely ones." He hesitated. "Tess, you know how Tom would think. . . . Why would be become involved in assaying a miner's find? Did he ever show an interest in financing a mining operation?"

"No, as far as I know, he didn't ever invest in a mine. Do you think that's what this is about?"

"I can't imagine why else he would take the sack of nuggets."

Tess's eyes were round. "Could it be that this was a mine of exceptional promise? A real bonanza?"

"You hear those stories," Jack agreed. "All miners like to think that there's one of those just around the corner. But in my experience, it hardly ever happens."

"If that's what it was, though, it must have been a mine of rare quality. I can't believe that Tom would have involved himself in anything less. Still," she mused, "if it were that extraordinary, it's strange he didn't mention it. He didn't tell me much about the Silver Dollar, but this—this is different. Surely he would have told me."

They went back into the saloon, Tess behind the bar and Jack in front of it. He felt just a little relieved. In the quiet confines of that small room, the attractions of the widow had become amplified—and she was a very recent widow, he reminded himself.

He drank his beer and set out on another round of the bars and music halls, and in particular the gambling saloons. Among his stops was the Green Bottle, where he asked for Shanghai Hanrahan. A waiter pointed. "Know where his office is?" Jack nodded.

Hanrahan looked up as Jack came in. "Close the door," he ordered. Hanrahan pushed aside the accounts book he was studying and stubbed out a distinctive-smelling cigar. "Got something to tell me?"

"I must be getting close," Jack said. "Two men tried to kill me and make it look like a sidewalk mugging."

Hanrahan's tough, no-nonsense attitude was typical as he said, "Looks like you survived."

"I did," said Jack. "Wanted to ask you something. Heard any word of a big bonanza mine? A really big one?"

Hanrahan shook his head slowly. "No. Is there one?"

"Maybe. Tom Tullamore was mixed up in some deal that may involve a high-value mine. Thought you might have heard whispers."

"This threat to the city can't be about a gold find," Hanrahan said impatiently. "Don't let yourself get sidetracked. You'll find you're wasting your time."

"There may be a connection," Jack said doggedly. "I have to follow this up."

"Well, okay," Hanrahan said. "But you'd better know when to drop it. Anything else to tell me?"

"Yes, I've established contact with Wyatt Earp. We're cooperating, in a way."

"Is he still in town?" Hanrahan sneered. "After the way he botched that fight, I'm surprised he hasn't lit out for Tombstone."

"He might run across a lead. If he does, I may get in on it."

"Make sure that he doesn't get in on any of your leads," said Hanrahan. "Don't tell him anything. All that blarney about the great lawman—he's a killer and a gambler and I wouldn't trust him an inch."

Jack merely nodded. Hanrahan's opinion was clear and Jack had no intention of arguing with him. He would continue to follow his own instincts.

"Who's Earp working for?" Hanrahan asked.

"He told me that he came here because Butch Cassidy and the Sundance Kid were heading this way after robbing the Denver stage."

"They do that?" Hanrahan sounded surprised.

"A couple of witnesses said they recognized them. So Earp came here to head them off. Then he was approached by an old friend of his, a former marshal now working for the government, to look into this matter of a threat."

"Did he give the name of the former marshal?"

"No, he didn't."

Hanrahan grunted. "After the way Earp bungled that fight, I wouldn't expect him to be able to find his pistol with both hands."

"Did you have any money on it?" Jack asked innocently.

"Yeah," Hanrahan snarled.

"On Fitzsimmons?"

"Never mind about that. Concentrate on this other matter."

Jack realized that Hanrahan must have dropped a bundle but he just nodded. "I keep running across this O'Sullivan," he said. "He still gamble here?"

"Yeah."

"Does he win a lot of money?"

"Not from me."

"He's supposed to have an infallible system," Jack persisted.

"If he has, it doesn't help him."

Jack rose. "Okay. I'll keep in touch."

"Remember what I said. Don't trust Earp."

Jack nodded, willing to let Hanrahan have the last word.

Chapter 17

The meeting of the Bohemian Club was held in the main conference room at the University of California at Berkeley. Chairs had been pushed to the walls, which were covered with pictures of the university football team. Tables were set up in the middle of the room for snacks and drinks. In addition, waiters circulated with loaded trays, and Jack stopped one and took a glass of beer.

It was a simple arrangement and Jack knew that the hosts felt that conversation of a civilized nature was the main object of the evening. In addition to literary figures, some of the show-business luminaries of San Francisco had been invited. Oscar Hammerstein was one of the first that Jack encountered.

The impresario pumped Jack's hand enthusiastically. "Jack, my boy! Changed your mind about writing for me?" Hammerstein had been pursuing Jack for some time, trying to persuade him to write material for his stage shows. He was a short, chubby man with a smooth, well-fed face. He was always smoking a big cigar and his arms were usually in motion, excitedly illustrating some aspect of his conversation.

"I haven't forgotten your offer, Oscar," Jack assured him. "Just been too busy. Houghton Mifflin wants to publish a book of my short stories."

Hammerstein took the cigar out of his mouth. "Is that right? Good for you! Say, you think any of those stories of yours could be turned into sketches for me?"

"I don't think so, Oscar."

"Too bad, too bad. You know who I'm trying to bring here to the Coast right now? Steens, that's who!"

"Should be popular," Jack said. Flo kept him informed about characters and shows, so he knew that Steens was a current sensation in New York. He brought a full-size guillotine onto the stage during his act. Members of the audience were invited to come onstage and examine it. All agreed that it was genuine, and branches of trees were chopped in two when the gleaming blade flashed down.

Then Steens came on in a glittering costume and laid his head on the block. An assistant grasped the release cord, and when Steens gave the order—in a hushed house—she pulled the cord. While the blade was hissing down, Steens extricated himself—just in time.

"Does the audience expect that maybe the next time Steens won't get out before the blade reaches him?" Jack asked.

"Probably," Hammerstein said airily. "He's talking about making the act more hair-raising. He wants to have his hands chained—then he'll have to release them before getting his head out of the way."

Jack shuddered. "One of these performances you're going to have a head rolling into the audience, Oscar."

The showman shook his head emphatically. "I don't think so. It sounds reckless but Steens is really a more sensible and careful person than he sounds. He insists that he doesn't take risks. His act is perfectly timed, he says."

"I hope he's right. By the way, what about these rumors of Lillian Russell coming here soon?"

"Bah! Nonsense! She's tied into a contract. She can't get away."

"Haven't I heard of contracts occasionally being broken?" Jack asked with a guileless look.

Hammerstein took another puff of his cigar, pulled it from his mouth and said, "Once in a while maybe. The Shubert brothers won't release her, though."

David Kavanaugh, the head of the drama department at

Berkeley, approached, saying, "Ah, Oscar, I think I have that actor you are looking for!"

"You always do, David, you always do," replied the showman, and with a nod to Jack, he walked away with the other man.

Nearby, nursing a glass of Sazerac and contemplating the room, was Ambrose Bierce. He wore a new frock coat and a white cravat. His fair hair, mustache and thick eyebrows were neatly brushed. Jack went to him.

"Ambrose, you look thoroughly at home in this bastion of knowledge."

Bierce acknowledged him with a flourish of his glass. "Not knowledge but education, not at all the same thing. Do you know what education does?" He did not wait for an answer. Most of Bierce's questions were purely rhetorical. "Education is that which discloses to the wise and disguises from the foolish their lack of understanding."

"Have you told that to David Starr Jordan?" The eminent educator was well known to have had numerous verbal contests with Bierce and the newspaper editor never missed a chance in his column to flay him with words.

"Many times," said Bierce. "So, how goes your battle to preserve American civilization as we know it?"

"Still fighting the good fight," Jack said.

"And preparing to combine a number of your short stories into a book, as I believe you told me on our last encounter."

"That's right," Jack agreed.

"Your next step on that shaky ladder to success—is that going to be a novel?"

Jack looked at him in surprise. "I didn't mention that, I don't believe."

Bierce smiled. "You didn't need to. It was an inevitable decision. After all, a novel is only a short story that has been padded."

"I don't agree at all," Jack said hotly. "A novel—"

"Save it for the debating society," Bierce cut in. "Few

writers can resist making the leap. Even journa~
done so. Richard Harding Davis, for instance."

Jack grinned. "All right, Ambrose, I know you are aw~
of my opinion of Richard's novels."

"Yours will be different, I take it."

"Yes, it will, it—" Jack stopped. Bierce was baiting him.
"All writers tell you that, I suppose."

Bierce cocked his head to one side as if the thought had
only just struck him. "Now that you mention it, they do."

Jack decided to switch subjects. "The last time we talked,
you told me that a famous lawman was coming to town."

"Yes, the former marshal of Tombstone."

"You didn't tell me that."

"Thought I'd let you read it in the paper."

"I met Earp. We talked."

"Did you now?" Bierce was interested, despite his pose of
indifference.

"Pity he made a wrong decision about refereeing the
fight. Thanks for the ticket, by the way."

"Ah, enjoyed the experience, did you?"

"More of an experience than a fight, certainly," Jack
said.

"Perhaps his decision to referee the fight was not so
much of a mistake as his decision to call a foul," Bierce
replied.

"A referee has to call it the way he sees it. I think Earp is
an honest man. The other papers are making him out to be
a villain."

"The other papers—bah!" Bierce said. "Who cares
about them? The *Examiner* is standing by Earp. He's faced
tougher battles than this."

"He could get out of them with a six-gun," Jack said.
"This may be more difficult. Aside from this probable end
to his career as a referee, he's still a lawman."

"And the case he's on is this strange threat," Bierce said
as he deftly took another Sazerac from a passing tray and
returned his empty glass.

"Heard any more about it?"

vague. Have you learned any more?"

sor here at Berkeley whose name keeps

an—do you know him?"

. Man with a system, is that him?"

'Hope to learn a little more tonight."

Plenty of his colleagues and students here, I imagine. At least you can gather opinions and criticisms—all equally unreliable, no doubt."

"You're a true cynic, Ambrose."

"A cynic," said Bierce, "is a man with faulty vision—it causes him to see things as they are and not as they should be."

"Are you making any headway with your mystery competitor?" Jack asked. "The one who wants to buy up publishers, small presses?"

"Not yet, no clue so far."

"The next you hear will be when he wants to buy you out, Ambrose."

The editor snorted indignantly. "I'd like to see him try!"

"It's probably a big New York chain," Jack went on. It was usually Bierce who roasted others, and Jack was enjoying reversing the process. "Willie Hearst would sell you off if the price was right, wouldn't he?"

"Not a chance," Bierce declared firmly. "He's a newspaperman, just like his father. He has all the money he wants and can get as much more as he'd ever need with a snap of the fingers." His gaze went over Jack's shoulder. "Ah, the Spreckels family is represented, I see." He nodded in the direction of a stately blond lady wearing some expensive-looking jewelry. "I wonder if they're speaking to me. I must find out."

He drifted off and an eager-faced man with slicked-down hair came toward Jack. "You're Jack London, aren't you?"

"Yes, I am."

"You were pointed out to me. I'm taking literature. I'm in my final year. I want to be a writer. Could I talk to you for a few minutes?"

One of Jack's frequent complaints was that he had received no advice and no encouragement in his earlier days. Even at the university, he did not consider that he had learned anything from his professors. However, he was always willing to help others, and he avoided communicating his own attitude to the enthusiastic young fellow, who asked, "Can I hope to make a living from writing when I leave Berkeley?"

"You need a job to survive," Jack told him, "unless there is no one dependent on you—and then you have to be prepared for hardships, especially not eating."

"What kind of writing is the easiest to sell?" was the next question.

"Humor is the easiest to sell, and it pays the most, but it's also the hardest to write. Not many can write it— use Mark Twain as an example. Fiction pays well and it sells best when it's of fair quality. Avoid the unhappy ending, the tragic, the brutal, the horrible."

The young man's eyes widened. "But I've read some of your stories and they are—"

Jack grinned. "Tragic, brutal and horrible—yes, I know. But this is a case of 'Don't do as I do but do as I say.' Find out what you write best and throw everything you've got into it."

"How do you write? Do you get inspiration all the time or do you find sometimes that ideas just don't come?"

"I don't wait for inspiration," Jack said. "It might never come. I set myself a goal of a thousand words a day. If I don't reach that number one day, I make it up the next, but I still have to write the thousand words for that day too."

They talked on, Jack trying not to discourage the zealous youth. Before the young man moved away, Jack asked casually, "You didn't have classes with Professor O'Sullivan, I suppose. I don't think he teaches literature, does he?"

"Math and geology are his subjects." He looked around the room. "He's probably here, though I don't see him. There's Cal by that table." He motioned. "He takes classes from Professor O'Sullivan. Calvin Cartland, his name is.

He wants to be a geologist." He thanked Jack for his advice and departed.

Cartland was a gangly redhead with a wide grin that was almost permanent. Jack approached him, introduced himself and said, "I understand you're the man to ask about earthquakes in California."

"It's a new field of study," Cartland told him. "It's not as rewarding as prospecting for gold or silver, so geologists haven't paid much attention to earthquakes. John Milne in England probably knows more about them than anyone else alive. He believes we are due for a big one because of the San Andreas fault."

"Is that like a crack in the earth?"

"Yes, it is. There are several such faults in California but the San Andreas is potentially the most dangerous."

"Why is that?" asked Jack.

"Because it runs right underneath San Francisco."

"Can you tell when there will be an earthquake?"

"No, we can't. That's because we don't yet know what causes them. But it may come soon, and it will probably be very powerful." He regarded Jack closely. "Why are you interested in earthquakes?"

"I heard a mention of how threatening they are in a speech some time ago, a speech by one of your professors here. I think his name is O'Sullivan."

"He's a professor of geology here, also teaches math. He gives quite a few talks. I didn't know he talked on earthquakes, though." The grin dissolved into a frown.

"It may have been just a casual remark," Jack said easily. "I think he was talking about mining."

"It would have been mining," Cartland agreed. "He has had mines of his own."

"Really? Gold? Silver?"

"Gold, I believe. He still acts as a consultant to one or two mines. But it doesn't bring him enough money to live," said Cartland, "so he likes to try out his mathematical theories at the gambling tables. The board of governors here don't like it but so far they haven't cracked down on him.

He probably wouldn't care much if they did. He's been different since his wife died. He dresses carelessly, even for classes. He was always a little sharp and sarcastic but he's a lot worse now."

"It's too bad when that happens. She must have been an important part of his life."

"She was," agreed Cartland. "Everybody here on campus liked her. A very popular lady was Maria Elena."

Jack was just emptying his beer glass. He put it down slowly. "What did you say her name was?"

"Maria Elena."

Chapter 18

"Cal! Can I talk to you for a minute?"

The greeting came from another young man, doubtless yet one more aspiring writer, thought Jack. "Go ahead," Jack said. "Talk to your friend. I'll keep your warning about earthquakes in mind."

His mind was whirling as Cartland walked away, and he had no chance to focus as William Kellaway, the head of the English literature department, came to shake his hand.

"Jack! Glad you could join us this evening. How are things going?"

Contact between them had been slight during Jack's time at the university, but with Jack's growing success, Kellaway had acknowledged the writer more and more and had even referenced him in the university's monthly newsletter. Jack told him of the book of short stories and Kellaway congratulated him sincerely.

"Thinking of a novel now, I am sure," he added.

Jack grinned. "I was just talking to Ambrose Bierce. He made the same comment. I suppose it's a logical step, though I hadn't really planned one yet."

"I think you're ready," Kellaway said, "and with Houghton Mifflin liking your work, you have a ready-made publisher. Make the most of it, my boy."

"I believe I will."

"With your background, you have enough material for a dozen books," Kellaway told him. "There's someone here you should talk to—he also loves to write about the outdoors. He recently published his first book and already he has several others being eagerly awaited by his publishers. Ah, there he is. His name is John Muir."

Kellaway introduced them and left. "What's the name of your book that just came out?" Jack asked Muir. He was a slight man, probably in his middle fifties, with a luxuriant beard that he no doubt allowed to grow when he was in the wilderness.

"It's called *The Mountains of California*."

Muir told Jack he was a Scottish native. "I grew up on a farm in Wisconsin and soon lost my accent. I have spent all my adult life studying the glaciers, forests and mountains. The Yosemite area fascinates me particularly and I go there often. What do you write?"

"I went to the Yukon and I've written a lot about it."

"You made a lot of money gold mining, I suppose."

Jack grinned ruefully. "No, I didn't, but what I got out of it was dozens of ideas and characters and situations that I'm using in my stories."

Muir nodded. "It's a very fertile field for a writer. I spent some time in Calaveras County—do you know it?"

"Not very well."

"It's a rough, gravelly area, rich in gold. You can find granite, slate, volcanic lava, iron ore, quartz and lime all within a few miles of each other."

"Were you mining?" Jack asked.

"No, I was tracing the channels of the old preglacial rivers. Many of them still have water, though many others have dried up or been diverted. They are of great importance to the miner, of course, as many of them are gold fountains. Over time, miners have cut and scalped the hills, ripped open gorges, gulches and valleys and exposed gold veins."

Jack's interest increased suddenly. "I suppose California has a lot of areas like that," he suggested.

"A lot of the state is that way," Muir said. "After Jim Marshall found gold on the American River, within the next five years more than five hundred million dollars' worth of gold had been taken from the mother lode."

"Were you ever in Sunset Valley?" Jack asked.

"I know it well. I live in Martinez."

"It's a rich region for gold, isn't it?"

"There are some mines, yes."

"Still operating?"

"Some of them are." Muir smiled. "Thinking of investing?"

"A friend of mine worked out there."

"Which mine?"

"I'm not sure I remember the name," Jack said hesitantly.

"The Jubilee?"

"No, that wasn't it."

"The Bear Flag, the West Point?"

"No."

"Barefoot Diggings?" Jack was already shaking his head as Muir said, "The Maria Elena?"

Jack paused. "Might have been," he said.

When Jack left John Muir, he was feeling the thrill of the chase and the exhilaration of success. For the first time, a number of leads had come together. Rosie, the waiter girl at Every Man Welcome, had said that Sam Hooper had worked a gold mine in Sunset Valley. Magnus Swenson had probably worked there too, and his last words were "Maria Elena." Professor O'Sullivan had a mine in Sunset Valley and his wife's name was Maria Elena.

Still, what did this add up to? Jack wondered. The professor was a respectable academic, his wife was dead and nothing indicated the professor still owned the mine. Or whether it was indeed a bonanza mine.

The clincher, Jack decided, was that three deaths seemed to stem from these same facts. Sam Hooper and Magnus Swenson had both died because of something they knew. One of them had passed on to Tom Tullamore a sack that probably contained gold. Tom Tullamore had died, very likely because of that gold. Was there really someone willing to kill to protect this secret?

Jack had thought about the possibility of an incredibly rich mine before, but now he had some incontrovertible evidence that it was a key factor in his investigation. He had wondered about visiting it. Now it seemed like a necessity. He had worked in gold mines in Alaska, in the Yukon. He would be able to make sense of what he found there to a degree that many other investigators might not.

"Meet George Dornin," said Ambrose Bierce, again joining Jack, who had been so preoccupied he had not heard Bierce approach.

"Like you," Bierce said, "George has done almost every job you can think of, and now he's a writer. It must be the last refuge."

Dornin smiled. Elderly, thin and stooped, he had sparse gray hair. His eyes were alert and intelligent, though, and his ready smile made him likeable.

"I read a piece of yours," Jack said. " 'Thirty Years Back,' wasn't that the title?"

"It was indeed," Dornin said. "Ambrose tells me you've tried your hand at a few ventures too, but now you're be ginning to hit the writing jackpot."

"I hope he's right. A gold miner, were you?"

"No," said Dornin. "That's about the only job I never tried. I've done laundry, sign painting, baking, wallpaper hanging. I was an express agent, a telegraph operator, had a jewelry store, sold insurance, worked in a restaurant, plus a dozen more."

"I remember your book. It was about your six-month voyage around Cape Horn."

"Yes, and Ambrose is helping me place another book now."

Jack knew that Bierce helped many people but took pains to prevent it becoming public knowledge, preferring the reputation of being a curmudgeon.

They talked about the problems of getting published, Dornin being optimistic, Bierce underscoring the odds against it and Jack, for the first time, able to bask in his own success.

"Books by young writers," declared Bierce, "are usually like promissory notes that are never met."

Jack and George Dornin looked at each other and smiled. "I was young when I wrote 'Thirty Years Back,'" Dornin said, "and as it described events of thirty years earlier, it referred to a time when I was even younger. I think, therefore, that your remark may apply to me, but Jack here is young and is already making a name for himself. I think he is a note that will be met."

Dornin was hailed by an acquaintance and stepped away to renew what was evidently a long-interrupted friendship.

Across the room, Jack noticed a thin, lean-faced man entering and recognized him as Professor O'Sullivan. Jack watched as the professor greeted David Kavanaugh of the drama department. Bierce followed his gaze. "Ah, there's the fellow you were asking about, Professor O'Sullivan. Let's join the two of them. Under the cloak of my respectability, you can ask questions to which you might not otherwise get answers."

Bierce knew nearly everybody and nearly everybody knew Bierce. The four of them shook hands politely. Bierce broke the ice by describing Jack as a potential novelist.

Kavanaugh looked interested. "We're going to have Richard Mansfield here to give a short course on the dramatic art next month. You must come and meet him. He is always looking for novels to adapt to the stage."

"Does he still want to bring *Cyrano de Bergerac* here?" asked Bierce.

"Oh, yes, he's just finished a run of *Dr. Jekyll and Mr. Hyde*." Kavanaugh looked at O'Sullivan. "You'll want to meet him too, Andrew. He's a true Thespian."

O'Sullivan looked a little sour at the suggestion. Jack wondered if that was his normal attitude.

"Andrew wrote a play a while ago and we performed it at one of our drama festivals. It was very well received."

"But you weren't lured away by the theater? Abandoning the prosaic academic life?" asked Bierce.

The praise from Kavanaugh mellowed O'Sullivan slightly, but before he could answer, Jack added casually, "Or the romantic life of gold mining?"

O'Sullivan's sour look returned. "A dirty business—mining, that is. Grubbing in the ground for a few handfuls of a mineral that ruins men's lives."

Kavanaugh laughed. "But he was almost lured away by the theater—you were right there, Ambrose. When we put on *The Merchant of Venice,* he played Shylock when our lead fell ill."

"My one and only appearance on the stage," O'Sullivan said. "A pallid profession, parroting the same lines night after night."

George Dornin came up with a friend he wanted to present to Bierce. The trio excused themselves and Kavanaugh hailed a colleague and was drawn away. Jack was left with O'Sullivan.

"Asking about me, weren't you?" the professor said.

His complexion was grayish, as Jack had observed when watching him at the gambling tables in the Silver Dollar. He had an unhealthy look and Jack concluded that he spent far more time gambling indoors than he did mining outdoors. He was a little taller than Jack but his rounded shoulders gave him a stoop. His eyes were light gray and emotionless.

"I was talking to one of your students," Jack told him affably. "When he said he was studying geology, I asked him about earthquakes and he said you were the expert and know all about them."

"No one knows all about earthquakes." O'Sullivan's voice was throaty but his words came easily, the result of years lecturing in the classroom. "Even experts know little."

"People say we're due for a big quake in San Francisco, is that true?"

"It is possible, yes."

"When will it hit us?"

"Possibly within the next few years. No one can say for

certain, but it will happen." His light eyes searched Jack's face. Did he know that this earthquake topic was a cover? Jack could not be sure. "Why do you ask?" O'Sullivan continued. "Are you afraid of earthquakes?"

"Of course," Jack said with an uneasy laugh. "Isn't everybody?"

"No, they are not. San Francisco would be a ghost town if they were." His testy response suggested that he did not encourage debates.

"Let's hope it won't be that bad," Jack said, wanting to engender an image of a lightweight thinker. "I just came back here from the Klondike, nearly lost a foot from frostbite. I was thinking I might do a little prospecting here in California's much nicer climate. I wouldn't want to be digging and find the earth opening up under my spade. Anyway, they didn't mine all the gold already, did they?"

"I'm sure they didn't."

"Do you do any prospecting yourself?" Jack was determined to edge the professor into divulging something useful.

"Why do you ask?" The question was frosty.

"Well, knowing so much about mining and prospecting, you'd have to know where gold was, wouldn't you? It would be hard to resist going and digging for it."

"Nobody knows where gold is. Geologists like myself know where it is likely to be but the earth is a vast place. Nobody can be sure; otherwise all geologists would be rich."

"Maybe you are," Jack said, relying on the brashness of youth to get away with that statement.

"It requires an immense amount of luck to find gold. I have tried it but didn't have that luck. I gave up trying years ago. That's why I expressed a negative opinion about the whole venture." He fixed Jack with a penetrating stare. "Were you a student here?"

"Yes, I was." Jack avoided elaboration.

"Were you in one of my classes?"

"No, I was an English lit student."

O'Sullivan's grunt was a dismissal. He turned away in search of a brighter conversationalist. Jack joined a few other conversations, but finally he disengaged himself and left the university to head toward the Barbary Coast, where his destination was the Midway Plaisance.

Chapter 19

A show was in progress and the master of ceremonies was introducing the Lightner Sisters, direct from Joe Bignon's in Phoenix, Arizona, as Jack made his way to the bar. The sisters sang and accompanied themselves on several musical instruments. They were a nationally known act and their professional attitude showed—which was just as well, for, as Jack knew, this crowd would tolerate nothing less.

Acts that offended through lack of talent would be pelted with oranges or eggs, an occasional cowboy in the audience would lasso performers and pull them offstage and, in a more extreme critical vein, pistol shots would be fired. Perforation of the scenery would result, and if the shooter was inebriated, anyone on the stage might be hit. The Midway Plaisance had one of the better behaved audiences on the Coast, but there was no knowing when an unruly customer might appear, and in any case, acts that appeared at any music hall were proficient in the art of entertaining with the motivation of gunfire.

Andrew Mack, the renowned Irish tenor, came on next and sang "When Irish Eyes Are Smiling." After three verses, he was prepared to go on, but Jack recognized the experienced hand of Flo in bringing on a chorus line of a dozen attractive girls in green costumes. Their flashing legs, tightly cinched waists, dresses cut low over the bosom and dazzling smiles restored the audience's faith in show business and applause soared up toward the ceiling, where smoke wreathed in thick gray clouds.

Glasses rattled as the thirst for more drinks was accentuated by the speed and excitement of the girls' number. A leprechaun played by a dwarf came onstage, seen by the audience but not by the girls. He pointed his long, gnarled stick at each one in turn, and as he did so, the lights went out abruptly. When they came back on, whichever girl he had just pointed out had lost most of her clothing. The strategically located fragments that remained were the same green color, maintaining the Irish theme. The yells became louder as each girl, mouth open, turned to look at the audience with mock dismay.

Finally, they joined in a provocative dance, during which the lights dimmed slowly. Near the end, the leprechaun reappeared and stood at the end of the stage. The girls had to pass him to leave, and as they did, what little remained of their costumes fell to the stage each time he pointed his stick.

The crowd roared its appreciation and pounded the wooden floor with booted feet, demanding the girls come back onstage in the same state as they left. Two more leprechauns came out, unraveling a long green banner. The girls reappeared obediently but they stood behind the banner, which was just wide enough for propriety. Shouts for the leprechauns to drop the banner remained unsatisfied, but then the pants of each leprechaun in turn fell down.

Reaching to pull them back up meant lowering the banner for a few seconds, and whoops of delight resulted. The tempo of alternate pants falling increased until it seemed inevitable that both leprechauns must be pantless at the same time, but somehow that never happened. The wide-eyed, openmouthed crowd accepted the momentary glimpses of feminine nudity in good humor and funneled their frustration into ordering more drinks.

Another of Flo's inventive numbers closed the show and got the usual enthusiastic applause. Jack waited at the bar until she came out after the noise had died and the atmosphere had settled down to the normal clatter of glasses and boisterous conversation.

He pushed his way through customers and waiter girls

and Flo greeted him with a hug. "Did you get here in time for the number?"

"I certainly did," he told her as he held her at arm's length. She looked enchanting in a close-fitting gown, light bronze in color and in a material resembling silk. It fit her perfectly proportioned body like a second skin and Jack got more than a few envying looks. Her shiny black hair was held in a silver bangle at the back of her neck and on her feet she wore only tiny black ballet slippers.

One of the waitresses motioned to Flo and directed them to a small table that had just been cleared. She also found them chairs and took their orders, Jack for another beer and Flo for a glass of white wine.

"You're a marvel, Flo," Jack said. "You can make even Irish farm girls look exciting."

"That's not costuming," Flo said. "It's the lack of it."

"It was a great number anyway. Was the leprechaun part your idea?"

"The whole number was my idea," Flo said. "Fritz gives me a free hand now, so I can do anything I want."

"Fritz is smart. How long does this show last? It was a big hit tonight."

"It lasts only until the end of the week. I'm just starting rehearsals for the next show."

"What about that show you were telling me about? The one that's set in the Marie Antoinette period."

"That's the one—it's next. We received the props today. Oh, there's Edith." Flo waved and a tall girl wearing glasses and a street dress joined them. Educated Edith had been a dancer but decided she could make more money with less effort by keeping the books. A wizard with figures, she also loved reading. She greatly admired Jack for his writing and was willing to do anything to help him or Flo.

"What about Drummond?" Edith asked as she came to their table.

Flo giggled. It was a knack of hers that she could giggle and still remain a sophisticated woman. "Hello to you too, Edith."

Jack smiled. Edith was always devouring books on psychology, history or philosophy. She had no use for small talk and loved to exchange opinions with Jack, for they had the same insatiable curiosity regarding such subjects.

"Henry Drummond has chosen a difficult task," said Jack. "He attempts to reconcile evolution with religion and I think the subjects are too far apart for that. Darwin and Wallace are the ones to read for a more accurate viewpoint of evolution."

"That's what I want to read," declared Edith firmly, "what these scientists think about evolution, not blending it in with another topic, especially religion—which is bound to be in conflict."

"The French writers Lamarck and Cuvier are others you should read, in that case," Jack told her.

"I will. Thanks, Jack."

She gave Flo a brief smile. "Sorry to interrupt, Flo, but I just had to ask him." She waved a hand and was gone.

"I hope you're not leading that girl astray," Flo said in a tone of mock reproval. "Filling her head with these abstruse ideas when she should be thinking about men and love and passion and . . ."

"Go on. Men and love and passion and what else?" Jack asked.

Their drinks arrived and Flo ran a finger around the rim of her glass. It sounded a mellow note. "We were talking about Marie Antoinette when Edith appeared. She fits right in with love and passion."

"She certainly does," Jack agreed. "You're still looking for themes for your show, I'll bet."

"I am."

"And you're thinking about Lillian Russell at the Silver Dollar at the same time?"

Flo sipped her wine. The orchestra—a piano, a flute, two violins and a viola—was playing musical tunes. Flo had to raise her voice a little so that Jack could hear her. "Oh, yes, certainly. I'm also thinking that it's a shame I couldn't combine the two. What do you think of Lillian Russell as Marie Antoinette?"

"I don't think she's ever played the role, has she?"

"Not as far as I know. But if we had the right vehicle for her, I'm sure she'd jump at the chance."

Jack drank some beer and nodded. "You know, you could follow that thought a bit further. If you want to put on Marie Antoinette here, why don't you consider Lillian Russell at the Silver Dollar as, say, Catherine of Russia."

Flo's eyes sparkled. "That's a great idea, Jack."

They continued to discuss the possibilities, Jack tossing out thoughts based on what he had read of the Russian empress and her seemingly unlimited sexual demands and Flo becoming more and more enthusiastic.

When their drinks were finished, Flo asked, "Want to see the props that came in?"

Jack took her hand. "Yes, I do."

They went through the crowd and backstage into one of the large rooms where props were stored. Flo lit a lamp, and as the light flickered into life, Jack's gaze fell first on an immense bathtub with gold-plated knobs and feet.

"What are you going to do with that?" he asked.

"Marie is going to take a bath in it, of course," Flo said carelessly. "I haven't decided yet whether it will be in milk or champagne."

"That needs a test," Jack said, studiously looking past Flo.

"I agree," said Flo, taking his arm and pulling him into the tub. "We'll test it now, but I don't intend to wait for either milk or champagne."

Chapter 20

The Southern Pacific Railroad train puffed out of the Oakland depot promptly at 8:05 A.M. Since engineer Theodore Judah's ingenuity and determination had conquered the Sierras and the last spike had been driven at Promontory Summit in Utah, the East had been linked to the West. The Central Pacific had gone east from the Pacific Coast and the Union Pacific had gone west from the Atlantic Coast. They had met in Utah, and though the last spike had been made of iron and not the alleged gold, a historic moment had been realized.

Jack was thinking of this enormous achievement as the locomotive shrieked a raucous warning to all to get out of its way. As it left the yards and headed toward Stockton, he felt a subdued thrill of excitement at the prospect ahead of him. He was now on his way to the Maria Elena gold mine.

Jack had no doubt that he would be faced with suspicion if some nefarious activities were being conducted at the mine. What would he say when he got there? The best approach he had been able to think of was to emphasize—maybe even exaggerate—his position as a writer. He would say he wanted to write a story, part of which took place in a gold mine. He would be vague on this, leaving it open to interpretation whether it was to be fiction or nonfiction. Then, if suspicion increased, he could fall back on a description of an article for the *San Francisco Examiner*. If pressed further on that assignment, he could mention Ambrose Bierce's name, confident that the crusty editor would back him.

Perhaps it would not come to that, but anyone with a true bonanza, a mine of extraordinary wealth, would be ruthless in protecting it. Ruthless enough to kill, even. Only how could that be a part of a plot that threatened the city of San Francisco? Jack had difficulty in reconciling those two ideas. It occurred to him that maybe large sums of money were needed to finance the plot. In that case, a bonanza mine was just what was needed.

The train puffed along, putting the miles from San Francisco behind it. White smoke streamed past the window as Jack worked on his plan.

The small township of San Lorenzo nestled around the railroad depot. Jack stepped out onto the platform and swung his leather bag onto his shoulder, the coach door slamming behind him. A uniformed man with a short beard looked up and down the train that stood puffing impatiently. He could see no other passenger than Jack and he raised his whistle.

A flag fluttered out of the caboose window, evidently indicating that the train could continue. No one wanted to join the train on its journey to Sacramento so the man on the platform waved his flag and blew his whistle. Jack watched the train move out, then walked up to the uniformed man and offered his ticket.

"I want to go out to Sunset Valley," he told him.

"You got the right stop, mister."

The stationmaster was elderly but his whiskers were well tended and he was bright eyed. He looked curiously at Jack, as if wondering what his business might be, but he did not ask.

"Is there any transport that way?" Jack asked.

"Some of the mines has a wagon every two or three days but I ain't seen any lately."

"I didn't say I was going to a mine."

"Nothing else out that way."

"I don't fancy walking," Jack said. He was physically capable of walking long distances but he disliked the idea of being on foot, which carried with it a certain vulnerability.

The stationmaster put his whistle in his breast pocket and tucked the flag under his arm. "Got a stable in town here," he said. "They might be willing to let you have a horse. Can you ride?"

"I sure can."

The other nodded. "Turn left out as you leave the platform," he instructed. "Keep walking. You'll go past the general store and the post office. Turn left again and you'll see the stables on the far corner."

Most blacksmiths of Jack's acquaintance were strong, big men accustomed to swinging heavy hammers and working long hours over hot metal. This smithy was no exception; he was a black-bearded, barrel-chested giant with arms like tree trunks. He gave Jack a nod. "Howdy. Lem Garton," the smithy introduced himself, assessing Jack from under heavy black brows.

"Good morning. Jack Drake," Jack said amiably. It seemed appropriate to be incognito until he knew more of what lay ahead of him. "I want to go out to Sunset Valley. Can you rent me a horse?"

"It'll cost you a dollar a day."

The price was high. "Fifty cents," offered Jack.

"A dollar." Evidently the only smithy in the area, Garton could charge whatever he wanted. Jack was nodding as Garton added, "Ten-dollar deposit."

"Five dollars," said Jack.

Garton shook his head. "She's a valuable animal. Anyways, you'll get it back."

"Let me have a look at her, see just how valuable she is."

"Sure, come on back."

There was only one horse in the stable. "Got three more but they're all out right now," Lem Garton said.

Jack looked at her. She was a quarter horse, a crossbreed, and probably used on a ranch for rounding up cattle. She was a bay with a brown coat and black points.

"Name's Betsy."

She raised her head and whinnied when she heard her name and Garton patted her on the neck. He evidently treated her well, Jack noted.

"Know anything about horses?" Garton asked.

"Some," said Jack. He took a foreleg and lifted it. The black-and-white stripes around the hoof indicated that she was part Appaloosa. He looked at the other hoofs in turn and saw that the shoes were fairly new. He looked closely at her eyes. They were clear. He pulled up her top lip and saw that her teeth were in good condition.

Garton watched all this approvingly. "Yeah, I guess you do."

"All right," said Jack, "I'll take her."

"Hell," said Garton, "you're only going a few miles."

"I know," Jack said. He did not add that he might need a reliable and fairly speedy horse to get away from the mine if the worst happened—well, the next to worst.

"Price'd better include a saddle," Jack said.

Garton appeared to consider Jack's remark; then white teeth gleamed out of his black beard. "Reckon I can manage that."

The nondescript area around San Lorenzo was not quite farming country and not quite ranch country. It showed no sign of being mining territory, but the range of mountains that Jack had seen on the map at the town hall began to the north. He rode toward the range so as to enter Sunset Valley from the southern end.

It was still midmorning and the sun was merely warm. The sky was light blue with a few wispy white clouds. The bay trotted along contentedly, glad to be out of the stable. Jack was an expert horseman and his mount seemed to sense this and respond. On one occasion, Jack had been riding a horse when he was spotted by an old seafaring buddy. "Well, lookee there!" the seaman had said. "A sailor on horseback!"

The mountain range rose gently at first, but as Jack drew

nearer, he saw that the peaks in the distance were much higher. As he entered the valley, the mountains on the other side became visible. The two ranges were very close, making Sunset Valley narrow and confined. They were clearly of volcanic origin, Jack realized, making this desirable mining country.

After two hours of steady riding, he stopped by a rocky outcrop. The bay sniffed out a patch of edible grass and munched happily. Jack had made sure that she drank her fill before leaving the stable so she could go without water for the rest of the day. He opened his leather sack and took out a can of corned beef, a loaf of bread, an apple and a flask of water. He sat, ate and drank.

Nothing was visible and nothing moved except a high-flying bird. The silence was complete. He took his old Colt pistol from the sack and checked that it was loaded and on safety. He put it back with the sincere wish that he would not have to use it. A compass was in there with the pistol, but the double row of mountains made it unnecessary at the moment.

He stretched his arms and legs, limbering up. He spent a few minutes with the horse, calling her by name and letting her get familiar with him. Then he remounted and pulled the reins in the direction of Sunset Valley.

At the entrance to the valley, a trail was just visible on the hard, rocky ground. Jack followed it and Betsy displayed a surefooted caution. The sun was high now and its heat could be felt. The temperature was ideal and there was no sign of rain. The silence was intense after the relentless clatter and noise of busy San Francisco.

After he'd gone on for another hour of steady riding, a cluster of buildings came into sight on the east side of the valley and a well-used track ran toward it. The buildings were at the foot of the mountains, just where they began to rise. A six-foot-high pile of rocks bore a sign: THE JUBILEE MINE—KEEP OUT.

Jack ignored the lack of friendly welcome and rode on.

As he closed on the nearest building, a wooden shack that looked near to collapse, a figure emerged. His gray hair was tousled and his beard was the same color. His clothes were old and ragged.

"Want somethin', stranger?" he asked in a cracked voice.

"Looking for the Maria Elena mine."

"This ain't it."

"Thought not," said Jack, "the minute I saw your sign. Can you tell me where the Maria Elena is?"

" 'Bout eight miles north. On the eastern slope. Easy to miss—got no sign on it."

"Thanks very much," Jack said. "Appreciate your kindness."

He rapped his heels against Betsy's flank and she trotted off. Jack did not look back but he could feel the old man's eyes watching him. From his own experiences in the Yukon, he knew how paranoid men could get from long periods of loneliness and disappointment.

He resumed his ride north. The trail continued, faint but unmistakable. The afternoon sun was warmer but the temperature was still comfortable. When he judged that six or seven miles had been put behind him, he kept a sharp eye on the slopes to his right.

The old man had been right. The Maria Elena mine was easy to miss. If Jack had not been alert to its approximate location, he would not have seen that the track led off to the mountain range to the east. It looked little used and the ground was still rocky and did not hold any traces.

After riding for a short time, Jack saw that the track turned into the foothills, thus concealing the mine buildings. They appeared old but still serviceable. Behind them, skeletons of steel equipment stood. They too were probably old, but there was no indication of rusting in the dry, desertlike air.

Jack could see no signs of habitation. As he rode in among the buildings, no one came to challenge him. He rode slowly past a wooden structure with shuttered doors then another that might be sleeping quarters. The air was still, the sun beat down and not a sound disturbed the silence.

He slid out of the saddle, led Betsy by the reins, and walked throughout the mine area, looking for signs of life. It seemed completely deserted. He gave Betsy her head, no longer leading her, letting her go where her more acute sense of smell might take her. Still, there was nothing.

He looped her reins over a broken steel girder protruding from a mangled mess of machinery and walked slowly past a wheelbarrow that had lost its wheel. Jack could see no sign of water, so this was not placer mining. He looked up at the rising cliffs and noted the quartz ledges, which meant it was all pick-and-shovel mining for nuggets.

He stood and listened. There was the faintest sound of the wind singing up into the canyon that cut into the mountains but nothing more. He walked on past the end of the camp, then came back. No question about it—this was an abandoned site.

Jack felt bitter disappointment. Without any clear idea of what he really expected to find there, he thought he would at least see mining activity that would yield some kind of clue. He wandered around, looking for piles of rejected rock. There were several but he could see no trace of gold in any of the jagged pieces.

He walked again to the mouth of the canyon. He stood, his eyes covering every inch of the cliff faces. At last, he saw it—a wooden door, almost completely hidden by loose rock. It was the entrance to a shaft.

A broken length of angle iron from one of the heaps made a convenient tool and he scraped away rock until the door was fully exposed. He tried to open it. It resisted at first, then gave way with a crunch. He pushed it aside and went in cautiously.

The outside light did not penetrate very far but Jack could see that the shaft was just barely big enough for a man to stand. As his eyes adjusted, he saw that it went out of sight, and he shuffled along, taking short steps. No gleam of metal was visible from the walls and roof, so perhaps the seam had been worked out.

He went on slowly, until he became aware that a wooden plank blocked the way. It was propped almost vertically in the center of the shaft and Jack thought it might support a roof beam. Consequently, he made no attempt to move it. He grasped it and started to squeeze past.

A noise began, the noise of sliding rock, and it grew louder immediately. It filled the small shaft, and before Jack could make another move, a loud roar came from behind him. The light filtering in from the mouth of the shaft disappeared at once and Jack was plunged into darkness. The roaring sound continued for some seconds then subsided. The silence was broken only by the rattle of small rocks and gravel.

The entrance to the shaft was blocked by an unknown amount of rock and he was trapped inside.

Chapter 21

The intense darkness was unnerving. Jack still had an image in his memory of those last seconds. It was of the mine shaft, just big enough to stand in, and then the beam that had propped up the roof. Nothing else.

The utter blackness seemed to shut down all his senses. It was only one short step from death. He forced himself to sit down and stay calm. He felt a panicky urge to open the leather bag, which was still over his shoulder, and feel inside for the box of matches that he knew was there. He did not know how many matches were in it, though, and he might need every one of them. He could not afford to waste a single one. When he lit one, he had to make the maximum use of it, so he sat and thought.

He was disoriented from the rockfall—where were the walls and where were the rocks that had fallen? By touch in the darkness, he might be able to judge which was which. Then he had to decide what his next move would be. There could be only two choices: either try to dig out or go on into the tunnel and see if there were any other exits.

Digging out was going to be a long, difficult and tedious job. It had the advantage that once he had determined where the shaft entrance was, it was only a matter of digging, however onerous that might be. Exploring the tunnel was an inviting choice but he cautioned himself that it might merely raise unreasonably optimistic hopes. An occasional air shaft was dug from mining shafts, but they usually went upward and a climb would be out of the question. A small mine such as this one most likely would not have any

air shafts and would probably peter out eventually. That
usually happened when the ore veins ran out or the diggers
gave up for external reasons.

Jack sat in the pitch-darkness, thinking. Carrying one-
hundred-and-fifty-pound packs over the Chilkoot Pass
through deep snowdrifts and howling blizzards had taught
him how to train his mind to ignore the physical and concentrate on the mental. He called upon all that ability now
and sat there for several minutes.

He stood, having made his decision. He would explore
the mine shaft for a limited distance. If he found nothing,
he would come back and start digging. It was a compromise
but it enabled him to embrace both hopes of escape. He decided against using matches for the moment. He could use
his sense of touch and would only need light when he had
exploited touch to the full.

He fumbled around. It was solid rock. He continued to
move his hands along the rock face and felt it receding from
him. He took two steps in the other direction and touched
the other wall. Between them was the tunnel. He followed
it, pushing one small step forward at a time.

He had gone about eighty paces when the rock face
curved away. He felt for the opposite face. It did not follow
the same curvature—there must be a recess in the wall. He
pulled his leather sack in front of him, opened it and took
out the box of matches.

When the match flared, it was like he'd stepped into another world. He had not realized what deprivation man suf-
fered when confined in darkness. The light from the match
revealed that a large recess did dip into the rock wall and he
held the match high to look into it. A stack of timbers of the
size known as pit-props stood there. He pulled one down.
He had it on the floor in front of him before the match
flickered out.

He did not light another. Instead, he took his trusty jackknife from the sack and whittled at the timber. Then he
pushed the cut strips into a pile and lit it. The light was
bright after the dim flare of the match and he looked into

the depths of the recess. Beyond the pit-props were chopped lengths of timber, cut by an ax into thin strips. Several were tied together to form torches. The miners who had used this tunnel must have lit it this way. Jack quickly grabbed one and lit it from his dying pile of whittled strips.

Holding the torch before him, he felt a surge of hope. What a difference being able to see made! He filed the thought in his head along with many similar impressions related to the theme he most loved to write about: man's struggle to master his environment.

He could now go farther into the tunnel than he had hoped. At intervals, he saw ledges cut in the rock face. They were blackened where torches had burned and enabled the miners to dig. He went on, more quickly now, deeper and deeper into the mountainside. He had brought more torch bundles with him and he had to light a second. When it burned out, he would have to consider going back, but in the meantime, he continued.

Ahead of him, he saw another large storage recess. He had counted one hundred thirty paces from the rockfall. To his delight, the first thing he saw was a shovel. He picked it up, but his delight turned to dismay when it fell into two parts. The steel pins holding the metal end onto the wooden shaft were missing. He looked for other tools but none were evident. He was putting the metal end of the shovel in his sack when a wooden box in a corner caught his eye. He opened it but found it empty except for a sheet of brown wax paper. He was about to turn away when it occurred to him that there was something underneath the wax paper. He pulled the wax paper aside and discovered two sticks of dynamite!

His luck seemed too good to be true, but then he reasoned that torches, a shovel and dynamite were all items likely to be found in a mining tunnel. When a mine was abandoned, many items were left behind. He put the sticks in his sack, dropped the metal end of the shovel in after them, then threw the sack over his shoulder and headed back toward the mouth of the tunnel.

On the way, his eye caught a glint of a reflection. There was virgin metal in the ore here and Jack could not resist. He used the shovel end to jab at the rock until he had dislodged several pieces. He sifted them, picking out those showing the most color and put them in his sack.

Back near the tunnel entrance, he lodged the torch in the rock pile. It was still burning well. He racked his brain for every scrap of memory relating to dynamiting. He had often been a helper to miners who were experts in its use but his own experience was limited. Still, it would have to do.

He was fully aware that what he was intending to do was extremely dangerous. In a routine dynamite blast, most of the dynamic energy generated by the explosion was expended in breaking apart solid rock. The rock pile blocking the tunnel consisted of loose pieces. Setting off a blast in it would mean that rock pieces loosened by the fall would come hurtling down the tunnel, and each one would have the power to maim or kill, and there were thousands of them. It would be like converting the tunnel into a gigantic shotgun, and he would be the target.

The first recess in the tunnel wall was the ideal place to shelter from the blast, but it was far enough away that he would need a long fuse. He took the two dynamite sticks out of his sack. They looked in good condition but he knew only one way to establish that. As for the tail, it was short and would burn for only a few seconds. Again, he thought back to the Yukon.

Jack had worked alongside an old-timer with decades of experience in gold mining and considered what the man would do in this situation. Jack decided to use his knife to cut a strip off the tail of his shirt; then he twisted this into a makeshift fuse. He placed a rock at each end to hold it in position and lit it, counting the seconds for it to burn.

It burned nicely, only to die out when it was halfway. Jack tore off another strip, wider this time, and counted again.

This time, it burned all the way, taking about twenty-five seconds.

He made a rough calculation. He should be able to run at ten miles an hour on the uneven rocky ground—say, seventeen thousand yards an hour, or about three hundred yards a minute. That meant a hundred and forty yards in twenty-five seconds. The nearer recess was eighty paces. That should be sufficient margin.

He cut another strip from his shirt, twined it into a length and twisted it around the tail of one dynamite stick. He was tempted to use both sticks to double his chances in case they were old and one did not ignite. But if the sticks were in good condition, the energy from both might be too much in the narrow space of the tunnel. He resolved to play it safe and use only one. The next problem was exactly where to locate it.

He held the head of the shovel in both hands and dug away at the rock pile. The rock pieces fell away only to be filled in by more rock from above. The biggest hole he could open was a foot or so deep. This would have the advantage that the blast would propel most of the rock outside, Jack reasoned. At least that would reduce the number of rocks hurtling in his direction.

He made sure everything was in his sack. He pushed the dynamite stick into the rock pile, took a deep breath and lit the fuse.

He waited at least ten seconds to make sure it was burning; then he grabbed the torch, snatched up his sack and ran as if his life depended on it. He was well aware that it might.

He dived into the recess, breathless more from tension and excitement than lack of air. The sound of his lungs pumping was all that broke the silence. He counted . . . ten seconds, twenty seconds, thirty seconds. As he went on counting he had a mounting fear that the fuse had burnt out before reaching the stick. What should he do? Go back and try again? How long should he wait? He had to be certain that the stick was not going to explode late.

Fifty seconds must have passed, then a minute. Something had gone wrong. He had taken a step out of the recess when there came a thump. It seemed to have no specific origin; it was as if the whole earth hiccuped. A sound followed, a distant roar like a train in a tunnel. He knew that sound well. When he was riding the rods, suspended underneath a railroad car, he still remembered vividly the terror of the first time he had heard that sound. As he was dozing from the sway of the car, the monstrous sound almost dislodged him from his precarious perch only inches from the track as the train raced along at sixty miles an hour. He grew to recognize it but he never forgot those earlier feelings of utter panic.

The sound was growing louder and louder. It became a gigantic whistle as the air in the tunnel was compressed; then it was like the shriek of a thousand banshees. The patter of small fragments of rock against the walls increased until it sounded like a colossal hailstorm. Then rocks of all sizes were racing past the recess, heavier pieces bouncing along the uneven floor, rumbling and thundering.

Jack had experienced several earth tremors, as had most inhabitants of San Francisco, but this dwarfed all of them in sheer volume of noise, amplified no doubt by the confines of the narrow tunnel. Jack thought he could hear the rock walls cracking and wondered if the blast he had set off had merely entombed him more securely.

Then it was over as suddenly as it had started. Small fragments skittered along the tunnel but the noise was fading. Creaks and groans from the violated earth persisted for a few minutes; then they subsided until the silence was almost painful.

Jack went out into the tunnel. His torch had flickered with the varying air pressure but it was still burning. He saw more and more rock piles littering the tunnel floor as he went on but he paid them no heed. He held the torch at arm's length, straining to see some light at the end of the tunnel. There was nothing but darkness ahead.

His heart sank. Had his efforts been in vain? He tried to determine how much of the rockfall blocking the tunnel had been blasted away but walls and rockfall looked the same. He wedged his torch into the rock and took out the shovel head. He began to dig. It was easy to remove the rocks in front of him. They were not large and were fairly loose. Abruptly, there was a slide from the top of the rocks and—he could hardly believe it—daylight!

Chapter 22

Jack looked across Mason Street at police precinct number eighteen. From where he stood, he could also see the Grace Cathedral, but finding what he was looking for took a few minutes.

Then he saw the ideal candidate: an alert-looking boy about twelve, clothes a little ragged but not unkempt.

"Want to make fifty cents?" Jack asked him.

The boy gave him a skeptical look. "What do I have to do for it?"

Jack held out a note. "Hand that to the desk sergeant in the station over there."

The skepticism did not abate. "That's all?"

"No. You have to wait for an answer. It'll take a few minutes."

"They won't arrest me, will they?"

"Only if you try to rob the bank," Jack assured him, keeping a straight face. "If you're not out in ten minutes exactly, I'll come in and get you."

He waved the note. The boy still hesitated, and it was the appearance of a quarter that convinced him. "Another quarter when you bring me an answer," Jack said. Five minutes later, the boy was back, proud of having entered a police station and emerged safely.

"He gave me this." He held out a slip of paper. Jack read it and handed the boy another quarter.

An hour later, Jack went into the Orion, a small melodeon with a dubious reputation. Only one bartender was on duty and Jack approached him. "Got a message for me?"

The bartender shook his head, surly and uninterested.

"I think you do. Name's Drake."

The bartender turned away, but before he walked off down the bar, he said over his shoulder, "The Red Monkey, across the street."

It was a dingy place and at first Jack did not recognize the man in nondescript clothes lounging at the bar. Captain Krasner was good at adapting. The police captain saw him and beckoned him over. The bar was almost empty and they were able to talk without fear of being overheard.

"Your message said you had some information for me."

"I had an exciting day yesterday," said Jack. "I want to tell you about it and give you something."

Krasner nodded. "Go ahead."

"I went out to a mine in Sunset Valley," Jack began. "It was booby-trapped, no question about it. I was lucky to get out. The people who own the mine have apparently finished with it but they wanted to conceal something there. They booby-trapped it so that if anyone did get into the shaft they wouldn't get out alive."

"What made you suspicious of this mine?" Krasner wanted to know.

Jack told him about O'Sullivan and the connection leading from his wife's name. "How did you get on to him?" Krasner asked.

"He kept showing up in the gambling places. He's a geologist and he owned, or part owned, a gold mine, and the clincher was . . ." Jack finished by telling him of Rosie's words about Sunset Valley, of Sam Hooper and of Magnus Swenson and his last words.

"You took a risk going out there," Krasner said.

"I know, but I'm here."

"I didn't mean that," said Krasner. "You took a risk of spoiling a good lead. If you hadn't found that dynamite, you might not have gotten out, and who would have known where you were?"

Jack grinned ruefully. "You're right. Anyway, here's what I brought you." He took from his pocket a sheet of newspaper rolled into a ball. He waited until the bartender went down to the other end of the bar, then put it in front of Krasner. The captain was equally cautious, opening the sheet of newspaper just enough to see what was in it.

"This is a piece of ore from the mine?"

"Yes, and it's from the shaft that was booby-trapped. It's not easy to hide a mine. The only way to guard whatever secret is there is to make sure that anyone who gets in doesn't get out."

"Do you have any idea what this piece of ore is going to tell us?"

"My only guess is that it's a bonanza, a really rich strike."

"So why would they abandon it?" Krasner asked.

"They may have worked it out. I managed to find these few pieces. They probably took out all they could then booby-trapped it to cover their tracks."

Krasner looked at the piece of ore in the crumpled newspaper. It gleamed with the lure and promise that had seduced men for centuries. He didn't attempt to flatten out the newspaper in order to see it better. Other, covetous eyes, might see it too. "All right. I'll have it assayed." He rolled it up carefully and put it in his pocket. "Find anything else there?"

"After I got out of the shaft, I looked around. The quarters where the miners lived had been abandoned fairly recently. The storage areas had been cleaned out. The piles of tailings had no ore of value—at least I couldn't see any color."

Krasner nodded. "Ah, yes, you did some gold mining yourself, didn't you? So you know valuable ore when you see it?"

"Yes, I do."

"This O'Sullivan—know much about him?"

"No." Jack looked at Krasner. There was a different tone in his voice. "Do you?"

"I've seen his name in the files. His wife, this Maria

Elena, died. She came from a very wealthy Mexican family. A cousin asked us to check on her death."

"You mean the family was suspicious?"

"Yes. I wasn't involved in the investigation, but like I say, I've read the files. The couple went out in their boat, ran into bad weather, and she was washed overboard. Her body was never found. Nothing showed up that suggested he might have murdered her but he did inherit a lot of money."

"He still works as a teacher at Berkeley," objected Jack.

"He lost a lot of money at the gambling tables."

"I see." Jack was quiet for a moment.

"Anything else?" asked Krasner.

"No."

"Be careful." The words were a dismissal.

In Jack's conversation with Tess Tullamore, he had told her that her husband, Tom, had taken the sack of gold nuggets to be assayed. He had brought back an empty sack and presumably left the gold samples with someone for that purpose. Tess had not known where he had taken the sample, but Wells Fargo and the Bank of Philadelphia were the two most likely places. Jack still wanted to follow up on that aspect, so he went first to the Wells Fargo office on Leavenworth Street.

It was still a magical name. Jack, with his writer's curiosity about a host of subjects, knew a fair amount about it. Henry Wells and William Fargo had founded the American Express Company in 1850, but when the company did not want to expand to the West, Wells and Fargo went to San Francisco in 1852 in order to capitalize on the massive migration to California resulting from the gold rush. They set up the Wells Fargo Company, which carried freight, passengers and mail and bought gold dust and bullion from the mines.

Banks in California were hastily formed, but most of them made risky investments in the euphoria of the gold rush, and in 1855, most of the banks collapsed. This left the

Wells Fargo Company in a unique position, and by 1900, they had more than three thousand offices. This one in San Francisco was the headquarters.

On Leavenworth Street, an endless parade of buggies and wagons rumbled by. Horse-drawn cars loaded with passengers honked their way impatiently through the traffic. Workmen in blue uniforms scraped up horse manure with shovels and filled sacks. Pigtailed Chinese peddled brown cigars wrapped in bundles and elderly men carried boards on poles advertising stomach remedies, cough cures, laxatives and corn plasters.

The guard at the door looked Jack over but said nothing. The first room was filled with desks, where agents were handling the shipment and receipt of goods. Some of these traveled by railroad but most were carried on the Wells Fargo stagecoaches, for the company had a firm hold on road traffic between cities, especially in the western states.

Jack went through into one of the adjoining rooms where he knew that the valuable metals were bought and sold. Transactions here were mostly on paper and desks were busily engaged. Jack made his way to the nearest one. "Is Franklin Boyd still here?" he asked. He had known Boyd at the University of California, and though their acquaintance had been brief, he knew that the mention of a name always helped.

The very young man at the desk was probably in his first job, Jack thought. He was fresh-faced and eager. "No, he isn't," was the reply. "Frank got transferred to St. Louis, a promotion. Can I help?"

"It concerns Tom Tullamore, who owned the Silver Dollar Saloon. He brought some ore here for analysis." Jack didn't know whether Tom had brought the ore there or not but he had learned that an assertive opening statement often paved the way. "He was mugged and killed and I'm trying to help out his widow, who has to run the saloon."

That was enough, Jack hoped, to elicit some sympathy. The young man looked appropriately helpful. "I'm not familiar with it but I'll see what I can find out," he told Jack.

He went off into another room and was gone for at least ten minutes. Jack was getting fidgety when he came back.

With him was a middle-aged man with a short beard and pince-nez glasses who wore a neat gray suit. "My name's Whitmore," he said, holding out a hand. Jack shook it. For a moment, he contemplated using his alias, but to do so here in San Francisco was probably not a good idea since too many people knew him.

"Jack London," he said.

"Come in and we can talk," Whitmore said, and to the young man he added dismissively, "Thank you, Edgar. I'll take care of Mr. London." As an afterthought, he went to a nearby desk, scribbled on a sheet of paper and handed it to the young man. "Take care of this too, will you?"

They went through into the next group of offices. These were mostly enclosed and evidently reserved for managers and supervisors. Whitmore led the way into one of the nearest of these. Jack noticed that the sign on the door read W. A. HETHERINGTON. Inside was a mahogany desk with two neat piles of papers and a brass nameplate bearing the name of Hetherington. File cabinets and bookshelves lined the walls and the hardwood floor was partially covered by a carpet that looked to be of Oriental origin. Mr. Hetherington was obviously at an elevated level in the Wells Fargo hierarchy.

When they were seated, Whitmore pushed the nameplate aside and said, "I'm using Mr. Hetherington's office while he is out of town. I'm with the State Treasury Department, spending some time here on an assignment. Now Edgar tells me that you are helping Mrs. Tullamore get over this very difficult period."

"That's right. Are you familiar with the circumstances of Tom's death?"

"He was mugged and killed in the alley behind the Silver Dollar, I understand."

"Yes," said Jack. He was not sure what he had expected to learn coming here, nor had he guessed how cooperative the Wells Fargo Company would be, but he had an uneasy feeling that there was more to both questions than he would have suspected.

Whitmore said nothing but gave a barely perceptible nod, waiting for Jack to continue. "As I told Edgar, Mrs. Tullamore told me that her husband had brought a sample of ore here and she wondered what the results of the analysis were."

It was a few steps beyond the literal truth but Jack wanted to move his investigation along. Whitmore must have something to contribute, he thought, and a show of confidence might be what was needed to bring it out.

"I see," Whitmore said. He continued to look at Jack for a few moments. "Do you know where the ore came from?"

"Mrs. Tullamore didn't tell me," said Jack truthfully. "But you could probably tell from the analysis." He awaited Whitmore's answer to that.

The Treasury man did not answer directly. Instead, he said, "What is Mrs. Tullamore's intention when she has this analysis result?"

Jack played dumb. "Intention?"

"Does she intend to go into the mining business?"

Jack shrugged. "She is running the Silver Dollar Saloon now. She didn't spend much time there when her husband was alive, he ran the place. Now she has a lot of learning to do, but she seems to be making a good job of it." It was not an answer to the question; he wanted to know how far Whitmore would press the point.

"So you don't think she has any interest in mining?"

"My guess would be no but she is a strong-willed woman."

Whitmore seemed to accept that. Jack pressed further.

"I suppose it's possible that if the analysis shows a mine of exceptional quality, she might be tempted to reopen it."

Whitmore raised his head slightly. "Oh, is the ore from a mine that is closed?"

Jack replied as smoothly as he could, aware of his error. "I assumed so. Tom Tullamore had nothing to do with the mining business as far as his wife knows." To get away from that topic quickly, Jack asked, "So what is the story on the ore? Mrs. Tullamore is quite eager to know."

Whitmore sat back in his chair. He was stalling, Jack guessed. Was he waiting for Jack to commit himself further?

Behind Jack's chair, the door opened. Whitmore glanced up and appeared relieved. "Ah, you got my message, good. This is Mr. London. He's inquiring about the sample of ore that Mr. Tullamore left here."

Jack turned.

"Mr. London and I are acquainted," said a man with a familiar Western drawl.

It was Wyatt Earp.

Chapter 23

They shook hands heartily and Whitmore invited Earp to sit down with them.

"Looks like you've been spending some time in the outdoors," Earp said, and Jack grinned. His light complexion tanned easily.

The famous ex-marshal was wearing Western garb, as it appeared he always did. The outfit looked new. The light gray shirt with a blue thread running through it looked as if it had just come from the store, as did the blue string tie. The boots and the belt were highly polished and the big silver buckle gleamed.

Whitmore seemed anxious to get on with the discussion. He took a sheet of paper from one of the stacks before him and scanned it briefly. "The ore sample that Tullamore brought here was analyzed in our laboratory," he said. "It shows some gold but barely enough to be commercially interesting."

"Not a bonanza mine?" said Jack. His disappointment was obvious.

"Not by any means," Whitmore said. "Tell me, what information do you have that made you think it would be?"

"Three men have been killed because of it," Jack said. "That makes it very important and suggests that it had to be valuable."

Whitmore nodded. "Yes, I suppose that's logical. But now that we know that the ore is not of exceptional value, why is it so important?" There was a moment of quiet. "You agree that this question is the natural one to ask?"

"Yes, it is," Jack said reluctantly. Next to him, Earp sat impassive. Why, Jack wondered, was he here?

"We need to find the answer if we are to make any progress," Whitmore said a little pompously. "Do you have any ideas?"

"I need to do some more thinking," Jack confessed. "I was hopeful that this ore would tell us something. If it's without any real value, then a whole new approach is called for."

Whitmore waited for further comment, and when there was none, he said briskly, "Well, I'm sorry to disappoint you. Good luck in your efforts."

Jack walked out through the other rooms with a farewell nod to Earp. The eyes of the guard were on him as he left the building. He walked along Leavenworth Street, past a vendor with a large notice board advertising Dr. Qualifer's Stomach Remedy and a small detachment of the Salvation Army soliciting funds for the homeless. He reached the next corner without considering which way he would head. Just as he paused to make that decision, a figure stepped out in front of him.

Wyatt Earp looked only slightly incongruous on the city street. San Francisco had more than its share of eccentric characters, many of whom dressed differently from the majority. Cowboys, miners, sailors, Mexicans and Chinese in traditional garb could all be seen rubbing shoulders with the local citizenry. It was only the newness of Earp's Western clothes that might attract a second look.

"How about a beer?" Earp offered.

"Okay," Jack said. "It's early in the day but I think I need it."

They found a small bar that was seedy but quiet. Earp ordered two mugs of beer at the bar and took them to a solitary table. He sipped off the foam, then took a large swallow. "Investigation's apt to be that way," he remarked. "Failures as well as its successes."

Jack drank some of his beer. "I suppose."

"Sometimes it can be misleading too. Failures can turn out to be more of a success than you think."

"You're in a philosophical mood today," said Jack. "What exactly are you saying?"

"From time to time, you find that you got to judge a statement by the person who said it. Makes a difference."

"Meaning Whitmore?" Jack frowned.

"He's been a government man a long time now," said Earp. "Guess I was one myself, being a marshal and all, but when you're out in a place like Tombstone, the law can be whatever you say it is. Whitmore's in state government and got himself a whole different way of thinking."

"Wyatt, I know you're trying to tell me something but I'm damned if I know what it is."

Earp gave out a rare chuckle. "Never was much of a diplomat."

"Especially when you ruled that foul by Fitzsimmons." Jack regretted the words as soon as they were out of his mouth but the disappointment of Whitmore's news followed by Earp's oblique approach had riled him. He had no need to worry. Earp smiled, a genuine smile of amusement even though it was at his own expense.

"I'm gonna regret that decision the rest of my life. Sure, it was the way I saw it, and sure, that's the way I called it. If I had to do it over again, I don't see how I could have done anything else. But it was a decision that's gonna follow me around wherever I go and I'll never get away from it."

"That's all a man can do, whatever he thinks is right." Jack was sincere and Earp nodded appreciatively.

"I know you believe that, it's the way your characters think and act," he commented.

Jack looked at him in surprise. "You've read my stories?"

"No, I'm not much of a reader. But I've asked around and everybody tells me those are the kinds of men you write about. Even the Eskimos putting their old folk out on an ice floe or leaving them to be chewed up by wolves, they're doing what seems right to them. Others may see it other ways."

Jack felt a pang of sympathy. "Are you getting a lot of criticism from people who lost money on Fitzsimmons?"

"Nasty looks and some nasty words—not too many of the words, I guess."

Jack grinned. Few men, if any, would express their opinions to Earp's face no matter how much money they had lost. His reputation was awesome even if he had never been known to shoot a man for his critical opinion.

"Take me a long time to live that down," Earp reflected. "If ever," he added. He shrugged. "Still, what's done is done."

"You could leave town," suggested Jack with a straight face.

Earp gave him a sudden angry look, then saw Jack's expression and smiled.

"But you wouldn't do that, not in a million years," Jack went on quickly.

"Guess not. Hell, I like it here. 'Course, it's a funny town in some ways."

"Name a few," Jack invited.

"Never saw a town so corrupt yet never saw a town where the folks were less inclined to do anything about it."

Jack nodded ruefully. "That's true. The way that works, though, is that politicians in San Francisco are mostly corrupt, but they do a good job and give people what they want. The honest politicians haven't been able to do that yet."

"In Tombstone, we shoot or hang villains," Earp said. "Here, you have 'em run the city." He drank more beer and set the mug down. He moved it around in small circles, ruminatively. "Same attitude can seep down through lower levels of government, all the way down from the top officials. Covering up and telling lies can be just as catching as chicken pox."

Earp was trying to tell him something, Jack knew. Something relevant. He tried to edge him along to a revelation that he could understand. "This Whitmore," Jack said, "think he would cover up or lie?"

Earp emptied his glass slowly. Was that so he could put his answer in the right words?

"Men at the top level in politics more or less have to lie and cover up. Men at the levels just below that have a tougher decision to make. They can follow the example of the men at the top and rise in the ranks or they can be real honest and find the upward path real steep. Down at the lower levels, they don't have to make decisions."

"A harsh assessment," commented Jack.

"Yeah," said Earp. "Maybe." He looked around for a waitress to refill his glass. There were none and the bartender tried to look away, but Earp fixed him with a steely look. Two more mugs of beer were brought and slammed down in front of them.

"Sometimes," said Earp, still in that same conversational tone, "a man gets caught in a dilemma. A cover-up or a lie may be the only way to get something done, if it's good—or not done, if it's bad. See, the outcome may be the best thing for the people. What's the harm in a little cover-up or lie in that case?"

"Everybody says you're a straight shooter." Jack smiled. "What are you doing now? Trying to shoot around corners?"

"Maybe I should have tried some of that earlier. Might have avoided all that trouble at the OK Corral."

"Aren't you trying some of it now?"

"Guess I am," Earp agreed pleasantly.

Jack was getting a little tired of this verbal fencing. It was not what he had expected from the legendary lawman from Arizona. Jack was a forthright, direct person with little use for subterfuge, but since had been a law enforcement officer himself, he had had to force himself to adapt. He decided to be blunt whatever evasions Earp might contrive.

"I was out at a mine the other day," Jack said. Earp showed surprise as much as he ever did, which was not much. "It was a gold mine. I had reason to believe that it was closely tied in with this threat. You know of the ore sample that I was asking Whitmore about, don't you?"

Earp nodded. "Sure. It was brought to Wells Fargo for an assay by Tullamore, the guy who owned the Silver Dollar. He was mugged and killed."

"Right. Well, I'm betting that ore came from this same mine that I just visited."

Earp was listening intently. His casual attitude had slipped away. Jack continued. "Now I hear from Whitmore that Tullamore's ore had little value. See, I had been thinking that the mine was a bonanza and it was being used to finance this threat. So here's my problem, and I'm going to put myself in your hands." He fixed Earp with a steady gaze. "I may be putting my life in your hands too. Three men have died already because of what they knew—or suspected—about that ore."

Earp was silent for a moment. Then he said, "Go ahead."

"I have some ore that I collected myself from this mine. I'm going to have it assayed. We'll see how it compares to what Whitmore told us." He paused. "What do you think the result will be?"

"Looks like I got myself between a rock and a hard place," Earp drawled. He pushed his beer mug to one side. "I'm gonna give it to you straight. I worked with Whitmore when he was a marshal and I never had reason to believe he was anything but honest with me. Since we haven't seen each other in a while, I don't know if he's been turned now that he's a big shot in government."

"Since you've been on this case, you must have talked to him enough that you can make a judgment," argued Jack.

"I've not seen or heard a thing that makes me suspect him."

"What about this ore assay?"

"I haven't seen a report on that. I guess when it came in to Wells Fargo, it was brought to his attention and he's kept it that way. He's the only one who's seen the results."

"All right," said Jack. "That makes me all the more sure that I want to get another assay." He flashed Earp a grin. "Appreciate your cooperation."

"Okay," Earp said. "Beers are on me. Watch your back."

Chapter 24

Jack had intended to go see Hanrahan and report on his findings, but in view of the uncertainty surrounding the value of the ore, he decided to postpone that, and so instead he went to the Silver Dollar.

Tess Tullamore was in the small office, poring over papers. She looked up and smiled. "Thank God! Some relief from all this boring office work."

"Didn't Tom have a bookkeeper?"

"Yes, but I'm doing as much of this work as I can myself. Get a better idea of the way the whole place runs this way."

"Good idea," agreed Jack, "if you can stand it."

"I'd rather be up front, pulling beer handles and gossiping with the customers," said Tess. "But if I have to get the Silver Dollar making money, this is how I have to do it. See where the money goes and where it comes from." She smiled brightly. "A lot's going to come from the appearance at the Silver Dollar of Miss Lillian Russell."

"You've got her all signed up?"

"Martin Beck has and she's really coming. He telegraphed me yesterday. Your friend Flo has been very helpful too. Got a whole chorus line under contract. She's starting rehearsals tomorrow."

"She knows her business."

"She's very fond of you," Tess said, looking him in the face.

"A great girl, looks and brains . . ." Jack changed the subject before Tess could continue talking about Flo. "You recall that sack we found, the empty one?"

"Yes."

"The ore sample that was in it went to Wells Fargo. Their assay office reported that the ore was not of good quality."

Tess's face clouded. "So that's a dead end?"

"Not altogether. I had an idea of where the ore might have come from. I went to the mine and got another sample."

"What did the people at the mine say?"

"The mine's been abandoned," said Jack. "It's deserted. Nobody to ask." He thought of telling Tess that it had been booby-trapped to guard whatever secret it might hold but decided it wasn't necessary. "I'm getting another assay, just to confirm."

Tess nodded. "You'll let me know?"

"Of course."

"Time for a drink?"

"Not right now. Good luck with the show."

She flashed him a smile. "I'm going to enjoy putting it on. With Flo's help, of course."

At the Midway Plaisance, the haze of tobacco smoke had risen as it always did during the day. It hovered now, a few feet below the lights, ready to be replenished when the evening crowds came in. One of the orchestra members was tinkling the keys of the piano but he was clearly not the regular piano player. Flo sat at a table with two men and an older woman. It was presumably a conference on some aspect of the coming show.

Jack went to the bar, where his friend Andy greeted him. "Beer, Jack?" He nodded and helped himself to the basket of shrimp in front of which he had strategically located himself. A few handfuls of these and some of the pickled calamari and a dozen oysters would make a satisfying lunch, and it was all free.

He chatted with Andy for a while. The big fight was still a hot topic in town and opinions flowed freely. The two were earnestly debating the method of choosing referees when Andy said, "Flo's meeting is breaking up, Jack. Don't know if she's seen you but you'd better catch her before she gets away."

Flo welcomed him with her customary vivacity and her large dark eyes smiled with joy. "Good meeting?" Jack asked as he kissed her.

"Costumes," Flo said. "Vera is the best dressmaker in San Francisco and the two men bring in material from New York and Paris."

"For the next show, the Marie Antoinette spectacular?"

"The next two shows," Flo corrected him. "That plus the Catherine of Russia spectacular at the Silver Dollar."

"You've got that all set too?" said Jack in surprise.

"Sure have."

"Martin Beck has signed up Lillian Russell?"

"Yes, and she's on her way here right now."

Jack patted her hand on the table. "You're a marvel, Flo. Can you really put on two shows at once?"

"Oh, yes."

"I thought you would have a problem getting girls for the Silver Dollar?"

"I thought so too but I had a stroke of luck. The show at the Alcazar finished early, and they have a good line of girls so I snapped up all of them."

"That's marvelous! Tess Tullamore will be delighted when she hears this."

"What makes you think she doesn't know?" Flo asked coolly.

"Well, I just stopped by the Silver Dollar—"

"Did you?" Flo's tone was cooler. "Before you came here?" She tried to pull her hand from under Jack's but he tightened his grip.

"I had something to tell her."

"You're working for her? One of your investigations?" Flo stopped trying to pull her hand away but she was no longer responding to Jack's grasp.

"No. I shouldn't tell you this—" Jack decided quickly that he didn't want to risk his relationship with Flo and that he had to trust to her discretion. "I'm working for the Saloon Owners Association. There is a threat to everything here on the Coast—in fact, to the whole of the city."

"What kind of a threat?"

"That's the problem—nobody knows just what it is."

"Somebody must," insisted Flo, ever practical. "Or else you wouldn't know there was a threat."

"It's possible that somebody high up in city or perhaps state government knows but they daren't let it be known publicly."

"Why not?"

"My guess is that it could cause panic."

Flo's eyes searched Jack's face. She knew him to be honest and she smiled softly. "Okay. So you're not working for the widow Tullamore. I suppose her connection is that Tom Tullamore was killed because of something to do with this threat?"

"Exactly."

She squeezed his hand. "Are you in danger again?"

"I may be," admitted Jack. It was better not to mention that he had been trapped in a mine by a rock slide designed to kill any trespassers.

"I know it's useless to tell you to be careful," Flo said.

"I always am. That's why I've survived."

"So far," said Flo. "Don't push your luck!"

"I won't," Jack promised, "especially with you. So the great Lillian Russell is on her way here, is she?"

"Yes, she'll arrive tomorrow. Have you ever seen her?"

"No, I haven't. When she was here before, I think I was in the Yukon."

"I haven't seen her either but I've been studying her," Flo said.

"You always do. You learn all about every star before they come here. She's from New York, isn't she?"

"No, Iowa. She made her debut in New York, though. It was in *HMS Pinafore* at Tony Pastor's and he billed her as 'the beautiful English ballad singer.' After that, she appeared in lots of other Gilbert and Sullivan shows and in operettas by Offenbach. Last year, she toured with the Weber and Fields burlesque show. A lot of people said that would be a mistake, but it wasn't. She got to be famous all over the country."

"And now Martin Beck has been able to sign her up to come here," Jack said.

"He says that when he told her he wanted her to play Catherine of Russia, that was what persuaded her to come." Flo gave Jack a big smile. "That was your idea, wasn't it?"

"I think we put the idea together between us."

"You're too modest," said Flo. "You'll never be a success in show business."

She looked over Jack's shoulder toward the bar. "Andy's making frantic signals. I think he wants to tell you something."

Jack turned. Several men were at the bar and Andy was pointing to one of them. "I'll be back in a minute," Jack said.

"All right," said Flo. "I have to go backstage and see how we're fixed in the hat department. Lillian Russell is crazy about hats. She wears as many as eight or ten in an act. I must see what we have and how many will suit the empress Catherine."

One of the men at the bar detached himself from the others and came to Jack. He saw that it was Luke Felson. His face was grim. "You've heard the news?"

"What news?"

"Matt's dead."

Jack was stunned. Matt had been a close comrade of both Luke and Jack. "I can't it," Jack said. "He was so full of life."

"I know. He was really enjoying spending the money he got for his boat, but he was getting a bit itchy, even thinking about buying another. He had taken to going down to the wharf. I heard he was down there and I followed him—it was the last time I saw him. Found him staring out across the bay. Spending too long on land didn't suit Matt."

"How did he die?" Jack asked.

"Stupidly. In a fight."

"A fight? I didn't know Matt was a fighter. He didn't used to be."

"All that money went to his head. Matt couldn't handle it," Luke said sadly. The death of his friend was clearly a severe blow.

"Where did it happen?" asked Jack, wanting to keep his friend talking and help alleviate the pain of the loss.

"The Blue Bull."

Jack nodded. It was a melodeon of bad repute. Fights and deaths there were not uncommon.

"Were you or Greg or any of the others there?" he asked. Most of the fishermen went out in groups.

"No. Matt went on his own."

"So you don't really know what happened? How he got into the fight?"

"No. I need another drink," Luke said, and Jack signaled to Andy, who promptly obliged. "It wasn't inside the Blue Bull," Luke said, gulping the whisky. "It was outside on the sidewalk."

Jack froze. "Outside? On the sidewalk?"

"Yes." Luke regarded him, puzzled. "Why? Doesn't make any difference. He's dead," he added savagely.

"Did anybody see the fight?"

Luke shrugged indifferently. "I don't know. When the law arrived, somebody told them two guys outside the Bull were having a fight. Matt must have joined in, probably had a few drinks too many."

Jack was already forming a different opinion. The story had an altogether too familiar ring. He waved urgently to Andy. "Tell Flo I'll be back."

Luke was looking at him bewildered. "Hey, where you goin'? Don't you want a drink?"

"Going to the Blue Bull," Jack said. "Need to ask a few questions."

Chapter 25

The Blue Bull was only a few blocks away and it was more than half an hour before Jack returned. Flo was talking to a table of out-of-town businessmen when he walked in, saw her and approached. Her usually serene features wore a slight frown.

"Take care of the hats?" Jack asked quickly.

"You told Andy you'd be right back."

"Took a little longer than I thought."

Two regular customers had been the only source of information at the Blue Bull, and such information as Jack gained was not helpful. Two men had indeed been seen fighting out on the sidewalk, as reported by a regular customer coming in. Another customer who evidently enjoyed watching fights without having to pay admission had left the bar to go out and watch.

Jack talked to both of them. The first could tell him nothing that was useful, but the second, a weathered old miner with thinning gray hair, was eager to talk when Jack bought him a whisky.

"Maybe the two of 'em had had fights before," he said in a crackly voice. "They sure wasn't doing each other much damage."

"Go on," Jack urged. This sounded exactly like the incident he had been involved in himself and the incident that had resulted in the death of Magnus Swenson.

"Then this young feller, 'bout your age, came out of the Bull. He'd had a few drinks"—Jack knew enough about drinking from his own dire experiences with alcohol that the word "few" had no exactitude whatever—"but he wasn't drunk. Leastwise, he walked straight enough. Looked like he was going right past the two fighting, but one of 'em pushed the other and he fell against the young feller, nearly knocked him down. Then the young feller joined in." The old man shook his gray head in bewilderment. "Don't know why. It wasn't his fight."

Jack knew why. The two had practiced their "fight" until it was as accomplished as a ballet. Jack listened to the rest of the story and it fit the pattern exactly. He bought the old-timer another whisky and went back to the Midway Plaisance.

When Jack finished giving Flo a carefully edited version of his dash to the Blue Bull, she was full of sympathy for the loss of his friend.

At the bar, Luke was still drinking, and Jack could see that he had better get his questions in fast while the answers would still be intelligible. First, he explained his hasty departure. "Luke, I just went to the Blue Bull and I heard one or two things that might fit in with Matt being killed and I wanted to check them out."

"Killed?" Luke was slack mouthed and glassy eyed but he was coherent. "He was in a fight."

"I know. But it might not have been an accident. Is there any reason for someone to want Matt dead?"

Luke looked alarmed then shook his head. "Dead? No!"

"Luke, this is important." Jack spoke slowly and clearly. "If there is a reason for anyone to kill Matt, then you and Greg are in danger."

Luke swallowed his whisky and ordered another. "That's crazy! Why would anybody want to kill us?"

"I don't know, but I want to find out. And I don't want you or Greg to get killed before I do."

Luke shook his head again. The alcohol had a strong hold on him but the threat of death was momentarily stronger. "What can I do, Jack?" he asked plaintively.

"This man Guilfoyle who bought your boats—have you seen or heard of him since?"

"No."

"Is he fishing them?"

"Nobody's seen him."

"You don't have any idea why he wanted your boats?"

"No idea."

"What did he look like?"

Luke strained to concentrate. "Forty, maybe fifty years old, didn't look too well—you know, bad complexion from not enough outdoors, thin, as if he didn't eat proper."

"Anything else? Any way to recognize him?"

His whisky glass, refilled, appeared on the bar and he reached for it. Jack put a restraining hand on his arm.

"Anything else? Anything at all? You must have noticed more—you sold him your boat."

Luke thought, then brightened. "Beard! He had a beard."

"What color?"

"White. Just a small beard."

"Eyes?"

"Blue, I think."

"Clothes?"

"I don't know, just ordinary."

"Voice?"

"Just a—well, a bit thin."

Jack persevered but that was all Luke remembered. Jack warned him to be careful where he went and asked him to pass the warning on to Greg. Luke had always been the leader of the group and Jack knew he would do that.

During the conversation with Luke, Jack had glanced across the room and seen Flo talking animatedly with a young man who was evidently a reporter from the *San Francisco Chronicle*. As he turned away from Luke, he saw that the reporter was leaving. Jack promptly rejoined Flo.

"Give him a good story?" Jack asked.

"He seemed pleased with it. Lillian's a big draw."

"Fritz doesn't mind you spending time here to talk to a reporter about a show you're doing at the Silver Dollar?"

"I told you, Fritz gives me a free hand here."

"He might think you should be bringing Lillian here to the Midway."

"He's a sentimentalist at heart. I laid it on about the struggling widow. Anyway, I'm working on a couple of big shows to bring here. Fritz is really enthusiastic about them."

"What are they?"

"Well," said Flo, "it's not public yet but Oscar Hammerstein is having talks with Caruso."

"Does that mean you'll be putting on an opera here?"

"We're working that out now. Caruso likes to do other shows too—he knows that audiences out here in the Wild West won't sit still for three or four hours of singing in Italian."

Jack grinned. "I can see the wisdom of that. You wouldn't want to have tomatoes thrown at the world's greatest singer."

"He'd never forgive us. So we'd never let it happen."

"You could really put the Silver Dollar on the entertainment map with your show, you know," he said admiringly.

"Lillian should be a big hit," Flo agreed.

"Will she bring Diamond Jim with her?"

"No, he doesn't leave New York."

"I can understand that," Jack said. "He's nearly three hundred pounds, isn't he?" Diamond Jim Brady was Lillian's usually inseparable companion and a source of innumerable stories.

"Yes, and of course, the *Chronicle* reporter wanted to know all about him too. They have a file on him naturally but the papers here don't give him nearly as much coverage as do the New York papers. I told him how Diamond Jim gives away everything he owns once a year, then replaces it all. That includes at least two hundred fifty thousand dollars' worth of diamonds and other stones."

"The two of them seem to be together a lot. Haven't they ever thought of getting married?"

Flo flashed him a look that suggested the question, *Haven't you?* but she didn't voice it. Instead, she said, "He has proposed dozens of times but she always refuses."

"Does she say why?"

"She says it would spoil a beautiful friendship. He still keeps proposing, though. A few weeks ago, he poured a million dollars' worth of diamonds into her lap to help her make up her mind, but she gave them back and declined once again."

Jack was realizing that he might be on insecure ground with this conversation, but he need not have worried. Flo knew exactly when to use the opportunity and she decided this was not it. "She thinks a lot of him, though—enough that she always takes him with her when she has dates with other men."

"Surely not!"

Flo laughed, a soft melodious laugh that caused her eyes to light up. "You don't think much of that idea?"

"I certainly don't."

"I was thinking of trying it," Flo said archly. "I like to keep up with modern thinking."

"I don't call that modern. I call it crazy." Jack was fervent in his response. In an effort to soften his tone, he asked, "In the meantime, you've solved the hat problem?"

"Yes. I've managed to round up some from the Odeon, some from the Bella Union and some from the Theatre Comique. Lillian Russell really does love hats. She likes to wear a lot of them in a show, especially big, gaudy, floppy hats."

Jack knew that those three were among the top locales on the Coast for lavish shows. "You know just where to go for them, don't you? Or anything else for your shows."

"I love it," Flo said, and it showed in her voice.

"I think I'd like to see these hats you got," Jack said.

"They are in the dressing room backstage."

"Any of the hats suit you?"

"I'll let you decide."

Hand in hand, they went to the dressing room backstage.

*   *   *

It was some time later when they heard noises out in the corridor. "Girls are arriving for the first show of the evening," said Flo lazily.

"I didn't get any writing done today," Jack commented as he groped for his shirt.

"You mean that you'd rather have been writing!"

"No, you misunderstand me. I—"

"You writers are easy to misunderstand. Too much fiction, I suppose," Flo said, reaching for her shoes. "You like to write every day, don't you?"

"Yes, but I missed today. I'll have to make it up tomorrow."

"Your discipline is amazing," Flo said admiringly.

"So is yours," said Jack. "It's just directed into a different path."

Chapter 26

The next morning, Jack was up early after his usual five hours' sleep, ready to make up for his previous day without writing. He had stayed at the Midway for the evening show, one for a packed audience that was fully appreciative of the music, song, dance and comedy.

He read his mail first. It was sparse, the first item of note being a letter from Bess Maddern. Jack had known Bess in his school days. She had helped him with his math and become engaged to Fred Jacobs, Jack's close friend. Just before they were to be married, however, Fred Jacobs died of a fever contracted on the ship taking him to Manila to fight in the war. Jack had established a correspondence with Bess as a small measure of consolation for her loss, and the intermittent flow of communication had continued in both directions.

The next item bore the impressive address of the *San Francisco Examiner*. Jack tore open the envelope, curious to see the contents. A sheet of notepaper fell out. The heading AMBROSE BIERCE, SENIOR EDITOR was printed at the top, and the note was brief:

> *Please stop by Luna's at your earliest convenience—*
> *the usual time.*

Such a note was rare and Jack wondered why Bierce wanted to see him. Their discussions at Luna's were usually of Jack's planning. He set the note aside and pulled some fresh paper in front of him.

The concept of writing a novel had been gestating in his mind for some time now and he had begun to put some of the components together. It would be set in the Yukon, the region he knew so well. His problem was that he had another literary goal—he felt a burning urge to bring public attention to the plight of the workers in so many industries and in so many countries. Starving and oppressed by inhuman management, underpaid, living in dreadful conditions—they needed a champion, someone to bring their predicament to the wide attention of those who could be sympathetic and helpful.

Jack was not sure how to do this. These were the same working conditions that he had discussed with Upton Sinclair, who had told him he was going to expose the atrocious environment of the meatpacking business through the medium of a novel. Having worked in the fish canning warehouses on the northern coast of California, Jack had personal experience of such barbarous and degrading conditions. He began to make notes.

Late in the afternoon, he heard a noise at the door, but he heard no knock, so he completed putting on paper the thoughts that were buzzing in his brain. When he went to the door, he found a terse note.

Martin and Horton at seven tonight.

So Captain Krasner wanted to talk to him. Had there been some developments or did Krasner merely want to know what Jack had learned?

Jack cleaned up his desk, a task that took some time, for he had sheets of paper strewn all over comprising a range of topics. He changed clothes and set off for the Oakland–San Francisco ferry.

The Martin and Horton Saloon was a large and unpretentious place with long bare tables and sawdust-covered floors. It was nearly always full, for the liquor and the free food were unexcelled anywhere in San Francisco. Prices were low and the barroom was the favorite loafing place of most of the queer characters in town.

The emperor Norton had been one of the most prominent figures there until his recent death. He had come from England with forty thousand dollars and, through shrewd real estate dealings, had quickly increased it to a quarter of a million. He put it all into one unfortunate gold-mine investment and lost every penny. The disaster unhinged his mind. He proclaimed himself emperor of the United States and paraded the streets in a dazzling military uniform. Every saloon and bar served him free food and drink, and when he needed cash, he issued bonds of fifty cents each and sold them.

The Martin and Horton Saloon was still the mecca of such characters. Jack had heard stories of others, including Herbie Cullen, who believed that he was George Washington. He wore a Continental uniform of tanned buckskin and came in every night to plan his battles and send communiques to his commanders. Another was Hallelujah Harlow in his high clerical collar and ministerial frock coat, who preached outside and inside and drank huge quantities of beer. He was frequently engaged in heated discussions with Calamity Cartwright, a freethinker who loved to tear apart Harlow's Bible quotations with the bellowed exhortation, "Now listen to the voice of Reason, friends!"

Jack was not a frequent visitor to the Martin and Horton, and for some minutes after his entrance, he stood at the bar enjoying the antics of the bizarre personalities who made up the clientele. He was not aware at first of the identity of the man who appeared next to him. He wore an old seafaring jacket and a small sombrero that effectively masked his face. With a start, he recognized Captain Krasner.

The other's eyes warned him not to express his surprise aloud. Jack nodded, as if to himself, and took another swallow of beer. Krasner waited until the men on one side became involved in a loud argument. On the other side was a pair of Cubans or Mexicans talking Spanish. Krasner said quietly, "Keep your voice down and we can talk here."

"All right," Jack said and waited for the other to continue.

"I have the assay on that sample you gave me. The ore is not of any value, I'm afraid." He drank beer, then went on to ask, "Does that surprise you?"

"I must have been on the wrong track," Jack said softly. "I thought that this threat was being financed by a bonanza mine. But you say the ore is of no value?"

"There is some gold in it but the ore is on the borderline of being worth mining. Could there have been veins of more value elsewhere in the mine?"

"I couldn't see any," Jack said.

"Perhaps all the ore of value had been worked out?"

"Maybe. But among Tom Tullamore's possessions, his wife found a sack that had held gold ore. He had presumably given that ore to somebody to assay. I figured Wells Fargo was the biggest and most reliable place to take it. I went in to ask about it. I was passed on to a man called Whitmore." There was a flicker in Krasner's eyes at the name.

"Know him?" Jack asked.

"Yes, a little. He's in the Treasury Department, State of California."

"He said the ore was of little value."

"The same as the sample you gave me," commented Krasner.

"Yes, but then there is the miner, Magnus Swenson."

"The man who was killed in that fight?"

"Yes. Also Sam Hooper, another miner and friend of Tom Tullamore. Swenson and Hooper had worked together in a mine. They had given the ore sample to Tullamore. Now why did they do that if it was useless?"

Krasner was silent, waiting for the conversation next to him to build up again. When it did so, he said, "I can only tell you that I have no doubt of the reliability of the assay of the ore you gave me. As for Whitmore, well, he's straight as far as I know. Furthermore, it doesn't seem very likely that Wells Fargo would be involved in any cover-up."

Jack felt deflated. He had risked his life in the Maria Elena mine. It seemed as if it had been for nothing. "What about O'Sullivan?"

"I had some more inquiries made about him. It seems that he did work as a consultant to a few gold mines and the last was the Maria Elena. It got into financial trouble and he bought it out. It didn't seem to make him much money, though, and he sold out some time ago."

"Was it still operating when he sold it?"

"Yes, but not showing much profit."

"Who did he sell it to?" Jack asked.

"A name we have no record of, know nothing about him."

"What is the name?"

"Guilfoyle." Krasner appeared to be drinking his beer but he did not fail to catch Jack's reaction. "You know him?"

"No, but I've heard the name."

"In what connection?"

"The fishing business."

Krasner put down his glass. "Fishing?"

Jack told him of the mysterious Guilfoyle buying the fishing boats from Luke, Greg and Matt, his old colleagues from his oyster pirating days. "And to add to that," Jack said, his voice rising with excitement, "one of those friends"—Krasner was pumping his hands in a downward direction above the bar and Jack lowered his voice—"one of those friends was just killed in a fight outside the Blue Bull."

"I think I saw that report," said Krasner. "Matthew Colman?"

"That's right, and the circumstances of the fight and Matt's death coincide with the way Magnus Swenson was killed. Then to cap all that, I was attacked in the same way. These are professional killers. They stage a fight on a busy sidewalk, then drag the victim into it."

"I've seen that method of operation in the files," Krasner said in a somber tone. "There must be eight or ten deaths that have occurred that way."

The two speaking Spanish next to them at the bar became louder. Jack and Krasner were quiet for a few minutes, each thinking his own thoughts and waiting for the argument to level off. Some noise was ideal for their own secretive purpose but too much encouraged them to speak louder, which was what both were trying to avoid.

"I think you need to increase the effort to track down this Guilfoyle," Jack said. "If he buys mines and fishing fleets, you should be able to find him."

"If a man wants to remain invisible in San Francisco, he can do so," Krasner said. "No matter what he owns or buys. He just has to have enough money. Of course, that's true anywhere, but it's especially true here." Jack thought he detected a note of censure in the police captain's voice. "But I will widen the search," he added. "Do you have any ideas?"

"Just one," said Jack.

"Want to tell me what it is?"

Jack expected the question as soon as the words were out of his mouth, and for a second, he wondered if it was wise to tell his intentions. But the death of Matt was still in his mind. He saw again that fresh, eager young face. "Why would this Guilfoyle want a fishing fleet?" he asked Krasner. "He has to have done something with those boats—they are difficult to hide. Even if they have been moved elsewhere, there must be a trail."

"Even in the water?" murmured Krasner, skeptical.

"Yes, even in the water," Jack said stubbornly. "Somebody, somewhere, knows where they are. I'm going to find them."

"It could be a dangerous search. The waterfront sees a lot of murders and a lot of disappearances."

"I know the waterfront," Jack insisted. "I've spent years there, some as an oyster pirate and some as a law enforcement officer."

Krasner nodded reluctantly. "I suppose you're better qualified than anybody." He finished his beer and tossed coins on the bar. "Be careful. I hate murder investigations where I know the victim."

"I've always hated the thought of being a victim," Jack countered.

They grinned at one another, then left, one at a time.

Chapter 27

Outside, it was raining slightly and the air was heavy with the promise of more rain. Fog hovered ominously just above the rooftops, held back only by the heat of the lights and the buildings. Jack turned up his collar, took out his cap and pulled it over his ears.

Shanghai Hanrahan was due for a report, he felt, and he also wanted to see if the proprietor of the Green Bottle knew of a man who called himself Guilfoyle.

Jack found him in conversation with a couple of well-dressed men. Jack waited. The three-man orchestra was trying out what must have been some new music—certainly it sounded new to them. After three tries on one number they moved on to the next, although Jack could not discern any improvement.

The two men left and Jack approached Hanrahan. "Let's go in the office," the saloon owner grunted.

When the door was firmly closed, Jack said, "I wanted to tell you what's been happening." He recounted the events of the past days.

"You've been busy," Hanrahan commented. "Cigar?" he offered, and as Jack shook his head, Hanrahan took one himself and lit it. "So the ore was a dead end," he said gruffly, his words more of a statement than a question.

"Yes," Jack said, "although I still can't understand why Hooper and Swenson thought it important enough to give Tom Tullamore a sample of it."

"It must have had some importance if they were killed because of it."

"I don't know. Now I'm beginning to think that they may have been killed for some other reason."

"What reason?" asked Hanrahan.

"I don't know yet." He had not mentioned the death of Matt Colman, since he could not prove it had any connection with the threat. True, assassins were responsible for Matt's death, as they were for the deaths of Hooper and Swenson, but that was their job—killing people. They might work for anyone who would pay them. Krasner had referred to eight or ten murders in the police files that could have been committed in the same fashion.

"Have any other items of information come in that explain something about the threat to the city?" asked Jack.

"Nothing that helps," Hanrahan said.

"Are you familiar with the name of Guilfoyle?"

Hanrahan shook his head. "Haven't heard it. We owe you some money," he went on, opening a folder and counting out some bills from a cash box.

Jack tucked them away carefully. "Thanks, I'll keep in touch."

"We don't know how much time there is left," Hanrahan said, his face stony as he watched Jack open the door. "Do all you can."

Jack walked up to Stockton Street and turned right, toward Fisherman's Wharf. He stayed on the edge of the sidewalk and kept a sharp eye out for scuffles or altercations of any kind. Fewer people were around as he left the entertainment district. Tendrils of white fog were snaking along the ground as he neared the wharf and they grew thicker as he crossed Jefferson.

The waterfront was never deserted, for ships could arrive or depart at any hour of the day or night depending on the tide. Nevertheless, during the hours of darkness, it was quieter, as loading and unloading were confined to daylight activities. A group of sailors passed him, heading for the fleshpots of the Barbary Coast. They were loud and boisterous, and when they were past, it was peaceful except for an occasional foghorn far out on the bay and the slap of waves against the docks.

Jack walked among the coils of ropes and stacked boxes of partly unloaded cargoes. The fog was thicker than ever here, twisting and writhing as gusts swept in off the water. He left the shipping docks and came to Fisherman's Wharf. The rank smell was one he had once become accustomed to and he inhaled it with nostalgia. It blended with the salt tang in the way he remembered so well.

He walked to the water's edge, where the fishing boats were tied up. In a few hours, they would be sailing out into the bay for their day's work. He strolled past them, looking at the names one by one. The name of Luke's boat, *Princess*, was one he recalled readily. He tried to bring to mind the names of the others.

Greg had named his after his hometown. Where was it? Iowa? Utah? No, it was in the midwest—Ohio, of course. *Columbus*, that was it. That left Matt, poor Matt. It was something from childhood, from school. It was a long name and Matt could hardly squeeze in all the letters when he had proudly painted it on the bow. *Rumpelstiltskin!*

Jack had all of them now and he examined the name of each of the fishing boats as he walked past them, stepping over heaps of nets and tarpaulins. Masts swayed in the choppy waters, ropes clunked and clanked. The smells of fish and salt seemed to get stronger—or was that just sentiment?

Painted letters had cracked and peeled, eaten by salt and time, yet all were legible. None were those Jack was looking for and he walked on to the next group. Soon, he reached the end of the dock. He stood, feeling the chill of the damp winds off the bay, the fog seething around his feet. He could walk back and look again but he was sure that he had not passed any of the boats he was looking for.

This was the end of the fishing boat moorings. The pleasure boats were in the next section, separated by an empty quay. Well, Jack thought, why not? That could be a good place to hide the boats. Until then, he had not thought of looking there.

He walked along, looking at some large yachts, then at some more modestly sized boats. Two vessels, side by side, caught his eye. They had short masts and long yards, the long, tapering spars that came out horizontally from the mast and held the sail. The sail on these fishing boats was of a triangular shape called a lateen.

These boats were feluccas, common in the Mediterranean, where they had been manned by the Italian and Greek fishermen who had recently come to California. Their design had changed little since the Arabs sailed them two thousand years ago.

Jack went to the water's edge to look closer. The names had been painted out recently. He had no doubt, though—these were the *Princess* and the *Columbus*.

He heard sounds in the fog behind him. He moved quickly, as far away from the water as he could. The source of the sounds came into sight, dim in the foggy darkness. A large wagon, four men clustered around it, rumbled by. What could it be? Such cargoes had no place on a pleasure wharf.

The wagon passed him and Jack followed cautiously. It went directly to the two feluccas. Loud grunts and shouted commands guided the unloading of several boxes. None of them was large but two of them must have been exceptionally heavy, for it took all four men to lift them out of the wagon and position them in the boat. Evidently, one boat was not enough and some of the boxes went into the adjacent boat.

Jack crept closer. The slowly rolling fog and the darkness provided intermittent cover.

He could hear scraps of conversation but could not make out any words. He hesitated over approaching closer but decided to risk it. If he stayed at the water's edge, he might be less likely to be noticed. He had just taken the first step when a slight noise behind him caused him to turn involuntarily.

The shapes of two men stood there, one very large.

"Hey, who are you? Why are you snooping around there?" came a rough voice.

They advanced toward him. Jack stood still. When they were a foot away, peering at him, Jack hiccuped. He swayed unevenly. "Never mind me. Who are you?" he demanded truculently.

The bigger of the two men had to be several inches over six feet and built in proportion. The other was about Jack's height and build but moved easily. The big man reached out and tweaked Jack's cap off his forehead. They both stared into his face.

Jack hiccuped again. His swaying took him off-balance and he lurched sideways. He corrected himself and stood stiff and upright, tight as a stick. It was a perfect imitation of countless drunks Jack had seen over the years and he was glad now that he had observed them closely enough to impersonate one. Of course, his knowledge of drunken behavior came also from his own earlier personal experiences and not entirely from watching others.

Maintaining his rigid pose, typical of a drunk determined to be considered sober, he repeated his words. "Never mind me. Who are you?" He enunciated precisely.

"What are you doing here?" the big man barked.

Jack regarded him owlishly. A stupid grin came onto his face. A body sway was noticeable but again he controlled it, only for it to return. He appeared to contemplate the question; then he answered slowly and with faultless articulation, "I am looking for the Rainbow Bar. I know it's here somewhere. Perhaps you know it."

A voice came from one of the boats. It had a querying tone. The big man called back, "All right, we're coming." To Jack, he said, "The Rainbow Bar's up there." He pointed over his shoulder. Jack knew that the Rainbow, the nearest bar to the waterfront, was in fact farther along, but he just nodded. The violent motion seemed to hurt his head and he winced. The smaller man chuckled but the big man just scowled and turned, motioning Jack past him.

Jack went, his mincing gait the cautious progress of a man who is intent on avoiding a fall. He continued on into the sluggishly rolling fog and did not look back.

When he was certain that he was out of sight, he stopped and turned. There was nothing but the darkness and the fog. It would have been useless to get into a fight. One man was too big and tough and the other was fast and agile. This way was better too as it left no suspicion.

He walked on. The two might be able to hear his footsteps and it was better they knew he was on his way to the Rainbow Bar. In fact, he turned and headed quickly for the Harbor Master's Office. He knew where it was, as he had been in it once. It was a glassed-in building with an upper story and a tower. On the ground floor were several offices, almost all of them empty at this time of night, but the port of San Francisco was one of the largest on the Pacific Coast and some activity occurred at all hours.

Jack went into the room where one wall was covered with a huge blackboard. Berth numbers of privately owned boats were painted in and boat names were chalked in the appropriate spaces. These changed frequently. A tired-looking man with unkempt hair appeared as if he had been sneaking an hour or two of unauthorized sleep. He picked up a sheet of paper from a table in an attempt to look busy.

"Looking for something?" he asked.

"Need to take a look at the board," Jack said. "I've forgotten the name of my friend's boat."

The other was too befuddled to offer help. He nodded and sat down at the nearest desk. Jack scanned the board. He knew the approximate berth numbers of the boats where he had been standing when the two men accosted him, and his task was made easier as many of the spaces on the board were empty. This was not the time of year for pleasure boating. He knew that the boats' names had been changed, and certainly neither *Princess* nor *Columbus* showed.

He looked at the slots on the board for two adjoining berths. Wavy lines had been drawn through them. He caught the eye of the sleepy clerk. "No names for those two?"

The fellow studied them. "They're being changed," he said.

"Whose boats are they?"

The man blinked. "Don't know."

Jack thought of pressing further but decided it was safer not to raise any suspicion by asking more questions. He knew where the boats were—that was most important. He nodded to the fellow, who appeared eager to get back to sleep, and left quickly.

Chapter 28

The long bar at Luna's was full at one end, and at the other end sat Ambrose Bierce. The renowned editor of the *Examiner* was alone and nursing a Sazerac. He watched Jack's approach through the long mirror behind the bar and waved an inviting hand.

Jack joined him. "Hello, Ambrose, nice of you to invite me."

A bartender loomed and Jack ordered a schooner of beer. "So, my young friend, how goes the great novel?" Bierce asked.

"I've made a start," Jack said carefully. He knew better than to expose himself to Bierce's barbed comments.

"You know why so few good books are written?" Bierce demanded.

"No," Jack said dutifully.

"It's because so few people write who know anything." Bierce brandished his glass at Jack. "I am sure that you will be writing about subjects on which you are well informed. The snow and the ice, the pain and the anguish, man's arrogance and brutality, the endless war against nature—these are what you know. Stick to them, Jack, stick to them!"

Jack knew how to handle Bierce's acid criticisms but he also knew that an altogether different approach was needed to handle his advice. "What if Jonathan Swift had followed that counsel?" he asked innocently. "We would not have *Gulliver's Travels*."

Bierce glared, then burst into explosive laughter. "You will recall the words I have said to you on more than one previous occasion: Rules are for the obedience of fools and the guidance of wise men."

Jack nodded. "The problem is that many of us are not fools, but as to how wise we are . . . that can be hard to determine."

"It's a wise man who profits from his own experience," declared Bierce, "but I would add to that the cautionary note that it is the wiser man who lets another get bitten by a rattlesnake."

Jack chuckled. "I'm glad you asked me here tonight, Ambrose. You have some new sayings."

"I always have new sayings, but I didn't ask you here merely so that you could enjoy my wit. This investigation of yours, how is it going?" His lowered tone was an indication of his serious intent.

"I'm not making the progress I would like to," Jack confessed.

"The way of the investigation, like that of the transgressor, is often hard," agreed Bierce. "I have had personal knowledge of that recently and that is why I wanted to talk to you. I have some fine reporters on my staff, although I never let them know that is my opinion. I set three of them onto this problem of mine—you recall that I was concerned about attempts to buy up small presses?"

"You said that someone was making offers to local newspapers," said Jack. "You were afraid of increased competition."

Bierce responded explosively, just as Jack had expected. "Competition? I'm not afraid of competition! The *Examiner* is the best newspaper in America! The idea of someone building up a small paper to be any kind of rival to the *Examiner* is preposterous. I get nervous, though, when I don't know who that rival is."

"And your best investigating reporters haven't been able to find out?"

"No, and I don't think they're going to. They seem to have run out of clues. I've harangued them, badgered them and used everything but a whip—and still they've found out very little." Bierce regarded Jack over his glass. "That's why I'm mentioning it to you again. You like to poke your nose into events and mysteries around our fair city. Keep a look out at the same time for a buyer of small presses."

"You say 'presses,' so it's not just newspapers?"

"My latest input is that a publisher of books has been approached. The evidence is that the same buyer is involved."

"And you don't think your reporters are going to get any further?" Jack asked.

"Maybe I'll have to get that whip out after all," said Bierce, putting on a ferocious look.

Jack grinned but kept Bierce from seeing it. The editor liked to regard himself as an ogre to his staff.

"Three of them working on it for a week," Bierce went on, still fuming, "and all they can find is a name that means nothing."

"They managed to get the name of the buyer?"

"Yes, but it was a dead end. A person who virtually doesn't exist."

"What was the name?" Jack asked, his interest increasing.

"Guilfoyle," Bierce said, then drained his glass and waved it in the air to get the bartender's attention.

"Jack," the editor continued, "you don't play poker, as I recall."

Jack was bemused at this sudden change of direction in the conversation. "No, I don't, Ambrose. Why do you ask?"

"I'm glad to hear it," said Bierce, finally getting the bartender to come scurrying over and take his empty glass. "You'd lose money."

"I would?"

"Yes. I noticed your reaction to the name of Guilfoyle. It means something to you. What is it?"

Jack chuckled and finished his beer. The bartender took his glass too. "I can't fool you, Ambrose, can I?"

"Better men than you have tried."

"Okay, yes, I have heard the name. You know that I was an oyster fisherman for a while—"

"Oyster pirate," Bierce corrected him.

"I was an oyster law enforcement officer too," Jack protested.

"You were a pirate first."

"Oh, all right. Anyway, some of my friends from that era sold their boats, sold them to a man called Guilfoyle."

Bierce slammed a fist on the bar. "Capital! We can trace him."

"No, we can't. None of the three know anything at all about this Guilfoyle."

"That's absurd. There must be a trail to him of some kind."

"If your star reporters can't follow it," said Jack, "then my fishing friends certainly can't. Who is this publisher, by the way?"

"Carlyle and Cannon—they're in Richmond."

"What kind of books do they publish?"

"Not your kind of book. Educational, school texts, college primers."

Jack shook his head, puzzled. Bierce waited until another Sazerac and another schooner of beer appeared on the bar. "Did this Guilfoyle say why he wanted a fleet of fishing boats?"

"No, he didn't. Not only that, but he appears to know nothing whatever about fishing."

"And you have been looking for this Guilfoyle?"

"No, I'm concentrating on the more important threat—whatever it is," Jack said. "No, my friends merely told me about it. They were paid handsomely for the boats. But there is a little more. . . ."

Bierce nodded. "Go on."

"One of those friends was killed."

"You mean murdered?"

"I believe so. Murdered in the same way as Magnus Swenson, a gold miner who knew Tom Tullamore. It was done in such a manner that it could be mistaken for a random mugging, but it wasn't."

Bierce's eyes were squinting under the bushy eyebrows. "Can these things be tied together?"

"It looks like it. What they all mean, though—that's the tough part."

"You'd better finish your beer, young fellow. Then you'd better get out there into those filthy dives you patronize and find some clues to this mystery."

"Yes, Colonel," Jack said with a mock salute. Then he added with a smile, "Although I'm beginning to regret that I volunteered."

"Volunteered, hell!" said Bierce. "This is an order!"

Chapter 29

On his way to the Midway, Jack's head was buzzing with the effort of trying to reconcile all these disparate factors. Fishing boats, a gold mine, schoolbooks—how could they possibly have anything in common? And how could a threat to the city of San Francisco arise from any combination of them? A threat that was so ominous that murders were being committed to protect it? Jack enjoyed a mystery, but this one seemed imponderable without more information.

The five-man orchestra was playing the popular "Playmates" as Jack walked into the Midway. Flo had used this number in one of her shows and had told Jack that it was one of many written by Harry Dacre, who had become famous for his "Bicycle Built for Two."

Dacre was one of several English songwriters, Flo had said, who came to America because they could get paid for their songs here. When they had written them in London, their numbers were pirated and played in America and they received nothing for them.

Next, the orchestra went into "Elsie from Chelsea," another song by Dacre.

The colored bunting behind the bar was a different color tonight, Jack noted as Andy came up with a wide smile. "Hey, if it ain't the man from the Yukon himself. Eager to spend all that money you made, Jack?"

"Just a beer, Andy."

"What? No whisky?"

"No, just beer."

Andy shook his head in disappointment. "Flo's in back," he said by way of consolation.

"Don't tell her I'm here," Jack said. "I may not be able to see her tonight."

Andy nodded and winked. He drew a beer and set it before Jack. "Anybody looking for me?" Jack asked. The trumpet ended the piece on a long note. The musicians looked appreciative as one of the waiter girls brought a tray of beers and set a brimming glass before each of them.

"No." Andy glanced toward the door. "But your friend Luke Felson just came in."

Jack waved him over and Andy took his order for a whisky. Luke was still in a stunned mood from Matt's death.

"I can't get over it, can't believe he's gone," Luke said.

"Neither can I," Jack said. They both drank. "You remember I told you that Matt's death might not have been an accident?"

"Yeah, but what—"

"I meant that it was probably murder," Jack said. "And here's what I wanted to ask you: Could Matt have been trying to find out something about this Guilfoyle who bought your boats?"

Luke nodded slowly. "He told Greg that he was curious about him. Matt had talked to some of the other fishermen and nobody knew anything about a Guilfoyle. It seemed strange to Matt that a man who knew nothing about fishing should be buying boats—particularly a man nobody knows."

"It seems strange to me too," Jack said.

"Yes, but you know Matt. He liked to chase reasons for everything, and after he'd sold his boat, he had time on his hands. I didn't see much of him. He could have been prowling around, trying to satisfy his curiosity."

"I'm afraid that's what may have got him killed," Jack said grimly.

"You know more about this, don't you?" Luke turned to look him in the face. "Tell me."

"All right. Yes, I do know more. I was down at the docks,

looking for any of the boats that you sold. I saw yours and I saw Greg's. They were berthed with the pleasure boats."

"The pleasure boats! No wonder nobody's seen them!"

"Right," Jack agreed. "Four men were loading cargo into them. Two more men came along and wanted to know what I was doing there. I made out like I was drunk and they let me go. Then both boats pushed out into the bay."

Luke digested this story, frowning. "You think they're smuggling something?"

"That occurred to me too. I don't know what it could be, though. Do you have any ideas? Any whispers about smuggling?"

"No," Luke said thoughtfully. "Some time ago, it was Chinese, but this doesn't sound like people smuggling. You say you saw boxes being loaded?"

"Yes, and two of them were very heavy."

"But that means cargoes going out," Luke argued. "Not coming in. Can that still be smuggling?"

"That puzzled me also," said Jack.

"Which way did they head?"

"I have no idea. It was dark and there was a fog."

"What part of the pleasure boat berths were ours in?"

"Now don't go getting ideas," Jack warned. "These are dangerous people. Some of them are professional killers. Besides Matt, they have killed three men that I know of—and they nearly killed me on two occasions."

Luke's mouth opened in astonishment. "Lawdy! What's going on?"

"I don't know but it's big, Luke. There is a lot at stake for these people. Human lives mean nothing to them."

Luke's eyes were big but his mouth snapped shut. He had a stubborn streak in him that Jack knew well, so he was not surprised when Luke said, "What can I do?"

"Nothing, Luke. You—"

"Matt's been killed. We're all in danger—you said so yourself." Luke's anger was building up. "We should do something. I'll get Greg and we'll go down to that dock and—"

"Hold on!" Jack was already beginning to regret having told Luke so much, but he had felt that Luke deserved to know how one of his closest friends had died. "Hold on, now, maybe you can help, but going off half-cocked won't do it. We'll put a watch on the dock and try to see where they go and what they are doing. I'll be there whenever I can, but if I'm not there, I don't want any of you doing anything reckless."

Luke still had a rebellious look, so Jack added in his most compelling voice, "I've lost two friends in this already. I don't want to lose any more."

Luke was silent for a moment. Then he said, "All right, we won't do anything without you."

Jack nodded. "Fine. You're in touch with Greg, aren't you?"

"Oh, sure."

"Good. Take it in shifts through the night. We'll meet by that crane, the abandoned one. Start about half an hour after dark. And remember," Jack said firmly, "just watch. These people are very dangerous."

Luke grinned. "Getting cautious, aren't you? Not the reckless oyster pirate I used to know, not the man who, single-handed, fought five Chinese, all with knives."

"No, I'm not that same man," Jack agreed with an answering grin. "That's why I'm still alive."

It was still early by Jack's reckoning, and after leaving Luke, Jack went to the gambling saloons, spending a short time in each one. He learned nothing beyond the fact that tables were active in each saloon and fair sums of money were changing hands. He could see no signs that hinted at anything abnormal and security measures looked no different from his previous visits.

His last stop was the Silver Dollar. A show had just finished and the place was crowded and noisy. Jack struggled through to the bar and finally caught Tess's eye.

"You've come back to us! What'll it be, Jack?"

"All quiet upstairs?" Jack asked.

"Games are still going on. The professor's playing, and Lucky Baldwin came in a little while ago."

"Are they both winning money?"

"One of our regulars, Joe Dean, was playing with O'Sullivan. Joe was just leaving but I caught him and bought him a farewell drink. During our, well, casual conversation, I asked him about the professor."

"Well done," said Jack. "That's the way to do it. What did he say?"

"The professor made a fair amount of money tonight— Joe thought near to a thousand dollars. Gold coins were flowing across the table, he said."

"Did you ask about the professor's system?"

"Yes, I did. Joe's a clever gambler, knows all the tricks. When I asked him about the professor's system, he said he couldn't see any sign of him using one. He didn't follow any particular pattern, simply played and kept winning."

Jack frowned. "Did Joe say anything else?"

"He said the professor's a very canny player. He often wins, but Joe also said that poker's a game of chance and that the professor went through occasional losing streaks too."

"Any of your other customers do a lot of winning or a lot of losing?"

"Lucky Baldwin has the most money out on the table most of the time."

"He can afford to lose more," Jack commented.

"Yes, but he wins more than he loses. We had Wyatt Earp in the other night, by the way."

"Did you?" Jack said offhandedly, not showing much interest.

"He lost some but not enough to hurt."

Jack was not surprised that Earp had been there but wondered if gambling was his main purpose. "Well, I'd better be on my way."

"Stay for the next show," Tess urged. "We can have a drink or two afterward, you and I."

"I'd like to," Jack said, "but I have a big day tomorrow. Need to catch up on some sleep."

"Maybe next time?" Her dark eyes glowed with promise.

"Sure," said Jack.

Chapter 30

The journey to Richmond was a tedious one. Jack had to take the horse-drawn omnibus from Oakland and then had to transfer to a second to Richmond. A half-hour wait between these protracted the morning and it was nearly eleven o'clock before he arrived at Oak Street.

He stood looking at the publishing house of Carlyle and Cannon from the opposite sidewalk. It was in a trim two-story building with large front windows composed of small square panes encased in black wooden frames. He had already viewed the rear, where a small yard opened onto another street. No one had gone in or out while he had been watching, nor was there any sign of movement inside.

That was a long enough appraisal, he decided. He walked across the street and rang the bell. On the second ring, it was opened by a small man with chubby cheeks and rimless glasses that sat partway down his nose. He opened the door only a few inches and peered out with an apprehensive expression.

"Yes?" The question floated out on the end of a breath.

Jack had spent the two omnibus rides preparing his story and he was able to produce it glibly. "I'm from Oakland, city hall. The company that prints most of the documents for us had a fire and we are looking for someone to take over until they get back into business. Carlyle and Cannon came highly recommended as someone who might—"

"Yes, indeed," breathed the little man. He talked breath by breath, it seemed. "That is, we do have a very good reputation—well, we did. Not that we still don't, but what I mean is, we are not in business anymore."

"I see," Jack said in the tone of one who doesn't see. He tried to peer over the little man's shoulder. It was not difficult but he could see nothing in the dim interior. He continued to try, however, and asked, "Are you Mr. Carlyle or perhaps Mr. Cannon?"

"No, I'm Mr. Beckworth. Neither of those gentlemen is here."

Jack continued to peer around as far as the few inches of open door allowed until Mr. Beckworth took the hint. "Would you like to come in?"

Jack did so promptly.

"The business has been sold, you see." Mr. Beckworth sounded sad.

Perhaps his sadness was due to the effect of the sale on his personal position, Jack thought. "Sold?" Jack said. "Goodness me, I had no idea. When you were recommended, we thought—"

"Well, it was very recent," Mr. Beckworth breathed. "Very recent. It took us all by surprise, I can tell you."

He closed the door behind Jack, who found himself in a bare room. Large discolored areas on the floor showed where equipment had been removed. All that was left were several wicker baskets, piled high with trash, mostly paper.

"I suppose you are continuing with the company, under the new regime, that is?" Jack said.

"I'm afraid not." There was almost the hint of a tear in the little man's eye and Jack realized his earlier assumption had been correct.

"That's most unfortunate," he said. "But the buyers will continue to operate the business, won't they?"

"Not in these premises." Mr. Beckworth's tone, formerly melancholy, now took on more than a touch of rancor. "They've taken all the equipment, as you can see." He waved a pudgy hand at the empty room. "Not to mention all of the supplies."

"Gracious!" said Jack. "They have cleaned you out,

haven't they?" He followed his commiserating statement with the vital question. "Tell me, where has it all gone?"

Mr. Beckworth shook his head. "I have no idea."

"But surely the buyers have a publishing company that—"

"I don't know. Mr. Carlyle and Mr. Cannon don't know either. But then, they don't have to care, do they?"

"You mean they got a good bargain out of selling the business?"

"Good? More than good, more than even very good."

Mr. Beckworth's words dripped acid and Jack figured that he was telling all he knew, however much that was.

"These buyers—either Mr. Carlyle or Mr. Cannon must know who they are, where they are?" As soon as the words were out of Jack's mouth, he saw the flicker across Mr. Beckworth's face. Had he been too transparent? He went on, as smoothly as he could. "Mr. Walters will be most displeased when I go back to city hall and say that I have failed to find such a prominent company."

Mr. Beckworth shrugged. The loss of his job was obviously the paramount consideration as far as he was concerned and his future was probably bleak. Jack felt a pang of sympathy for the little man.

Beckworth sighed and went on. "More than that I cannot tell you. Mr. Carlyle and Mr. Cannon are both advanced in years and the offer they received was, as far as I understand it, beyond their fondest hopes. The company has been sold, the employees dismissed, and I am left here to clean up and then close up. Then I go too."

Jack shook his head and his regret was sincere. "I am sorry. I am sure you enjoyed working here."

"It was a fine company, with a good reputation throughout the trade. No company in the Bay Area had a wider range of products—textbooks, schoolbooks, legal documents, local government records, deeds—every one of these requiring different inks, different paper, different print."

"Your customers will miss you," Jack said.

"They will, they will," agreed Mr. Beckworth whole-heartedly.

"And now they will have no idea where to go." Jack made one last try.

"I fear that we can't tell them."

"And you have nothing, not even a name?"

"There was a name," said Mr. Beckworth. "I heard Mr. Cannon mention it. Guilfoyle, I think it was. But I don't know if he was the real buyer or just a representative."

Jack had no difficulty concealing his surprise. It was the name that he had been expecting.

Mr. Beckworth looked around him unhappily. "This is all that's left, I'm afraid. The other rooms are just the same as this one—stripped bare."

Jack gave him what consolation he could as they walked to the door. He shook his hand firmly and wished him the best of luck. The door closed on his sad smile.

The horse-drawn omnibus rattled over an uneven stretch of road on the way back to Oakland as Jack reviewed the morning. He had learned little but at least it was full confirmation that the shadowy Guilfoyle had bought all the equipment of Carlyle and Cannon, and at a price a lot higher than its true worth. Where it was going was still a mystery, but there might be an opportunity to pursue that lead if he and his two friends from oyster pirating days could find out where the fishing boats went when they left the dock on San Francisco's waterfront.

Back home, Jack opened his mail. The first envelope had the name of *Youth's Companion* on it. Jack had sold them stories on previous occasions and he had sent them the revision on "Dutch Courage" they had requested. It certainly took them a long time to decide they didn't want it, he thought. A check fluttered out. It was for twenty-five dollars! Enthusiastic as he always was every time a piece of writing was accepted, he went at the day's work with renewed vigor. The rewriting of "The Son of the Wolf," which he intended to be the lead story in the collection for

Houghton Mifflin, came a little easier. By early evening, he read it through. It wasn't quite the way he wanted it yet but he had made progress.

He put on his oldest clothes, picking the darkest in color. The he went down to the ferry, crossed the bay and walked up Pacific Avenue into the Barbary Coast.

His first stop was a place he had not visited for a while. Doc Lewis's was known far and wide as a gambling saloon where a man could get fair treatment. Tonight was quiet, though. No well-known characters were at the tables and the atmosphere was calm. Jack watched, then moved on to the Haymarket, then to the El Dorado, where he went to the bar and ordered a beer while he studied the tables. The first face that caught his eye was bearded, with a high forehead and deep-set eyes. It was Lucky Baldwin.

He was a man who kept appearing, Jack reflected. He kept showing up as a gambler and as a man with interests in gold mining. Jack watched him play poker. His style was bold and resolute and Jack could understand why the man despised the nickname Lucky—he felt that luck had nothing to do with his success, just hard work and determination.

Baldwin reached out and pulled in the rewards of another winning hand, gold coins, chips and banknotes. Jack regarded the other players at the table. Though Jack did not recognize all of them, they all looked well able to sustain the losses. He did know that the big, portly man with jowls and a majestic beard was a vice president of the Denver and Western Insurance Company. He had a scowl on his face now.

Jack felt someone squeezing in at his side at the bar. He turned. It was Wyatt Earp.

He wore his habitual Western garb and his belt and boots were the usual shiny leather. "Learning how to play poker by watching Elias Jackson Baldwin?" Earp drawled. He leaned comfortably on the bar.

"I'm watching him but I'm not sure how much I'm learning," Jack admitted.

"Lucky don't take much to the idea of losing."

"I was thinking," Jack said, "how he shows up at the gambling tables and in gold mining."

"That he does," said Earp.

"What are you drinking?" Jack asked, waving for the bartender's attention.

"Nothing at this minute." He noted Jack's surprise. "And you better finish yours. You and I are going for a walk."

Jack waited for a further explanation but Earp just jerked his head toward the door. Jack finished his beer and they walked out.

Earp led the way along Montgomery Street, familiar to every San Franciscan as being named after Captain John Montgomery, commander of the USS *Portsmouth*, the man who raised the United States flag here to fix the boundary between the United States and Mexico.

"Going to tell me where we're headed?" Jack asked, increasing his stride to keep up with Earp's long legs.

"Wells Fargo Bank."

"Open at this time of night?"

"It'll be open for us," said Earp. He kept up his rapid pace. The evening air was damp, bursting with rain to come, but the sidewalks were still busy with pedestrians. Horse-drawn carts rattled by with night deliveries. "I had a talk with Whitmore this afternoon. The upshot of it was that I told him it was time he came across. I wasn't prepared to blunder around in the dark any longer. I told him he was holding back. I said he might have a good reason for that as far as he was concerned but that wasn't good enough for me."

Jack glanced at the ex-marshal as they hurried along. His profile was grim. "I promised to take my case to a higher level if I had to," Earp continued. "He didn't want that and agreed to reveal some facts that he had had to keep under cover. He had one condition—he wanted Captain Krasner to be present so that he could be made aware of these fresh facts too. I told him my condition—that you be there as well."

Neither spoke as they covered the few short blocks to the Wells Fargo Bank. The three-story building had a few lights on but only on the ground floor. A night guard stood on duty, a strapping fellow who blocked the door. Earp identified himself and the guard took in the Western clothes and boots, then peered carefully into his face. He gave a reluctant nod. "Yeah, saw you at the fight."

"Too bad if you lost money," Earp sympathized.

"I did," the guard grunted. He stared at Jack.

"He's okay," said Earp, and a steely note of authority was in the words. The guard unlocked the door and pushed it open.

Another guard inside immediately blocked their entry. Earp frowned. "The security's good but we're coming in." He pushed through the doorway and Jack followed. Both stopped.

Captain Krasner stood there, wearing a dark blue fisherman's sweater and cap. He turned to look at Earp and Jack but their gazes were locked on a desk that had been cleared to allow a body to be spread across it. The body was unmistakably dead.

It was Whitmore, the man from the California State Treasury.

Chapter 31

Several stab wounds were clearly visible in Whitmore's stomach and chest. "When did it happen?" Earp asked in a low voice.

"Not much more than ten minutes ago," Krasner said.

"You got here fast," said Earp.

"I was in the neighborhood when I got the message about this meeting. Came over here right away but I wasn't in time to prevent this."

"Didn't the outside guard see it?"

"Both guards were inside and the door was locked. Nivens here heard a struggle outside"—Krasner nodded to the guard who had been outside when Jack and Earp had arrived—"but by the time he had the door open, Whitmore had been stabbed and whoever killed him had gone."

Another man moved to join them. He was white haired and looked every bit the bank executive. His face was nearly as white as his hair. "I'm Carter McCaffrey, I'm the president. This is terrible, terrible." He looked from Earp to Jack. "You're the two men that Whitmore wanted here?"

"There was three of us he wanted here," drawled Earp. "Captain Krasner got here ahead of us." He turned to McCaffrey. "Did Whitmore tell you why he wanted to see us?"

"No." The bank president was shaking but with a firm effort controlled it. "I haven't talked to him many times, as a matter of fact. I received instructions from our branch in Washington to make facilities available to Mr. Whitmore— whatever he wanted."

"Did he tell you what this was about?" Earp asked Krasner.

Krasner shook his head. "No. He said you had been to see him. He said he felt it was time to tell you and me some important information. Perhaps he had kept it to himself too long, he said, but it had been in the best interests of the city." He turned to McCaffrey. "Where was he going to talk to us? Perhaps we had best go there."

The front door rattled and one of the guards unlocked it. Several men were there—some in police uniforms, some not.

"Just a minute." Krasner went to talk to the newcomers. When he came back, he said, "While they are starting the investigation, we'd better talk."

"The office that we had set aside for Mr. Whitmore is over here," McCaffrey said and led the way. It was the same office that Jack had been in before, the office that belonged to a Mr. Hetherington.

Inside, McCaffrey looked at Jack. "I don't believe we've met."

Krasner introduced them. "He's helping us," he told McCaffrey briefly.

Seated at the big mahogany desk, the bank president said, "This was the office Whitmore used when he was here. You are, of course, free to look around. There may be some leads that will help you find who killed him."

Two trays were filled with papers. Krasner pulled the first one to him and pushed the other over to Earp. After a few moments, they looked up. Krasner was shaking his head; Earp was impassive as usual, but said, "Not much here."

"I'd like to ask a question," Jack said, aware that the age and experience of the others greatly exceeded his own but he was determined not to be intimidated by that thought.

"Go ahead," Earp drawled.

"The first man to be killed was Tom Tullamore, the owner of the Silver Dollar. He had brought in an ore sample given to him by Sam Hooper, a miner. Hooper was killed right after that. I'd like to know more about that sample."

"When you say 'brought in,'" McCaffrey asked, "you mean here?"

"I didn't know where Tullamore took it," Jack said. "But if it was important enough that the two of them were killed over it, then it seemed that Tullamore would have taken it to the most reliable place he knew. I figured that would be the Wells Fargo Bank. I came here and asked about it. I talked to a young man named Edgar and he went off and Whitmore came out. I told him the story and he said the ore was not of any value."

"Mr. London here has been very active in this investigation," said Krasner. "He gave me another ore sample that he had, er, obtained. I passed it on to one of our technical experts and he had it analyzed in one of our laboratories. It too was of no value."

McCaffrey was getting impatient. "All this talk about ore seems to be leading us away from Whitmore's death and the important issues here."

"Maybe," Jack said stubbornly, "but I'd like to know more."

McCaffrey shook his head testily. "We shouldn't be wasting time on—"

Earp's calm voice cut in. "Hold on here now. Looks to me like Whitmore wanted to tell us something pretty vital for him to call us in this way. We gotta find out what it is. Maybe it's to do with these ore samples and maybe not." He turned to McCaffrey. "Did Whitmore work close with anybody here?"

"No," McCaffrey said. "He was not a cooperative type of individual." His tone was reprimanding. He was obviously used to running a bank where everyone was part of the team.

"We'd better look through the rest of this office," said Krasner. "Police officers will be doing this as part of a routine murder inquiry but they will not be aware of the ram-

ifications of this case and they won't know what is significant."

"Do we?" drawled Earp, but no one answered.

Jack remained in his seat and allowed the others to go
through the desk drawers, the file cabinets and the cup-
board. "Much of this is Hetherington's," McCaffrey murmured.

Krasner lifted a metal cash box from one of the drawers
in the desk. He shook it and it rattled. McCaffrey looked
over. "I think that's Hetherington's too," he said, but Krasner pulled open the desk drawer and selected a key from
one of several. It fit the box and he opened it.

Jack went over to look. McCaffrey and Earp stopped
their searches and looked. Krasner took out a handful of
coins and looked disappointed.

"Petty cash," said McCaffrey.

"Nothing else," Krasner said after examining the box
carefully.

They continued their hunt until McCaffrey called out,
"Ah, here's a sheet. This is not Hetherington's writing. It
must be Whitmore's." They all crowded around to look at
the sheet, which contained a short list of dates.

1893
1894
1895
1896
1897

"What does that mean?" asked Earp. No answer came,
and twenty minutes later, none of them had found anything
of merit.

A police officer came and rapped at the door. Krasner
answered, talked briefly and came back. "Multiple knife
wounds were the cause of death," he reported. "He died
quickly, probably stabbed three or four more times after he
was dead."

"Similar to the wounds that Tullamore and Swenson and Hooper died of?" Jack asked.

"This officer didn't see those bodies but it sounds like it. They will confirm that."

"What did Whitmore do while he was here at the bank?" Earp asked. "Don't seem like there's much sign of activity."

McCaffrey said, "He wasn't here that much, and when he was, he had little contact with anybody."

"I'd better get back with the team outside," Krasner said.

"I'm not doing any good here either," Earp grunted, unwinding his tall frame.

"A terrible business," muttered McCaffrey, and all agreed silently. "Oh, I almost forgot," McCaffrey said suddenly. "Yesterday, Whitmore gave me some papers to put in my safe. I think they were duplicates but I didn't look at them."

"Now's a good time to do it," said Krasner.

McCaffrey went out and returned in a few minutes with papers, which he spread out on the desktop. The other three left their chairs and gathered to look.

One sheet was an analysis of gold ore, marked SUBMITTED BY THOMAS TULLAMORE. The next was another analysis of gold ore marked SUBMITTED BY POLICE LABORATORY. A third was still another analysis but this one was marked GOLD EAGLES. Each sheet had a code number in one corner.

Captain Krasner was the first to comment. "This is the ore that Jack here gave me for analysis. I recognize the code numbers. I gave it to the police laboratory—why is it here?"

"Our laboratory at Wells Fargo is the best on the West Coast for ore analysis," McCaffrey said proudly. "The San Francisco Police, the U.S. Army, the Department of the Interior—they all send material here for analysis."

"These numbers don't mean much to me," Earp said, "but even a dummy can see one thing."

"Yes," said Krasner slowly. "It's very obvious."

McCaffrey too was thinking as he spoke. "I spent one of

my earlier years in the Wells Fargo division that bought ore from the mines. I remember some of what I learned."

"The analyses are almost the same within a few points," Jack said. "They all show only fifty percent gold."

"Yes," Krasner agreed. "Which is why the ore was described as not being worth mining."

"But look at the analysis of the supposed gold eagles," said Jack. "These have only a little more than half gold in them too!" He looked at McCaffrey. "The rest of the analysis must mean something—they're supposed to be one hundred percent."

"It certainly does." The bank manager had recovered the composure he lost after the discovery of Whitmore's death. "Lead is heavier than gold so it makes up the weight difference."

"The lead content is thirty percent," commented Krasner.

"Yes," said McCaffrey, "but lead would give the coins a different color. They'd be paler, duller than genuine eagles. Look at the other main element in the analysis."

"Copper," said Earp, determined to make his contribution.

"Ten percent copper," McCaffrey said. "That restores the color. When I was in the mining division, we used to get a wide range of the elements in an analysis. The volcanic mountain ranges in California contain an amazing number of different metals. The ore coming from this mine was rare—it contained close to the exact percentages to give the coins their color yet not change the weight and feel."

"Making it real easy to cast phony coins," said Earp. "And with only a little more than half of the gold that's in a real eagle."

"And nobody can tell the difference," said Jack. He looked from Krasner to Earp. "Now we know why the gambling tables are of such interest. These phony coins are being fed into circulation that way."

"Goddamn," said Earp with feeling. "Better check my

winnings. They may be worth only half of what I thought they were."

"That cash box!" Jack said. "Weren't those gold eagles?"

Krasner quickly retrieved the box from the desk drawer, found the key and opened it again. He held out a handful of coins.

"I did think it looked kinda rich for petty cash," said Earp. The coins were all gold eagles.

"That list of dates—I wonder if it refers to the coins?" asked Jack excitedly.

Every one of the coins had a date that was on the list.

"Recent dates," said McCaffrey. "So the newness of the coins wouldn't arouse any suspicion if the dates were checked."

"We can see why Whitmore wanted to keep this information quiet," Krasner said. "It could cause a panic. I wonder how much money they've put into circulation already?"

"The next step is to find out where they are producing these coins," Jack said. He turned to Krasner. "Any clues?"

"No. Do you have any ideas?"

"Maybe." Jack told of his encounter on the waterfront. The three listened intently.

"Fishing boats?" Earp asked, puzzled.

"Friends of mine," Jack explained, "sold their boats to a man called Guilfoyle. I went looking for the boats. I found two of them being loaded with boxes but I wasn't able to find out what was in them or where the boats went."

Krasner sounded irritated at not being informed. "So you have no idea where the boats went?"

"They went in the direction of the moorings of the cargo ships out in the bay. My guess at the time was that some kind of smuggling was going on."

"You could check with the Revenue Cutter Service," Earp suggested to Krasner.

Krasner nodded. "I will, although I haven't heard of any smuggling activities recently that might fit in."

"What about O'Sullivan?" Jack asked. "Are you going to arrest him?"

"That the professor fellow you asked me to keep an eye on at the tables?" asked Earp.

"Yes," said Krasner, "but we don't have a thing on him. He sold his share in the mine and we have no proof of any involvement in counterfeiting eagles." He turned to look at the others. "Well, we've learned a lot today, gentlemen, but we still have a lot to do. I have to bring the commissioners up to date and, Mr. McCaffrey, you have to do the same with the Wells Fargo directors and also with the Treasury Department. Between the police department and the banks, we will have to issue warnings to the bars and saloons and the other businesses in the city. We will have to be cautious—we don't want to start a panic of the kind that Whitmore was trying to avoid."

To Earp and Jack, he said, "You two gentlemen have your agendas too. I trust that you will keep this under wraps a little while longer. Perhaps between us we can end this quickly."

"Maybe we can leave by another door," Earp said. "The front door might be watched."

"Before you go, however," Krasner added, "I need statements from all of you regarding Whitmore's death. Just routine . . ."

Chapter 32

Routine it may have been but it took more than two hours before the police team was satisfied that they had extracted every last detail. Jack thought about what a difference it made when the victim of a crime in San Francisco was a government official. The murders of Sam Hooper and Magnus Swenson had not merited more than half an hour. Krasner subjected himself to the same investigational procedure as Earp and Jack, pointing out that he had been the first on the scene.

Jack felt drained by the time it was over and he was allowed to go. Yet another death had affected him deeply, and he collapsed into bed and for once shut off his alarm clock and slept until late morning.

He had a busy schedule ahead of him. Shortly after noon, he jumped off the ferry from Oakland and went to a café near the San Francisco waterfront. He knew the owners well and remembered that fishermen often brought them some of their catch. Jack enjoyed a large plate of fried fish, then went to the Green Bottle.

Shanghai Hanrahan was loudly berating a bartender, and although he cut short his reprimand when Jack came in, it was clear that the cash register contents and the number of empty bottles and barrels did not coincide. The bartender took off his apron, flung it on the bar and walked out.

"Hard to get honest help," grunted Hanrahan. "Let's go in the office."

Seated at his desk, he lit up one of his cigars, and when

he was puffing smoke clouds, he asked, "Found out anything?"

He did not sound hopeful but his eyes widened and he forgot the cigar in his fingers as Jack told of the gold eagles and the ore from which they were made. Hanrahan knew nothing of Whitmore, though his brows contracted when Jack told him that Whitmore had been with the Treasury Department and had been killed in front of the Wells Fargo Bank.

"So the state government has known all the time what this threat was all about!" he stormed. "They didn't tell us. They just let us keep losing money! God knows how many phony eagles we're taking in. Are they going to reimburse us for those?"

"Whitmore wanted to keep the story quiet as long as possible," Jack said. "The police will be making an official statement to you and the other saloon owners. They want to minimize the impact on the public too."

Hanrahan ranted on about police inefficiency and government ineptitude for some time, then asked, "Do they know where these coins are being made?"

"Not yet."

"Or who's behind it?"

"We don't know that either." Jack subtly transformed the "they" into a "we."

Hanrahan remembered his cigar and recommenced his puffing. Jack waited until the saloon owner had calmed down before continuing. "Now that we know what this threat is, I suppose my job for you is terminated?"

Hanrahan squinted at him through the smoke clouds. Then he took the cigar out of his mouth and snapped, "No, by thunder, it's not terminated!" He rubbed his chin thoughtfully. "I guess I'd better tell you, some of us in the Saloon Owners Association think that one of us—a saloon owner—is mixed up with this threat."

"Do you suspect anyone?" Jack asked in surprise.

"I can't say that right now. Meanwhile, keep on nosing around."

* * *

At the Silver Dollar, Tess Tullamore was wrestling with the books and looking frustrated. She blew at a strand of hair falling over her nose and pushed a big ledger away from her. "Relief at last! I'm glad to see you, Jack. This paperwork has convinced me I need a new bookkeeper."

"I have some news for you." Jack pulled a chair forward, sat and recounted the events of recent hours.

Tess listened in silence. "So that's why Tom was killed," she murmured.

Jack nodded. "I'm afraid so. And Sam Hooper and Magnus Swenson."

"And now this poor Treasury man."

Jack was thinking too of Matt Colman, a simple fisherman who had died as part of the same plot.

"So we have to watch out for counterfeit eagles?" asked Tess.

"Yes, but don't spread the word any more than you can help. It could still have a damaging effect on the city's economy."

Tess was frowning, thinking.

"What is it?" Jack asked.

"Remember those coins we found in that box of Tom's? I'm going to get them."

She was back at once and spread eight of them, all eagles, on the desk. Jack looked at the dates. They ranged from 1894 to 1897. "These are most likely counterfeit," he said, weighing a few in his hand, "even though they feel like the real thing."

Tess examined one of the coins. "I wouldn't know the difference."

"Very few people would," Jack told her.

"I'll return these," said Tess, "and make sure they don't get back into circulation." She forced a smile. "On a more cheerful note, Flo is making great progress on the show. In fact, she'll be here shortly for a rehearsal. You'd probably like to wait for her."

"May as well," said Jack.

* * *

Half an hour later, Flo came in, eye-catching in a blue satin dress with Oriental styling. Jack greeted her with a kiss. "I hear you're making fine progress with the show. How's Madame Russell to work with?"

"She's been very easy, so far," Flo said.

"It must be hard, putting on a new show like this with so little time for rehearsal."

"We seldom get much time for rehearsals," said Flo with a smile, "so that's nothing new. We're using some of Lillian's numbers—ones she's already done in Broadway shows—so they don't need rehearsing. What we have to do now is let her get familiar with our orchestra and our chorus line."

"Does she like the idea of being Catherine of Russia?"

"She loves it. She played Mary, Queen of Scots, once. She thinks this role is similar."

Jack grinned. "I don't think your audiences here will either know or care if she plays the Queen of Scots and you call her Catherine."

Flo raised her chin. "Our audiences are very sophisticated. They know the difference between a Scottish accent and a Russian accent."

Jack decided not to argue with that. "Lillian won't mix them up?"

"She's not trying for one or the other. She was a great hit in New York last year with Dubarry, so she's making a lot of use of that character."

"Any songs like 'On the Banks of the Volga Far Away'?" Jack asked mischievously.

"Our audiences are familiar with the songs of Paul Dresser—and besides, everybody who lives along the Wabash would be up in arms."

"Tess is very enthusiastic about the show," Jack said.

"You've been talking to her?"

"I had some news. I told her. Now I'll tell you."

He gave Flo a brief description of the murder of Whitmore and the revelations concerning the counterfeit coins.

Her eyes widened, and when he finished, she murmured, "Another murder? When will this be over?"

"Very soon now."

"You know who the counterfeiters are?"

"We're very close."

She regarded him suspiciously. "You're still in danger, aren't you?"

"The police can do most of the work from now on," Jack said.

"That Mr. Whitmore who was murdered—you said he was with the Treasury Department?"

"That's right," Jack said.

"There was some big news about the Treasury Department in the New York paper the other day."

Jack knew that Flo was an avid reader of the New York papers, mainly so that she could keep up with the performers appearing on the stage, but she was also interested in other news too.

"What was it?" Jack asked.

"I can't remember. It didn't seem too important at the time. I have the paper in my dressing room. I'll take a look and let you know."

Her suspicions had not lessened since she knew that Jack downplayed the risk he was in so as not to alarm her. But she knew better than to voice those feelings. Jack had a stubborn streak and would finish any job he started.

Jack stayed to watch the rehearsal. The chorus girls looked delectable in their uniforms and he was not surprised to see that Flo had completely disregarded sartorial convention and dressed them as Cossack guards. It was improbable that they would have been recognized as such in Russia, for the very short skirts and the bare arms and shoulders were quite inappropriate for the climate of the icy steppes.

But for the stage of the Silver Dollar and for the purpose of supporting Lillian Russell, the shining star of Broadway, the chorus line was perfect. The dazzling blue uniforms with their glittering gold braid, buttons and epaulets, the silver swords and the elaborate headpieces that failed to conceal flowing hair, created an eye-catching spectacle as the smiling girls whirled and twirled.

An occasional line of music from "The Volga Boatman" punctuated the score and reminded the audience that they were at the Royal Palace in Moscow. Jack thought that many other lines were reminiscent of other musical scores too, but that was normal for a Barbary Coast show, where plagiarism was not an acknowledged word, where the tune was paramount and the show was everything.

Bare legs flashed and posed, figures pirouetted and bosoms jiggled provocatively. The girls took a practiced bow and applause sounded hollow from the sparse audience. The Cossacks trouped off the stage to reappear minutes later as gypsy girls.

The costumes were scanty and enticingly precarious. Skirts swirled and heads tossed, portraying the abandon traditionally associated with Bohemian girls. Bangles on ankles and wrists clashed like cymbals, mingling with the cries of the girls depicting frustrated desire. The orchestra increased the tempo and trumpets blared while violins screamed musical passion.

As the number reached its climax and peaked, the perspiring girls applauded the orchestra while the musicians slapped bows against fiddles and trumpets waved triumphantly.

The girls left the stage. A waiter girl brought the orchestra foaming schooners of beer. Flo came out to join Jack. "What did you think?"

"That was great, Flo! Lillian Russell will have to give her all to match up to that!"

"The girls did very well," Flo agreed.

"They were up to your very high standards," Jack told her.

She smiled as she spread a newspaper on the table. "Here's the article on the Treasury Department I told you about."

It reminded readers that, only months ago, Congress had passed the Gold Standard Act, which put the nation on the gold standard. This meant that gold had become the official medium of exchange in a move to stabilize the economy and encourage growth. The article went on to point out that the issue had long been a bone of political contention. In the 1896 election, William McKinley had run on a platform firmly supporting the gold standard while his opponent, William Jennings Bryan, was equally against it.

However, the newspaper reported, entrance into the twentieth century was bringing about many changes, and among these was an expansion in the use of paper money. The Bureau of Engraving and Printing within the Treasury Department was planning to introduce increasing amounts of paper money. Metal coins, based on gold, silver and copper, it added reassuringly, would continue to be used.

Flo watched Jack read this through twice. "Does this have anything to do with these counterfeit coins?" she asked.

"Very likely," Jack said. "The counterfeiters must have stepped up their campaign to get more eagles and half-eagles into circulation while gold is still in wide use."

The piano player tinkled a few variations on one of the rousing gypsy melodies. A bartender clanked bottles, restocking the shelves for the evening trade.

"Going to stay around for the show tonight?" Flo asked.

"I have to go down to the wharf and talk to a man," Jack said. "If I can, I'll be back." He stood, leaned across the table and kissed her.

Gusty breezes were blowing around Fisherman's Wharf when Jack arrived. Darkness had already fallen but the winds had swept away the fog and under a bright moon the night was clear. Jack preferred to approach the pleasure boat moorage this way, and no one was around as he walked along near the water's edge. The day-shift workers had gone and the reduced numbers of men on the night shift were already at their posts. A swarm of seabirds coasted in and strutted to and fro, picking up fragments of food.

The wind picked up and the air was cold edged. Jack passed all the fishing vessels and came to the commencement of the section where the pleasure boats were moored. He slowed his pace. Either Luke or Greg should be here, according to their arrangement. He stood, watchful.

A figure detached itself from the large disused crane and Jack tensed. Then he relaxed as he saw it was Luke. His friend greeted him in a low voice.

"I hoped you'd be here tonight. We kept watch all last night but nothing happened."

"Are the boats there?"

"Only the *Princess*. Others are out."

"Let's stay under the crane," Jack said.

For an hour they stood, conversing only periodically and then in soft voices. Between the conversations, they watched and listened. The seabirds were noisy at first but quieted as they ate their fill and drifted off in groups to their nests. The water lapped against the wharf, whipped up by the gusting wind. Moorings rattled and once in a while a sound drifted in from distant ships in the bay.

Jack stuck his hands deep into the pockets of his seaman's jacket as the night became chill. Stars glittered in the pitch-black sky.

Then came a different sound. Jack and Luke froze, looking at each other and moving deeper into the cover of the old crane.

Wheels rattled over the uneven surface of the wharf and squeaks came from ungreased axles. A wagon came into sight, four men with it. One of them was berating the others for not greasing the axles. The wagon rolled closer to the crane, where Jack and Luke crouched motionless.

"Won't have to worry about it after tonight," one of the men commented. "This is the last trip, ain't it?"

A response came but it was lost amid the creaking of the wagon and the rumble of the wheels. It went on past and

Jack breathed a sigh of relief. "Let's keep it in sight," he whispered to Luke, and they followed at a distance.

As expected, the wagon stopped at the mooring of the *Princess*. There was grunting and gasping as the men placed the load in the boat, but none of the items seemed particularly heavy. All four men climbed aboard and then came the splashing of oars. The mast of the *Princess* moved slowly away from the wharf.

"It's clear enough tonight," said Jack quietly. "We can watch where they go."

They moved to the edge of the wharf. The boat did not show a light, as was required by the nautical laws, but the moon was brighter than ever now and they could see the boat clearly. It moved over the water, where waves reflected the silvery glow of the moon.

"It's not going to where any of the big vessels are anchored," Luke said, his voice puzzled.

Jack had just reached the same conclusion. "But where can it be going?"

They continued to watch the boat as it moved in a straight line across the bay. It did not hoist a sail and Jack supposed that was because that would make the vessel too visible. It continued to move at a rowing pace. Farther and farther out into the bay it went, still in a straight line. It grew smaller and smaller but the moonlight held and Jack and Luke, never having taken their eyes off it, were able to see it, a tiny speck in the distance.

"In a few minutes, we won't be able to see it any longer," Jack said.

Luke was looking up and then down the wharf.

"What's the matter?" Jack asked. "Hear something?"

"No," Luke said, "I'm getting oriented."

Jack was aware that Luke had spent his entire life as a fisherman on this bay. He knew it like the back of his hand. He waited for Luke to continue.

"She's on a course of three hundred fifty degrees," Luke said. "She hasn't deviated from it." He squinted into the night. "She's still on it."

"Go on," urged Jack.

"She's not going to any of the anchored ships. She's not going up into San Pablo Bay—that's too far. On a three fifty course, she can be going only to one—"

There was no warning. Jack never heard Luke's further words. A massive weight crashed against the back of his head and all was swallowed in darkness.

Chapter 33

The cold was intense. It bit into the very marrow of Jack's bones, freezing all movement and all resolution. Strange, though, that with all this snow and ice, there was no accompanying wind. He could not understand that—the merciless wind usually augmented the chill until it cut into the body like a hundred sharp knives.

He tried to move but his limbs were inert. He tried to open his eyes, but when he did, he could see nothing. A momentary panic flooded over him. It was the fear that every writer experienced but suppressed: the fear of being blind.

What was that sound? At least his ears were operating. It was a low wailing sound, like mourners at a funeral. He tried to see where it was coming from but still could see nothing. Movement was still impossible; his body was as inert as a bag of sand.

Was that sunrise? It seemed to be getting lighter—or was that another symptom of his condition? He felt an immediate resurgence of his normally ebullient spirits. He moved an arm and it obeyed. It was painful but he could tolerate pain now that he realized he was still alive. For a few moments there, he had thought . . .

With a firm effort of will, he pushed all such pessimistic thoughts out of his head. He moved his arms and legs and tried to sit up.

Pain shot through every muscle in his body, but as he finally wrenched himself into a sitting position, the pain abated, or perhaps was less noticeable. His hand touched a wall and he turned his head. The dim light showed a rough stone wall and he used it to scramble to his feet. Again he heard that sound—it was near. The first thing he saw as his eyes adjusted to the gloom was a body.

It was Luke. His own problems forgotten, Jack put an arm under him and propped him against the wall. He felt his neck. A faint pulse still beat, slowly but regularly. He slapped Luke's cheek, shook him gently. Luke groaned, then jerked suddenly and started to move. He groaned louder with the effort but came to his senses. His eyes opened and he half smiled as he recognized Jack.

Five minutes later, Luke was rubbing the back of his head as they both stood at an iron-barred window.

"Funny," Jack said, "my head doesn't hurt any more than anywhere else. My whole body aches, though, as if I'd been kicked by an army mule."

"Mine does," Luke said, still wincing. "Feels like the back of my skull is crushed in."

"It isn't," Jack assured him. "No bones broken. We were hit by an expert." He gestured out of the barred window. "But where are we?"

A quick examination of their immediate surroundings showed them to be in a cell. The floor was uneven rock. The walls were rough stone and one had a big wooden door with iron straps and a monstrous lock. The only outside light came through the small iron-barred window.

It was early dawn. That was the light that Jack had seen when he had first recovered. Strings of orange lights decorated the view and puzzled him. They ran here and there in peculiar patterns. They looked vaguely familiar, and Luke said, "You've forgotten. You used to know that view, coming in early mornings after a night's oyster poaching. I guess I've seen it so many times and more recently than you."

Jack's head still ached and the effort of thinking made it worse. He felt a flash of dizziness but it faded quickly.

"That's San Francisco," Luke said.

Memory flooded back. "Of course!" Jack said. "But that

means that we're—you were just about to tell me when we were both hit on the head—we're on Alcatraz Island!"

"Three hundred fifty degrees from Fisherman's Wharf." Luke nodded. "I should have realized it sooner. A three fifty course goes only to Alcatraz. It passes all the anchored ships, and in a small boat, it's the only possible destination."

"I've never been here before," Jack said. "Have you?"

"No."

The two of them reviewed what they knew of Alcatraz. It had been uninhabited except for pelicans until 1854, when a military fort was built there. That had been abandoned in 1861, when the building had been converted into a military prison. Again, it had been abandoned, then rebuilt and opened once more as a military prison in 1868. It had continued in this role, a political football most of the time. Politicians in power always wanted to rebuild it and the opposition always fought the suggestion.

Jack contributed most of the information. He soaked up any information about San Francisco and its surroundings like a sponge. Luke was less interested. "Maintaining this island as a prison," Jack explained, "has been the theme of all critics of local government. Everything here has to be brought out by boat, which makes it enormously expensive to keep open."

"Right now, it's closed again," Luke said. "I know a fellow who's a guard here. He asked me about the fishing business when he got tired of being without pay every time the prison closed down."

"A perfect place for a counterfeiting operation."

Luke stared. "What operation?"

"Oh, I haven't had a chance to tell you about recent happenings," Jack said, then proceeded to tell his friend of the events at the Wells Fargo Bank.

Luke took hold of the iron bars in both hands and shook them. They remained immovable. He stared out at the lights, less bright now as a weak sun came up in the east.

"So that's why Matt was killed," he said grimly. "He got

curious about what his boat was being used for. He learned too much and they killed him."

Jack made no reply. He was thinking of Tom Tullamore, Sam Hooper, Magnus Swenson and the Treasury officer, Whitmore. They too had died because they knew too much, but he did not want to depress Luke's mood further by mentioning them at this time.

"That's not going to happen to us," Jack said with all the cockiness he could muster. "We've survived more desperate situations than this. Let's see how we can get out of here."

"They've emptied our pockets," Luke said, turning one inside out. "Even if we'd come prepared, we wouldn't be any better off. Still, it was a bit reckless to suggest going to the docks. I'm—"

"Forget it," Jack said.

The barred window was small, but because it admitted some of the sunrise, the cell grew lighter. As the two examined it in detail, though, their spirits sagged. No change from the earlier assessment. They stood by the window, silent and disappointed.

"There's only two ways in or out," Jack said. "The window and the door. We can work on these bars and we can try the door."

The same thought occurred to both of them at the same time. They stood on tiptoe to look down through the bars. A strip of rocky cliff dropped off almost sheer to the water, where angry waves pounded.

"Must be nearly a hundred feet," Luke said, dejected. He shook the bars again. "Even if we could get any of these loose."

They went to the door. "The hinges are on the outside," Jack said. "That leaves the lock." They studied it. It was a massive iron affair, very old and probably dating from the original construction. Despite its age and the humid atmosphere, it was sturdy and showed only traces of rust.

Luke put out an arm and moved Jack back a pace. He raised his leg and lunged at the lock with all his body weight. Luke let out a gasp. Nothing yielded. Jack peered through the big keyhole. "The key's not in it."

They sat on the rocky floor to consider their next move.

It was a long and annoying day. They pushed and pulled at the iron bars in the window. They poked and pried at the lock, all to no avail. Jack reflected that fifty years of military prisoners must have used exactly the same measures trying to find a means of escape from this cell. According to the stories that circulated, there had never been a successful escape from the island.

No one came, no food was brought and no sound could be heard other than the beating of the waves and the shrill cries of the seabirds. Jack wondered if they would simply be left here to die from starvation like in the oubliettes, the forgotten cells in French castles in the books that he had read.

Sleep was difficult during the ensuing night. Both still ached in every limb, hunger and thirst gnawed at their insides and the rocky floor was painfully uncomfortable. Fog wreathed the cell window and its damp cold leached in to chill their bones. Still there was no sound to indicate the presence of humans on the island.

Dawn was gray and gloomy as befitted the mood of the two captives. Luke tried the door once more. It was a forlorn hope. "Better get some exercise," Jack told him. "When our chance comes, we don't want to have frozen muscles."

He did some of the exercises he had done when on long sea voyages, and Luke reluctantly joined him. When they were finished, they went to the window, but all they could see was whitish fog.

Two hours later, they had alternately sat and walked around irritably. Now they sat by the window, silent. A pelican shrieked ear-piercingly as it floated past; then came a different sound. . . .

A key squeaked in the lock.

Both tensed. The key made a grinding sound as it turned; then the door was pushed open. For a few seconds, they stared; then a figure appeared and stood in the open doorway. Neither Jack nor Luke had seen the man before but he was big and tough-looking. He took a step into the cell and another man came from behind him and stood framed in the doorway, a Colt pistol in his hand.

"Come with us," ordered the first man in a gravelly voice. The man with the pistol, smaller but equally formidable, seemed comfortable holding the weapon. He stepped well back to keep plenty of space between them and prevent either Luke or Jack from jumping him.

The first man led the way along a gloomy corridor, its floor the same rock as the cell. Jack and Luke followed, and the man with the Colt brought up the rear, keeping a distance behind and not coming close. They went out by way of a heavy wooden door and on to a well-used path that looked like it might date back to the earliest days of the island's use as a military fort. It was rocky and uneven, and as they went on, it twisted around a small promontory. As it dipped, the path was on the outside of the cliff and they encountered the full force of the battering wind.

At another building, they entered and turned into a corridor. It was dim and dismal too, the only light coming from skylights chopped through the rock above. They climbed some rough stone steps, and at a rough-hewn wooden door, the first man knocked and went in, pushing the door wide. He took a dozen steps into a room that was much lighter and waved Jack and Luke forward. Jack looked back at the man with the pistol but he stood outside, the gun leveled. There was no choice but to obey. Jack and Luke went into the room and the first man went past them and out of the same door, closing it behind him.

"No need to sit down," a man's voice said. "You won't be here long."

Chapter 34

During the building's last period as a military prison, this room had apparently been an office. File cabinets and bookshelves lined one wall. Boxes—some open, some sealed—were piled against another wall. The open boxes contained papers. Bunk beds were near the third wall. A desk remained along with a few chairs. The wall with the boxes had a long window with a view of the bay and a part of the city of San Francisco. Despite wispy fog, the land looked surprisingly close.

No footsteps could be heard outside and Jack concluded that the two men were out there on guard. One chair had been pulled up to the desk and another chair faced it. Both were unoccupied. A faint odor hung in the room, an odor that Jack found vaguely familiar, but then his attention was immediately captured by a figure before them.

A man stood by the window, looking out. The silvery glare of the morning sun was directly in the eyes of the two captives—a ploy that Jack assumed was intended to intimidate them.

"You don't look surprised to see me," the man said. His voice was weak and crackly.

Jack was about to respond that he had never seen the man before but Luke spoke out first.

"You're Guilfoyle. You bought our boats."

Jack studied the man with interest. So this was the shadowy Guilfoyle. He conformed to the description that Luke had given him: about fifty years old, stooped and round-shouldered, with an unhealthy complexion and a wispy gray-white beard. He leaned heavily on an ivory cane.

He was not, at first sight, an intimidating figure, yet Jack felt a slight shudder of apprehension as he looked at him. There was a hidden menace there, a sense of unsuspected power behind the fragile exterior. It was as if he were a coiled spring about to release enormous energy. Jack, in his writer's imagination, envisaged a reptilian presence under that cloak of frailty.

Guilfoyle half turned toward them and gave them a perfunctory glance from pale eyes. "And a very good deal they were," he said in that cracked, forced voice. "They are sturdy vessels, ideal for our purpose, and you got a very good price for them. So we all gained." He licked thin lips before continuing. "A pity your colleague got inquisitive and started nosing around."

Luke took a step forward, his face angry, but Jack laid a hand on his arm to restrain him.

Guilfoyle went on, unperturbed. "Now you've done the same thing and learned more than is good for you."

Jack wondered if the other was uncertain about how much they did know and if this was his way of probing. He decided to go along and perhaps learn more himself. What he and Luke would do with the information was a problem to be tackled later. He spoke out.

"We've learned that you are counterfeiting gold coins using the metal from the Maria Elena mine. It has an unusual blend of alloys that makes the coins almost indistinguishable from genuine eagles and with only half the amount of gold in them."

Guilfoyle's lips twitched. "Ah, yes, the mine. The booby trap in the tunnel worked very well but the fools who set it up didn't have enough sense to search carefully. You must have found some old dynamite sticks and been lucky with them. Very lucky, in fact. The blast might have killed you."

"And now, although you're still putting out counterfeit coins and spreading them around San Francisco, you're worried because there's going to be a big switch over to paper money," Jack said. "You've stepped up your campaign to turn out more coins as there will be a lot of people who don't have faith in paper money who will be anxious for coins."

Guilfoyle nodded slightly. His eyes, expressionless, regarded them with an unblinking stare. He reminded Jack of a rattlesnake about to strike and Jack tried to push aside the thought that he was probably even more dangerous.

"So you're satisfying some of those who want metal money," Jack continued, "by spreading it through the gambling tables in the saloons, which account for a significant amount of the money going into circulation in the city. Most gamblers and perhaps even dealers wouldn't notice the difference. Some of the saloons prepared to take gold and turn it into gambling chips have a man and a scale. Most of those men are familiar with counterfeit coins and can spot them easily. Yours are more difficult to identify. So by keeping an eye on those saloons, you would get confirmation of how good your coins were if no alarm was raised."

Luke was listening, wide-eyed. Guilfoyle said nothing and his implacable gaze did not waver.

"You covered your trail well at the beginning, but when you bought the fishing boats, you made a mistake." Jack paused.

"Go on," whispered Guilfoyle.

"You paid too much for them. They may have suited your purpose, which was ferrying goods and equipment out here to Alcatraz. But these were just ordinary fishing boats. Not knowing their true value, you paid too much. You should have bargained and negotiated, like everyone does in San Francisco. But you were in a hurry, weren't you? The fishermen who sold those boats to you told me about it and then one of them started nosing around, asking questions."

"Yes, Colman, wasn't it? He was asking everyone along the waterfront about me." Guilfoyle's voice was almost a hiss now and the venom in it again reminded Jack of a snake. Still, the eyes remained cold and emotionless.

Jack said nothing. He could sense Luke fuming impotently at his side and hoped that he would control himself a little longer so that they might learn more.

"Then that Whitmore committed the error of meddling in my business too. Another inquisitive fool asking questions. I had to have him eliminated. I hope it was before he could alert people in Sacramento or Washington," Guilfoyle said. "Do you think Mario was in time to do that?"

Mario would be the Latino assassin, Jack supposed. He only shrugged, having no intention of aiding the other.

"And now Mario has another task—to eliminate my partner. He'll do it at the show." Guilfoyle's voice had changed. It was an evil croak now, as if the act of ordering men's deaths was enjoyable to him. Perhaps it was, Jack thought. He could hear Luke's breathing getting heavier and flashed him the briefest of warning looks.

"Your partner?" Jack asked. The longer Guilfoyle talked, the more they might learn and the longer they might prolong what had to be an inevitable execution.

"He's getting to be a nuisance," Guilfoyle said testily. "He is no longer contributing to our alliance. In fact, he hasn't done so since he was able to put this place at our disposal."

"I've heard enough of how clever and ruthless you are," Luke burst out. "I don't care how many partners you want to kill. You already killed one of mine and you're going to pay for it." Before Jack could stop him, Luke was across the room and reaching for Guilfoyle's throat.

Guilfoyle did not move. He rapped twice on the floor with the ivory cane, and instantly the door flew open and the same two men who had brought them here grabbed Luke and pulled him away. One jabbed him viciously on the side of the neck and evidently hit an intended nerve, for Luke sagged to the floor.

Guilfoyle looked down at Luke, not with contempt but with an indifference that Jack found even more chilling.

"Put them both back in the cell," he said and turned away to resume staring out the window. "A couple of days without food or water and they'll tell me all I want to know."

Jack knew that their time was running out. He and Luke had to make a move soon or their chance would be lost. On the way out, Jack watched for the least chance of escape, even though the risk might be high. But the two men were experts. They covered one another, allowed no attacks, even though those would be barehanded, and they were alert every second. One of the men dragged Luke the first few steps but then he recovered.

He struggled to get to his feet and Jack reached out to help him. One of the men pushed Jack away but he persisted and, with one arm around Luke's waist, helped him to walk.

They walked along a corridor, the walls beaded with moisture. This led to a cellblock, where they walked between two rows of tiny cells, and Jack shuddered at the thought of being incarcerated in one of them. His cell in the Erie State Penitentiary had been a palace compared to these. All were empty but the bars looked impregnable and the reputation of Alcatraz of being escape-proof was surely well deserved.

Their footsteps echoed with a hollow ring—a ring of finality it seemed to Jack. The cold chill of the air here changed abruptly as they went into the next area. As they walked through, it was obvious that the heat came from a furnace that emitted a dull red glow from under its lid and at a charging hole.

Jack guessed that this was where the ore was smelted. A number of sacks stood against a wall and presumably contained ore. Pouring ladles stood in a rack nearby, and at the other end of the area, a pair of stamping presses gave off faint plumes of acrid smoke.

He had seen similar machines to these in the prison workshop at the Erie State Penitentiary, where they forged horseshoes and other small items. The air reeked with a smell of burning oil. A wire basket was half full but the stamped pieces in it were not iron. They reflected the dim light with a radiance that told what they were: gleaming gold eagles.

One machine stopped and the man operating it cursed. He pulled open the clamps that held the die, pried it out and examined it with a magnifying glass that sat on a bench. Jack wanted to observe more but the two guards hurried them on through. Then one of them pulled open a door and the cold, damp air from outside hit them.

Chapter 35

Jack found it invigorating rather than cold and he breathed in deep lungfuls. They went back along the same rocky path and Jack flashed a look at Luke, who nodded imperceptibly. This harsh terrain might yield an opportunity.

They could see the waters of San Francisco Bay more than a hundred feet below. It appeared to be late afternoon, judging by the yellow glow in the sky that was the sun behind thick clouds. A chance might occur under these conditions, a momentary imbalance or diversion of attention of either of the guards.

The spaces between Jack and Luke and their captors had lessened and the thought that there was slim opportunity for escape had barely crystallized in Jack's mind when the nearer of the two guards stumbled.

Jack was on him in a flash, concentrating on getting both hands on the other's right hand as it reached for his pocket. His full weight held the arm paralyzed. He heard the second guard shout something, probably a warning to Luke, but Luke had already turned on him. They grappled and swayed; then Jack lost sight of the struggle as he had to focus his full mind on his own duel.

The man's eyes gleamed as they came face-to-face, inches apart. The guard grunted, trying to pull his hand free so that he could reach in his pocket for his gun, but Jack held on, tightening his grip on the other's wrist. For long seconds, they stood immobile, both tense, straining. Then Jack let go and crashed his right fist into the other's face. The man fell away, blood streaming from his nose, no longer reaching for the gun but using his hands to protect himself against the fall.

He hit the edge of the flat area they were on and tried to grab something—anything—his hands flailing wildly. But there was only rock and none of it protruded enough to grasp. Pawing madly, he slipped over the edge and gave a cry as he disappeared from sight.

Jack took time for one deep breath and turned to help Luke, who had already traded blows with his adversary. Luke had a smear of blood on his mouth and his opponent was gasping as Luke jabbed a one-two combination below the man's belt. He made the mistake of throwing a long glance in Jack's direction, probably having seen his colleague slide over the cliff edge. He was justified in being wary of a second opponent entering the fray, but Luke took advantage of the man's temporary lapse and smashed a pile-driving left hand into his solar plexus.

The blow to the stomach pushed the breath out of the guard in one gigantic whoosh and the man staggered, off balance. Jack lunged at him and the man jerked his head around—a mistake. Luke swung another left, speed being more important than aim. It was only moderately powerful but it was enough to send the man reeling. He glanced desperately down to see how near he was to the edge of the cliff but it was too late. One foot was already sliding off the edge, and limbs flailing, he toppled out of sight.

Luke stood gasping but managing a grin. Jack clapped him on the shoulder. Neither needed to say a word. Jack went to the edge and looked down. The cliff was not sheer but the waves foamed where they broke and re-formed. Jack could see no sign of the bodies.

"We'll have to find our own way down," Jack said. Luke nodded and they hurried down the path. It was steep in places but it leveled out occasionally, then dropped again. Finally, they came out at a small dock. Jack held up a warning hand. The dock was about thirty yards away. It too looked old but was still serviceable. One boat swayed against ropes, its name painted out.

"The *Columbus*!" gasped Luke.

They examined the dock and its surroundings with scrupulous care. There was no indication of anyone else being there. "Guess they don't see any need to have a guard down here," breathed Luke, and Jack nodded slowly. They approached cautiously, scanning the rocks above and around them. There was no beach of any kind. It was a natural mooring, a small sheltered cove.

"Must be the only shelter for small boats of any kind on the island," Jack said.

Luke nodded. "It's big enough for the supply boats—that's for sure. It could hold all three of our boats easy as well."

Jack uncleated the midships and bow spring lines and flung them onto the deck. "Two oars," he commented as they climbed aboard into a half inch of water, evidently from splashing waves.

"All we need," said Luke as he pushed off the dock.

They rowed slowly out of the tiny harbor. Jack scanned the surroundings but saw nothing move. He found he was still holding his breath and he let it out.

As they came into the open bay, they were hit with the pounding wind. The waves slapped forcefully at the side of the boat and it rocked severely. Both men steadied it with the oars, but that delayed their rowing, and both were eager to put as much water between them and Alcatraz as fast as possible.

"Better not put the sail up yet," gasped Luke, straining at his oar. "It's too easy to see from up there on the cliffs."

Jack agreed. The wide lateen sail would stand out against the choppy sea and there were still three hours or so of daylight. They pulled on the oars, full deep thrusts that took their toll on Jack's unaccustomed muscles. Still, he was experienced enough to know how to use his body strength to the maximum. Luke sat in front of him and Jack admired his easy, fluid motion and his smooth stroking.

They rowed for about half an hour; then they took turns, each resting and getting his breath while the other continued rowing. Jack used his rest period to gaze at the formidable heap of rock behind them, and especially the water that separated them from it. He could see no sign of a sail and turned his attention to the cliffs.

Alcatraz didn't seem very far away. It was disappointing how little distance they had covered. Jack resolved to row harder when he resumed. The cliffs, though, showed no sign of any activity. He wondered if the absence of the two guards had been noticed yet. Maybe they were going to be lucky and not have any pursuit. True, no other boats were in the small harbor, and they were not aware of any other harbors, but that was not certain.

Luke rested on his oars and Jack took over. Farther out into the bay, the waves were bigger and rougher. The current here seemed to be amidships, but they were setting a course for the mainland, wherever the nearest point would be. San Francisco's north beach would probably be ideal but they were at the mercy of current, tide, waves and wind and would have to go where those took them.

Luke now resumed rowing and Jack felt the slight additional surge forward as his friend's forceful stroking made a difference. They rowed for another half hour. The sky had clouded heavily and it looked like rain but none fell. The coastline of San Francisco seemed to be just as far away, and when Jack threw a look over his shoulder at the rocky mass behind them, he was dismayed to find that Alcatraz appeared to be just as close as it had before.

Luke stopped rowing and turned, panting. "We're not making much headway," he gasped, "and we're taking on water."

Jack looked down at his feet. There were two to three inches in the bottom of the boat. It had been a half inch when they had left.

"Must have a leak," he said to Luke. "She was in good shape when sold to Guilfoyle, wasn't she?"

"Sure. Wouldn't have sold her any other way."

"We could put up the sail," Jack suggested. "There's no sign of anyone coming after us."

Luke shook his head. "That would bring in more water," he objected. He was feeling below the water in the bottom of the boat. His face clouded. "It's more than a leak! She's been run onto the rocks! She's part stoved in!"

"No wonder she was left there," groaned Jack.

"We'll just have to keep rowing," said Luke. "It's going to be hard to make headway with this water coming in. Let's put our backs into it anyway. At least we can get back even if we're full of water."

"I don't think that cunning devil Guilfoyle intends us to escape," Jack said.

"Why do you say that?"

Jack pointed. A ragged, gray-brown triangle was slicing through the water toward them from the north. "Guilfoyle doesn't even intend to do his own dirty work," he said, and his arm moved thirty degrees to where another fin cut the surface. Near it, tails whipped the water.

Both men were fishermen. Both knew that San Francisco Bay teemed with sharks.

Chapter 36

The wind was growing stronger. Waves whipped higher, slapping against the *Columbus*. The sky had darkened, casting an aura of gloom over the waters. Even though the bay was almost completely surrounded by land and was like an inland sea, it was connected to the mighty Pacific Ocean. Ocean tides influenced the water in the bay and mountain ranges to the north of San Francisco caused rapid wind changes.

The deep waters of the bay, while enabling San Francisco to boast a harbor that could easily accommodate all the ships in the world many times over, were volatile in their activity. Jack knew this well from both his seafaring days and his days of oyster poaching. Storms could blow up very quickly and a boat the size of the *Columbus*, sturdy though the lateen-sailed felucca was, could be in danger of capsizing within minutes.

"We're going to have to put up the sail if we're to make any headway," said Luke.

"We can't worry about it being seen from Alcatraz any longer—that's for sure," Jack agreed, "but if this blows into a real storm, having the sail up could turn us over."

It was a dilemma. Both men were uncertain, worried about making the wrong decision.

"I have an idea," Jack said. "Let's cram the sail down under the seats. It won't stop the water but it might slow down the rate it's coming in. Then we'll have to row like hell."

Luke sat, staring at the school of sharks. More tails and

fins were visible now among the gray waves. Every bay fisherman knew about sharks. Most of the more than one hundred different species were fierce predators. They would eat anything that lived and anything that was dead.

Jack had heard that, in the course of gutting dead sharks, many extraordinary objects had been found in the stomachs: knives, harpoon heads, hatchets, iron cleats, gaff hooks, bottles and chunks of wood. Tales were told of rings, boots and coins, but seldom bones—the ferociously effective digestive system of the shark dissolved even those.

Most of the time, though, the sharks' diet was the fish that populated San Francisco Bay. Sharks depended on the same fish as the fishermen who set out every day in their boats from Fisherman's Wharf. The main fact about sharks that Jack remembered from his fishing days was their unpredictability. When an expert made a statement about any aspect of shark behavior, another authority would quote an instance of the reverse.

Some maintained that sharks did not attack people, but others insisted that dozens of swimmers died every year, eaten by sharks. Jack had heard the same stories as everyone else in the San Francisco Bay region: Although some prisoners had found a way out of the military prison on Alcatraz, none had ever lived to reach the mainland. It was universally believed that all had been eaten by sharks.

Jack saw the direction of Luke's gaze. "The sharks are an immediate threat," he said. "A storm might come or it might pass us by. We'll worry about it if it comes."

Luke stood up and reached for the sail. It was old, still serviceable but stiff and unyielding. They pushed it under the seat in the stern and squeezed it forward. They struggled and heaved and eventually got it into place. They stamped it firmly down with their boots.

"It's not much," Jack said, "but it'll help."

They picked up their oars and resumed rowing. It was hard to tell whether the sail staunched the incoming flow of water or not but Jack refused to worry about that. The boat contained nothing else that could be used so the sail had to be the choice.

They moved past the school of sharks. It had evidently found other food, probably some bluefish, and was still feeding. They rowed and rowed, straining over the oars, fatigue and tension forgotten. All that mattered was to reach the shore.

It still looked far away. Jack ignored that realization and just kept rowing. In front of him, Luke's back continued to bend in a smooth tempo, clean strokes cutting the water. As they rowed on, the weather improved. The waves were not as high or as insistent and the wind dropped. The sky remained overcast but they seemed to be making progress toward the coastline.

A bump disturbed them. It came from under the boat. Luke looked back but Jack shrugged. They kept rowing. Another thump came from below, although nothing could be seen on the surface. Luke kept rowing but Jack knew there could be only one source.

"We're bow heavy," Luke called back, resting on his oars. "I've been in this boat too many times. She doesn't sit like this."

"Maybe there are cracks in the bows," Jack said.

Luke stretched forward, feeling the bottom of the boat. "No, don't think so." He continued to grope, then stopped and slid into the bow of the chunky vessel. "There's a rope here," he said, feeling around the prow. He pulled and a rope length came into his hands. He pulled farther and Jack climbed forward to help him. Together they heaved and a sack came into sight. Sodden as it was, the stench of rotting fish assaulted their nostrils.

"The rotten bastards!" Luke shouted. "No wonder we're surrounded by sharks!"

"Guilfoyle's way of protecting against theft!" gasped Jack.

Lacking anything to cut the rope, Luke had to untie it. An expert had evidently combined several tight knots and Luke cursed as his cold fingers tried to pull them loose.

A heavier bump shook the boat, and then to Jack's horror, a huge gray head rose out of the water an arm's length away. Blank eyes stared at him, a silvery-gray snout opened in a mocking grin.

The shark crashed into the boat, as if it were trying to climb in, and it hung on the gunwhale. The boat shivered and rocked from the impact. Spray flew everywhere. By the time it had cleared, the shark was slipping away; then it was out of sight as if it had never been there.

Luke resumed his struggle with the rope. At last, he picked apart the final knot and pushed the remains of the tattered sack and its contents into the water.

"Did you see the size of that brute?" Jack gasped.

"Plenty bigger than that," Luke said matter-of-factly. "Ten to twelve feet, some of them."

Jack climbed back to his seat, still shaken. They resumed rowing. After a few minutes, Luke shouted, "Can't shake them off. They're on to us now and not gonna leave us."

Off the bows, to both port and starboard, fins crisscrossed the undulating surface. "How do they know we're food?" Jack asked.

"They probably don't," Luke said. "We're different and their curiosity about us has been roused. It's easy for them to keep up with us. They can swim faster than a horse can run."

Jack looked back. More than a dozen fins clustered around the place where Luke had dropped the sack of fish. The water boiled in the frenzy of feasting. "That won't last long," Luke said. "They'll finish that any minute and be after us, looking for more."

They put their backs into rowing. The bow rose a little higher out of the waves now but they were still taking in water. At Jack's feet, it was up to his ankles. Forward movement continued but the shore did not appear any closer. The sharks circled them. A drizzling rain started, soaking them, but they kept rowing. A few whitecaps appeared, cresting at the tops of the waves. In addition, they both became aware of a rolling swell that periodically blotted out their view of the coastline ahead. A thin line of fog traced the shore and looked to be growing.

Another thump came at the stern. The sharks were getting aggressive. One broke clear out of the waves, right alongside the boat, and there was a tremendous swoosh of noise. It seemed to hang in the air, then crashed down, throwing up a mass of water that drenched Jack and Luke and showered into the boat. They stopped rowing momentarily and Jack saw that the water was now up to his calves.

They both resumed rowing. Aching backs, tired shoulders, protesting muscles were all forgotten and they rowed—literally for their lives. The water rose. It was near the bottoms of the seats now. Jack flung a desperate glance ahead past Luke's figure, which almost disappeared as he bent forward to commence his stroke. The coast was invisible now and the fog was getting thicker by the minute. Another thump on the port side made the boat rock, and it was followed by two more near it. The gunwhale on the other side almost dipped below the water but the stalwart boat righted itself and rolled level.

They rowed on, everything forgotten except the next heaving stroke. Existence became a nightmare of agonizing pain, utter exhaustion and blinding sea spray as they smashed through the waves.

More thuds shivered the boat, first against the port side, then immediately afterward against the starboard. More followed, seeming to grow in strength, and Jack thought he heard cracking wood, but he tried to persuade himself that he would not hear such a sound from underwater. Luke must have heard the shocks too, as he increased his rowing pace and Jack strove to match him.

This was a fishing boat. It normally moved under sail and oars were not usually used for going any distance. Two men rowing, even two strong men, could not expect to make much headway, particularly in bad weather conditions. Both Luke and Jack were aware of this and of the increasing desperation of their plight. Yet they rowed on.

The water in the boat was now touching the bottom of

the seats and it surged over them as the boat rolled. The water was bitingly cold. A heavier thump came from amidships, and to Jack's chagrin, a plank a few feet in front of his eyes splintered, exposing a hole into which water spurted. Another crash came and the rest of the plank fell inward.

It was followed by a battery of blows and another plank snapped with a report like a gun. Water poured into the *Columbus* and rose before their eyes. Rowing was useless.

The dorsal fin of a shark cleaved the water and the smooth gray snout came above the waves. It had to be a huge specimen. It seemed to keep coming out of the water, endless, mighty, destructive.

Chapter 37

Jack was seventeen years old. He and young Scratch Nelson made a massive haul of oysters, the most they had ever gathered in one night. They celebrated with a colossal drunken spree that lasted three weeks. At one o'clock in the morning, dead drunk from the latest round of the waterfront bars, Jack tried to stagger aboard his sloop at the Benecia Pier.

He fell into the water and was instantly swept away by the powerful tide that raced through the Carquinez Straits. He knew no fear. In his befuddled state, the water felt wonderful and he was ready to die, the alcohol still coursing through his consciousness to keep him in a state of euphoria.

Yet that was years ago, so why was he living through it again? The water was colder now. It was unfair that he had to relive that earlier experience. One of his favorite books was Herman Melville's *Moby-Dick*. Ever since reading it, he could see in his mind that terrifying white whale surging out of the water, the eye gleaming, for the creature was so huge that only the eye on one side could be seen. Melville's magnificently graphic prose came back to him in all its frightening detail.

This shark was almost that large. A shark? How had the whale become a shark? It was more terrifying, a man-eater accompanied by a dozen others nearly as menacing. Its jaws opened wide enough to swallow a man. The others swarmed after it, all intent on their prey.

The past and the present merged into one. Images of

Luke using his oar to batter at the sea monster, the oar breaking into pieces and being torn away by the wind that had blown up again. The rain had resumed too as the *Columbus* sank deeper into the waves.

A face swam into Jack's vision. A woman, pleasant featured, fair hair, a soothing smile.

Beyond her, Jack found trouble with his focus. As his eyes fought to adjust, hunger pangs battled with aching arms and legs.

"That's better," the woman said.

"Where am I?" Jack groaned. His whole body felt numb with cold and pain, and as he got out the words, he had to spit out salt water.

"You're in the Salvation Army Rescue Center. A fisherman trying to get back before the storm saw your mast. He dragged you aboard just before your boat sank."

"I remember now. The boat was attacked by sharks."

"One fishing boat had already sunk. They think sharks got its crew. That made them more fierce than usual."

Jack's memory was recovering. His previous recollections of the Carquinez Straits had terminated with his rescue by a Greek fisherman. It seemed that history had repeated itself and he had again been saved by a fisherman, this time one hurrying back to the safety of the shore. Another thought struck him.

"Luke!" he gasped. "My friend in the boat with me!"

The nurse shook her head. "I don't know. Let me ask." She called another woman and spoke to her in a soft voice. The woman nodded and left.

Jack fell back. The pillow was warm and comforting. He strove to stay awake, though the lure of sleep was hard to resist. He was drifting away when the nurse returned.

"He's all right, your friend. He's in another room."

His mind at rest on that score, Jack found his strength returning. He tried to sit up but the nurse restrained him.

"You must wait until you're stronger."

"Then you have to get a message to the nearest police precinct."

The nurse studied him, evidently trying to decide if he was coherent or still suffering from exposure.

"It's urgent," Jack said and didn't wait for her response. "Tell them to contact Captain Krasner and have him come here. My name is Jack London."

The nurse nodded. "I will if you'll rest."

"I'll rest if you'll swear to me that you'll have the message delivered."

She nodded again. "All right, I will."

"And take good care of my friend."

Captain Krasner was there in less than an hour and by then Jack was sound asleep. He awoke with Krasner shaking his arm and the nurse protesting. "It must be urgent or he wouldn't have called for me," Krasner was saying to her.

He made sure that she had left and that there was no one within earshot before he had Jack tell his story. He listened intently then asked several questions. Jack felt drowsiness overcoming him on a couple of occasions but he fought it off. Finally Krasner said, "If Guilfoyle was talking about removing his partner, who do you suppose he meant?"

"Professor O'Sullivan would be my guess."

"Mine too. We'll pull him in, see what he can tell us. Now you'd better get some more sleep. You've done well. I'll talk to you again tomorrow. I'll see if I can pull in a few extra men tonight."

"Tonight?" asked Jack. "What's tonight?" Then it all began to flood back into his mind. "Opening night! Lillian Russell! Of course, I'd lost track—"

"It's understandable," Krasner said. "Now you just sleep. Leave it to us."

Jack had his mouth open to protest, but the stern look on Krasner's face told him that it would be a waste of time. He nodded and closed his eyes.

It took a tremendous effort of will to keep his eyes closed

until Krasner had left and not succumb to sleep, but he suc-
ceeded. Then he waited until the nurse's footsteps had re-
ceded before he slid out of bed. A wave of nausea overcame
him but it lasted only a minute or two. The other cots
around him were empty and he quickly found his clothes,
still wet, in a closet.

He put them on and left quietly.

His wet clothes brought a few curious looks from other
ferry riders, but he reached home at last and used a couple
of rough towels to thoroughly dry himself and restore his
circulation to near normal.

Pangs of hunger assailed him, worse than he remembered for a long time, perhaps as far back as his hobo days.
How long had it been since he had eaten? It was another
score he had against Guilfoyle; he had not given him or
Luke a single mouthful of food or drink.

Jack raided his larder. It held several thick slices of roast
beef, one of his favorite foods. A half loaf of bread was
there too, and he cut it into a few hunks. He lathered mus-
tard onto the beef and ate ravenously. Four large glasses of
water followed and he felt better.

He took out his best clothes and laid them on the bed.
They were not very grand for such a gala occasion, but San
Francisco was still a frontier town in many regards and fash-
ion was left to a handful of families on Nob Hill.

The Silver Dollar was a riot of noise and color. The tables had been rearranged, crammed close together so as to
squeeze in the maximum number of people. Jack was early,
even though he had stopped at city hall on the way there.
He had spent an hour there, starting with Ted Townrow, an
aide to the mayor and an acquaintance from their university days at Berkeley. Jack had undertaken an investigation
for the mayor recently and Townrow had been his liaison.
It had had a very satisfactory outcome and Jack did not
need to emphasize that to get the information that he
needed.

At the Silver Dollar, the tall figure of Wyatt Earp loomed

above many of the early comers. When Earp saw Jack he came toward him. "Haven't seen you around for a few days, young fellow," the lawman said.

"I've been out of town," Jack said.

Earp eyed him shrewdly. "I'd say it was a successful trip," he commented.

Jack grinned. "Hard to fool you, Wyatt."

"That's maybe why I've lived this long." Earp paused, still looking at Jack. "You look like a man who's getting close to the end of the trail."

"Is that where the villains get captured?" Jack asked lightly.

"Sometimes they do. Other times they get a bullet."

"I'm glad to see you're here," Jack said, and Earp nodded, acknowledging the sincerity in Jack's tone. It tightened the unspoken bond between the two men.

"I'll keep a sharp eye out," Earp said. "Not that there will be any shenanigans in a place like this on a night like this." The sentence ended on an unfinished note, almost a question.

"No referee here tonight," Jack commented.

Earp looked puzzled.

"So nobody'll be taking away your six-shooter," Jack explained, nodding to the leather belt that hung so naturally from the lawman's waist and the big pistol that nestled in the tooled holster.

Earp gave a rare chuckle. "That was a one and only. Ten thousand fans howling to see a fight—I wasn't going to do a thing to take that away from them. When Captain Wittman asked me to hand over my iron, I gave it to him. It was the first time I'd ever handed my gun over to any man and it'll be the last."

"Is it loaded now?" Jack asked. A slight smile was on his lips but a seriousness lurked behind the words.

"A six-shooter ain't worth a damn without bullets in it," drawled Earp.

"The first time we met, you said something about San

Francisco never ceasing to amaze you," Jack said. "Maybe it'll amaze you tonight."

"That Lillian Russell is a great entertainer."

"All the entertainment may not be on the stage," Jack said. He lowered his voice. "See that man who just came in?"

Earp turned. "Sure, Professor O'Sullivan."

"There may be an attempt to kill him tonight," Jack said, and Earp's eyes narrowed. "I can't tell you the whole story now," Jack went on, "but I have good reason to believe that. I've told Krasner."

"Haven't seen him yet," Earp said, "but I know he's going to be here." He looked over the room. "Okay, I'll keep both eyes peeled."

He left to join a party at a distant table. Jack saw Hap Harrison and they exchanged waves. Some saloon owners were fiercely independent and never patronized another saloon, no matter how important the star of the show might be. Hap was one of those who believed in cooperation and support and frequently attended other shows.

Martin Beck was near the front, Jack noted, with a large group. The place was filling up fast and already arguments at the door had begun because people without tickets sought admission. Three members of the orchestra came out. They adjusted their chairs and their music stands and, after tuning up, played some popular numbers, although their efforts were heard only intermittently over the rapidly swelling chatter of the crowd. Smoke clouds were rising, disappearing into the dark recesses above. Glasses clinked and waiters hurried to and fro with loaded trays, filling orders.

Tess had offered Jack a table but he had declined and asked instead for a reserved place at the end of the bar. He was less visible there, yet he had a clear view of the whole room.

A stocky figure pushed through the growing crowd. It was Ambrose Bierce; he headed for Jack.

"Doing your own reporting tonight, Ambrose? Don't

trust any one of those fine journalists of yours to cover the event properly?"

Bierce showed his teeth in that wolfish grin. He looked prosperous in a dark gray frock coat, a gleaming white shirt with white lace trim down the front and black trousers with shiny black leather boots. His beard looked to have been trimmed for the occasion.

"The last person I talked to suggested that I was too cheap to buy a ticket, so I am pretending to be here writing a review," he replied.

"You'll probably do that anyway," said Jack. "You won't be able to resist a few barbs, no matter how great the show is."

"As a matter of fact, I am going to describe this evening as a milestone in San Francisco history."

"It may very well be exactly that," said Jack.

"Oh? Do you know something I don't?"

"Oh, no, Ambrose. No one knows anything you don't. You are the eyes and ears of the city."

"And the conscience," added Bierce. "Don't forget the conscience."

More musicians were drifting in now and joining in with those attempting to entertain the customers before the show. Their task was becoming increasingly more difficult as the noise level rose. A shrill note from a violin cut across the panoply of sound, and Jack felt a frisson of . . . was it fear? Or just apprehension? He tried to suppress a shiver.

"Got a chill, Jack?" Bierce asked in an unusual moment of concern for the young man.

"Comes from swimming in the bay," Jack said.

"In December?"

"I didn't get to choose the month."

"I sense a story. Are you ready to give it to me?"

"Not quite. Maybe before the evening is over."

"Here?"

"Possibly."

Bierce knew when to press and when to ease up. He said

briskly, "Very well, I have to rejoin my party. I'll talk to you later."

The orchestra was complete now. They finished playing a selection of catchy melodies from the latest Sam Shubert show. The waiters were struggling to cram in late arrivals who had tickets and turn away others. The dozens of conversations were becoming more and more desultory. They died altogether as the lights dimmed. The Silver Dollar dissolved into darkness.

Chapter 38

Jack found that it was always a magical moment when theater lights dimmed and the audience waited in excited anticipation. Tonight was no different; that thrill was still there, but at the same time, Jack had another concern that gnawed at him. Before the lights dimmed, he looked carefully over the room.

Shanghai Hanrahan was at a front table near O'Sullivan, and Jack also spotted David Belasco, the flamboyant theatrical impresario known as the Bishop of Broadway who loved to bring New York shows to San Francisco, the city of his birth. Rudy Spreckels of the immensely wealthy sugar family had a table too, and Jack also saw a well-known California congressman with some prosperous-looking companions.

When Jack had told Captain Krasner of his ordeal on the island of Alcatraz, he had told him also of Guilfoyle's statement that he was going to have one of his killers, Mario, eliminate his partner at the show.

"At the show" hadn't meant much to Jack at the time. He had completely forgotten about Lillian Russell's opening. It had been wiped from his mind by all the desperate events leading up to the confrontation with Guilfoyle.

Jack told of the knife in the bullet-headed man's chest that he hoped had put him out of action at least. So the man to watch for was Mario, the Latin man who had been behind the murders of at least four people.

Jack studied the crowd in the vicinity of their target. He scanned faces but was unable to see anyone resembling the assassin. The police were still trying to accumulate more evidence against O'Sullivan, Krasner had said, but he had a background that was vague in places and his academic record provided a shield that made people unwilling to contribute any information that might be incriminating.

Jack had looked for Krasner too, but had not seen him. Although he recognized many people here tonight, some were faces that Jack did not know. Some of these could be detectives. Meanwhile, he tried to concentrate on the show.

The opening scene was set in a ballet school in Moscow and Flo's well-trained dancers got loud applause as they performed risqué versions of *Swan Lake*. Jack observed Flo's touch in some of the music too, for she loved to adapt, and the music of Rimsky-Korsakov and Tchaikovsky was evident in many of the numbers. The scene ended with the entry of the empress Catherine, played by Lillian Russell.

The star was greeted with tempestuous cheers from a crowd that was highly appreciative of the number she sang, "I Love to Dance." The second scene used an opulent version of the Royal Palace, where the empress's lover, Count Orlov, was protesting at Catherine's alleged affair with an officer of the Imperial Guard. La Russell accompanied her song, "How Could You Think That?" with sidelong glances at the front tables. She maintained her innocence to Count Orlov while bringing in the audience to sympathize with her urges, which she described as "irresistible" when she sang "How Can I Help It." These songs were parodies of currently popular numbers, and Jack admired Flo's deft adaptation of them.

The first intermission came early. No doubt Tess's intention was to sell as many drinks as possible, and though some places served drinks during a performance, many did not. Stars, particularly those from Broadway, often insisted on a clause in their contract that forbade it.

Jack stayed at the bar rather than circulate, as many were doing. He wanted to keep out of sight as far as he could and let Guilfoyle and his men continue to believe that he was no longer a threat to them, that the sharks had done Guilfoyle's work for him.

He saw Adolph Sutro presiding over a large table near the stage. Sutro had made a fortune drilling long tunnels under the Comstock Lode in Nevada, providing them with drainage, ventilation and improved ore-handling facilities. He had used most of this to buy land with a magnificent view of both the Pacific Ocean and the Golden Gate.

There he had built himself a small house and then used the rest of the land to erect several large buildings. First was the spectacular Cliff House Restaurant, next to it a huge saltwater aquarium fed by a hundred-fifty-foot tunnel from the ocean, and then a gigantic bathhouse, where ten thousand swimmers could enjoy the warmed seawater. A philanthropist at heart, Sutro had built several of the cable car lines in the city and even served a period as mayor of San Francisco.

The waiters were doing an unusually efficient job of serving drinks, Jack noticed. Impatient calls from thirsty customers were much fewer than usual and soon the crowd was settling down in eager anticipation of the second act.

They were not disappointed. No one was on the stage as the lights came on but there was applause for the scenery—the spires and towers of the Kremlin buildings, the onion-shaped top of St. Basil's Cathedral and gently falling snow. An old wagon creaked across the stage, pulled by an elderly mule. Figures began to drift into view and the villains of the piece appeared. They were trying to whip up support for a revolution and their evil intentions were cleverly depicted in a scene that ended with a rousing men's chorus.

Shows of this type primarily featured girls, though, good-looking, shapely girls. Jack had told Flo on one occasion that she could work girls into any plot or situation. She did so now with a location on a farm where the girls pitched hay, milked cows, shod horses and reaped fields. They performed all these tasks in scanty and unlikely costumes but the audience didn't care about sartorial inaccuracies.

The story moved on to the Royal Palace and brought

back the star, who entered to vociferous cheers. She sang a song that she had to reprise again and again before the audience would let her go.

The second intermission was noisier, with more people moving around and chatting with friends, and once again, Jack saw how rapidly drinks were being served. Again, he looked for assassins but could see them nowhere. He watched for other henchmen of Guilfoyle and for Guilfoyle himself, but equally without success.

The next act carried the story along showing revolutionary sympathizers in the palace and guards masquerading as revolutionaries. Lillian Russell sang two songs, the chorus numbers were raucous but tuneful, and Flo's girls received well-deserved ovations. The third intermission was short. Patrons had now had enough drinks to feel happy, though the waiters circulated as efficiently. Everyone was ready for the last act, which neatly solved all problems and ended with Lillian Russell, magnificently gowned and breathtakingly bejeweled, assuring Russia of her love for it.

Historical accuracy had been forsaken, thought Jack, but the song and spectacle were what this audience wanted. They had received it in full measure and the star had to reappear three times to take bows. She brought on the hardworking chorus girls for the last bow.

Many in the audience rose to talk to friends. Jack remained in his unobtrusive spot, his gaze roving over the room. The orchestra played a few of the tunes from the show, then finally finished and carried off their instruments. The hubbub of conversation was louder than ever.

Tess Tullamore made her way through the throng, stopping at tables to receive congratulations. Her eyes glowed with excitement and she looked radiant in a black satin evening dress with a tightly cinched waist and a dipping neckline. She saw Jack and gave him a hug.

"That girl of yours is wonderful! Didn't she put on a wonderful show?"

"She surely did," Jack agreed, "and Lillian Russell rose to the occasion too."

"Isn't she great? It's been a marvelous evening! Tom would have loved to see this."

"Congratulations are due to you too. Your staff has done a fine job."

"Yes, even the extra waiters we hired from outside have worked very hard."

"Where did you get them?" Jack asked.

"Hanrahan was very helpful. He lent me several. Look, Jack, stay around. We'll have a drink later."

"You go ahead. A lot of people want to compliment you," Jack told her.

Some patrons were leaving. The night was still young and many of the seasoned veterans of the Barbary Coast had more drinking spots to visit, places where they needed to be seen.

Jack watched for a few minutes, then decided to move into the crowd. He still had a feeling of alarm but it was disturbing that he could not locate its cause. He wanted to go backstage and tell Flo what an outstanding show she had put on but he felt his place was out here in the crowd as long as the threat remained.

While keeping an eye on O'Sullivan's table, Jack talked for a few minutes with New York impresario Martin Beck, who was effusive in his praise of Flo. Jack was making his way up front when he was stopped by one of the organizers of the longshoremen's union, a man who never missed a show on the Barbary Coast.

A cry came from the front of the auditorium. Somehow, it penetrated the chatter of the crowd. Perhaps it was its shrillness or perhaps it held a note of terror. Jack pushed forward. A gunshot ended the chatter and brought a stunned silence.

Jack shoved his way through and saw a waiter, a pistol in his hand, smoke spiraling from the muzzle. The weapon was aimed at Professor O'Sullivan, who stood immobile, a strange expression on his face.

Chapter 39

Behind O'Sullivan, Shanghai Hanrahan was trying to clutch his chest, blood spurting between his fingers. He staggered, then fell. Horrified gasps arose.

Jack recognized the waiter with the gun as the Latin henchman of Guilfoyle and one of the team of assassins. Mario swung the gun in a menacing arc and the crowd shrank back. Then he ran for the exit by the stage and disappeared.

A man standing by O'Sullivan examined him anxiously. "Are you all right? He was aiming directly at you!" Another was kneeling by Hanrahan.

O'Sullivan nodded, dazed. The noisy buzz of the crowd was resuming normal proportions already. Murder in a music hall was not common, but anyone who visited the Barbary Coast was aware of its reputation, and sudden death was a regular part of life there.

Krasner appeared, pushing his way through the awestruck onlookers. Someone apparently recognized him and called out angrily, "You're letting the man who did this get away!"

"He won't get far," Krasner replied without looking at his critic. He looked O'Sullivan over and finally said, "You're lucky. The bullet must have grazed you."

O'Sullivan blinked and shook his head as if to clear it. "I thought I was done for," he muttered. "When I saw him pull that gun, I just happened to be looking right at him. When he aimed and fired, I was sure I—"

"Hanrahan's dead," said the man kneeling by him. "Must have died instantly. Bullet right through the heart."

Tess had joined them by now. Her face was pale and strained. "Shanghai—is he—is he dead?" She looked at the faces around her. "He is, isn't he?" The silence was her answer.

Jack took her arm. "Tess, we need to use the room behind the bar." Krasner was about to speak but Jack cut him off. "We can clear this business up now. I believe the professor is ready to tell us what he knows."

Krasner was about to reply but the look in Jack's eye gave him pause. "I didn't think the Salvation Army would be able to hold you for long," Krasner said.

O'Sullivan's head must have cleared. He flashed a glance at Jack; then another figure came out of the milling crowd.

"Get him?" asked Krasner.

"Yup," said Wyatt Earp. "He's unconscious back there. One of your men cracked him across the head with a pistol barrel."

"Will he survive?" Krasner asked.

"Dunno," said Earp carelessly.

"You'd better join us," said Krasner, and Jack led the way behind the bar.

The four of them almost filled the small office. Krasner sat on a corner of the desk, Earp leaned against the wall near the door and Jack stood by the wall of shelves. O'Sullivan stood, uncertain, and Krasner motioned to the single chair. O'Sullivan hesitated, then sat in it.

Krasner looked invitingly at Jack, who said in a conversational tone, "I just visited Alcatraz."

No one spoke.

"It wasn't voluntary," Jack said. "I was taken there because I'd stumbled onto something I shouldn't have with my friend Luke. We were lucky to escape. The sharks were about to make dinner out of us but a fishing boat saw us and picked us up."

Earp leaned by the door, impassive but wary. Krasner

was alert and waiting. O'Sullivan was the only one to show no emotion, seemingly still in a state of shock.

"While Luke and I were out on the island," Jack continued, "we were taken through the rooms where they were stamping out gold coins. I had previously been out at the mine where the ore came from, inferior ore worth barely half the value of true gold. It was the Maria Elena mine, owned by the professor here."

"I sold it," said O'Sullivan in a weary voice. "Sold it some time ago to a man called Guilfoyle."

"When I saw that operation," Jack went on, "I was a little puzzled because the mine hadn't been operated for some time. I wondered why the counterfeiting operation didn't need more metal. The ore I saw looked good."

Jack paused but no comment was offered. "When Luke and I were taken to be questioned by Guilfoyle on Alcatraz, I noticed an unusual odor in the room. It was only tonight at the show that I smelled it again at Hanrahan's table. It was the smell of the cigars he smoked, which he said were blended just for him. And before coming here, I stopped at city hall. They told me what I wanted to know—that recent work on Alcatraz, repairing some of the buildings and general maintenance to keep it up to government standards, was done by a San Francisco company owned by Hanrahan. So I realized that he had to be a partner in the whole counterfeiting ring."

"But if it was Hanrahan's company doing work on the island, why wouldn't he be there?" asked Krasner.

"With Guilfoyle? Then he had to know Guilfoyle—but he told me that he had never heard the name. Another thing I just learned," said Jack, "is that Hanrahan lent Tess some waiters. One of those was Mario."

"Ironic," commented Krasner. "The man who shot him."

Faint sounds filtered in from the auditorium, where a few musicians had evidently been persuaded to return and contribute their talents.

"Hanrahan hired me to investigate what he described at that time as a threat to the city," Jack explained. "He hired me on behalf of the Saloon Owners Association, but what he really wanted was to keep track of what I was learning."

"And did you keep him informed?" asked Krasner.

"Sure," said Jack, "sure I did. Then these two professional assassins worked me over. They didn't want to kill me, just wanted to get me to ease up on my investigation. I was short of money and Hanrahan figured I'd just keep taking the pay from him and not try too hard." He grinned wryly. "I thought I was lucky to escape. I've puzzled ever since why professional killers were so effective in killing Tom Tullamore, Sam Hooper, Magnus Swenson and Matt Colman and didn't finish me off."

"The gold coins they were forging," said Krasner. "I suppose Hanrahan was passing them into the city through his gambling operations."

"Right. It couldn't all be kept quiet even so. Tom Tullamore, Sam Hooper, Magnus Swenson—three innocent men, all found out about it and all were murdered."

"On the orders of Hanrahan," contributed Earp.

"Hanrahan and his partner," said Krasner.

"Yeah," drawled Earp, "time to bring in his partner."

"At first, I thought his partner was the professor here," said Jack. "He had a gold-mining background. He owned the Maria Elena."

The professor spoke up. "It was an unprofitable mine. The ore was inferior, you said so yourself. Like I told you, I sold the mine to Guilfoyle—and was lucky to do so."

"The shadowy Guilfoyle," Krasner said. "We kept hearing about him but nobody ever saw him."

"I saw him," O'Sullivan said. "Our negotiations didn't take long. I had no idea of his intentions and I was anxious to get rid of the mine. He was an unpleasant character, I thought, but then there are plenty of those around this city."

"I guess he stayed shadowy," said Jack, "that is, until he had to buy a fishing fleet. He must have had some of his men do the preliminary work, but he had to emerge to clinch the deal himself. Then he had to transport more equipment to Alcatraz, along with supplies. So he bought these fishing boats from friends of mine. One of those friends, Matt Colman, with money in his pocket and not much to do, got nosy. He wondered why a man would buy fishing boats and yet not send them out fishing. He found out about Guilfoyle, who had him killed."

Earp said, "The feller out there with the bleeding head is one of the killers."

"Hired by Hanrahan," Krasner said.

Earp nodded. "Or his partner."

"Guilfoyle."

"Yes," Jack said, "Guilfoyle."

Krasner half turned to face O'Sullivan. "What can you tell us to help us catch this Guilfoyle?"

O'Sullivan shook his head. "I really don't know. I only saw him that one time. I realize that some suspicion must have fallen on me and I can see that this was due to Guilfoyle. I'd like to help you catch him but I don't know what I can tell you."

"Seems to be a slippery character," Earp drawled, "unless we catch him in the act."

There was a silence.

Jack's brain was racing. "In the act," he murmured, and Krasner turned to him. "I was thinking out loud. Do you think we should see if Mario has recovered consciousness? He might be persuaded to tell us something."

Earp had his eyes on Jack and something unspoken passed between them. Earp uncoiled himself from his position by the door. "I'll do that," he said and left the room.

Jack's mind had returned to the scene on Alcatraz when he was standing facing a window, sunlight streaming in. . . . He probed his memory for every detail.

Krasner was persisting in his interrogation of O'Sullivan. "Tell us more about the sale of your gold mine. How did he pay you?"

"It was an open draft on a San Francisco bank," O'Sullivan explained. "I can give you details of the draft. Maybe they will help."

"It seems this Guilfoyle only shows up when there's some kind of a transaction to be concluded," Krasner said. Jack was hardly listening. He was still trying to piece together the truth.

The door opened and a blast of music and singing swept in as Earp entered and closed the door. Krasner looked at him expectantly. "Is he alive?"

Earp came as close to a grin as he ever did. "Singing like a bird." He resumed his leaning position by the door.

Jack caught Krasner's eye on him. The police captain had come to know him very well, Jack decided. He was able to tell when Jack had something to say and he was ready to let him say it. Most of the pieces were now in place and Jack decided the rest would follow while he talked.

"You triggered it off, Wyatt," he began, "when you said we needed to catch Guilfoyle 'in the act.' It was the word 'act' that pulled it all together in my mind. No wonder Guilfoyle was shadowy—he wasn't real."

O'Sullivan frowned. "Not real?"

"No. He was somebody else who acted the role of Guilfoyle. You know, when I saw him, it was on Alcatraz. Guilfoyle stood against the window. At first, I thought that the sun was in my eyes to intimidate me. But it wasn't—it was deliberate, so that I couldn't see him clearly. He didn't want me to be able to get a good look at him, because I knew him in his real persona. None of the others who had seen him had met that other person, so they were no risk, but I was."

"Go on," urged Krasner.

"Seems very unlikely," O'Sullivan commented, "but it's fascinating. Please continue."

"I asked myself," said Jack, "who I knew who had done any acting." He turned to face the man in the chair. "The answer was you, Professor. You were the only actor."

No one spoke.

"The head of the drama department at Berkeley told me that you had played Shylock. With a small grayish-white beard, some pale makeup and a hunched appearance, I could see you as Shylock—and I could see you as Guilfoyle.

That forced voice too—that must have given you the most trouble."

O'Sullivan smiled. It was a smile without mirth. "You should succeed as a writer, young man, as you have a vivid imagination."

Jack went on. "When Guilfoyle told me he intended to have his partner killed, I thought he meant you. But he really meant Hanrahan."

"Seemed odd to me that Hanrahan took that bullet," Earp stated. "The killer was a professional. He couldn't have missed the professor at that close range. You're saying he didn't—he was truly aiming at Hanrahan?"

Jack nodded.

"You know," Earp went on in a conversational tone, "the way it looks to me is, both Hanrahan and Guilfoyle planned on having Mario kill the other. Guilfoyle must have offered more."

"And all the time, O'Sullivan was succeeding in establishing his own innocence by shifting blame onto Guilfoyle," added Jack. "The once-shadowy Guilfoyle, who O'Sullivan had brought out from the shadows to front for him as the villain."

"Intriguing," murmured O'Sullivan, "but preposterous, of course."

Jack ignored him. "You had done all the groundwork for the scheme. You recognized the ore as being only half gold and you realized that the other metals in the ore made it almost indistinguishable from the real thing. You saw a great opportunity. With Hanrahan as a partner, you set up the counterfeiting operation.

"It would be hard to conduct it safely, but Hanrahan had the contract for the rebuilding work on Alcatraz and he knew the schedule for shutting down the prison operation while the work was done. The island was an ideal place for counterfeiting—no prisoners, no guards, no visitors, nobody to see or suspect what was going on there.

"Pretending to have a gambling system, you unloaded a lot of gold eagles through the tables. Despite the fact that many money-handling experts saw the coins, none of them spotted any as counterfeit. To cover yourself, you sold your mine to a man called Guilfoyle, who didn't exist. The government decision to increase the paper money in circulation must have been a shock but you took care of that by buying printing presses. It must have been hard to find the right kind. And, of course, you needed boats to get the equipment out to Alcatraz."

O'Sullivan shook his head sadly. "So much talent. What a pity it isn't confined to the pages of fiction." He took a step toward the door. Earp did not move but his hand hovered above the big six-shooter in his belt.

O'Sullivan glared at Krasner. "You can't intend to detain me! You don't have an ounce of proof!"

"We can search your rooms," Jack suggested. "A makeup kit and a false beard that several people can testify makes you look like Guilfoyle will turn up, I'm sure."

"You'll be wasting your time," O'Sullivan sneered.

"Perhaps we'll find them on Alcatraz," said Krasner. "A team is out there right now, turning the place upside down. Meanwhile, there's the bank that handled the deal between you and Guilfoyle," said Krasner. "I'm sure we can uncover something there."

"Ridiculous!" O'Sullivan stormed. "This is all theoretical."

"Oh, it's a durn sight more than that," said Earp in his easygoing manner. "Now that Mario out there, like I said, is singing like a bird."

O'Sullivan moved with remarkable speed. In two long steps he was at the door. He pulled it open and headed out of the room.

"Sergeant!" Earp's voice burst out like a shotgun blast. "Hold that man!" To Krasner, he said, "Took the liberty of putting a man outside, just in case."

There were sounds of a scuffle, then a thud, followed by a silence that coincided with a lull in the music. "The biggest man I could find," Earp added.

Chapter 40

They were having a celebratory drink in the Silver Dollar—Captain Krasner, Wyatt Earp, Tess Tullamore, Ambrose Bierce, Flo and Jack.

"Should we invite Lillian Russell?" Earp had said. He had described himself as one of her fans.

"I don't think so," Tess had said. "She doesn't like violence and I don't want her scared enough that she might want to cut her contract short."

Across the room, two or three dozen patrons who had stayed on after the show were still whooping it up. "It takes more than a sensational murder to thwart the dedicated revelers in this town," observed Bierce dryly.

Two waiters were keeping busy bringing them drinks, and though all the other musicians had left, the piano player remained and was going through his repertoire for a second time.

Krasner had watched O'Sullivan being taken away under strong guard and had talked to the officer recording statements from eyewitnesses to Hanrahan's shooting. Jack had suggested quietly to Bierce that he remain and get the biggest story since the big fight. Bierce hardly needed any persuading after being an eyewitness—or so he claimed—to the shooting of Shanghai Hanrahan, and he listened attentively to the conversation.

"Tell me, Wyatt," Krasner said to Earp, "which officer told you that Mario was singing like a bird? I haven't been able to find a man who corroborates that."

Earp looked pleased with himself and waved for another

whisky. "Guy's still unconscious. I thought it might put a little pressure on the professor if he thought that his man was going to squeal on him. Not that it was altogether untrue," he added. "Just the timing. I'm sure he will tell all." He looked at Krasner. "Let me know if he doesn't want to cooperate. We had a few fellers in the jail at Tombstone who felt that way—at first, that is. We found ways to persuade them."

"So those stories about you are true." Bierce's eyes glinted; then he waved a conciliatory hand. "Don't worry, though, Wyatt. If I can get enough other material out of you, we can gloss over a few of your, er, bad habits."

Tess was shaking her head. "I still can't believe it about the professor. I mean, he was always a bit of a cold fish, but him and Hanrahan . . . they had this city in a real turmoil, didn't they? It could have been a disaster, all that phony money around."

"It may be best if the population of San Francisco doesn't learn just how disastrous it might have been," Bierce agreed.

"You mean temper the truth, Ambrose?" Jack asked, never wanting to miss a chance to ruffle Bierce's feathers.

"Not at all," Bierce said loftily. "I mean, protect the people. Men like the Big Three and Hanrahan and O'Sullivan want to exploit the people. It's the duty of a newspaper like the *Examiner* to shield them."

"You know what's best for the people," Flo suggested slyly.

"Yes," said Bierce, "I'm very fortunate in that."

"Well, I'm glad it's all over," said Tess, "even though it had to end in a shooting in the Silver Dollar."

"A terrible thing to happen," said Bierce, lapping up every moment of it. "One of our most prominent citizens, gunned down just after the final curtain. An evening full of drama indeed."

"And before that happened, a great show," said Earp. "Really great."

"A spectacular show," Bierce said in a rare display of praise. "Lillian is a true star."

"One of Flo's best shows," Jack said, "maybe the very best. Wonderful musical numbers, great sets and costumes, clever songs—well done, Flo!"

Congratulatory words came from all at the table. Flo smiled her pleasure at the acclaim. Captain Krasner rose to his feet. "Well, I must go. I'm anxious to hear the first report from the team that went out to Alcatraz."

"Me too," said Earp.

"I can just catch the morning edition," Bierce said. "Our readers will love this—we may have to rush out an extra."

The three of them left and Tess said, "Another drink, you two?"

"Not for me," said Flo, although Jack knew she had drunk only one glass of wine. She got to her feet. "It's been a long day."

"I envy you, Flo," Tess said, her large eyes soft and luminous. "Not only your dancing and your ability to teach it to others, but your sense of costuming and set design. Not to mention your musical ability and the way you conjure up catchy numbers." Tess's gaze turned to Jack. "As for your man here, if I were a few years younger, I'd be giving you some competition."

"You're young enough," said Flo, reaching for Jack's hand to pull him with her. "Don't think I don't know it."

She smiled sweetly and the two wended their way through the still-noisy tables and past the stage. In the rabbit warren that comprised the dressing rooms and the storage areas, a door was open. The two of them stopped, looking in.

A huge bed dominated the room. It had a massive gilt headboard bearing what looked like an imperial emblem.

"Isn't that the bed you used in act three?" Jack asked. "Catherine's bed in the royal chambers?"

"That's it. Enjoy that scene?"

"I felt sorry for Count Orlov," Jack said, "when Catherine had one of her temper tantrums in that bed and kicked him out of it."

Flo moved slowly into the room. "That doesn't have to happen in this bed," she murmured. "It was just a play, after all."

"Still," Jack said, matching her tone, "I'm not sure I'd want to take a chance."

"What? You? Not take a chance! Your life is spent taking chances."

"But this one's different," Jack said. "This is a real risk."

Flo pulled him into the room and kicked the door shut behind them. "Let me show you just how much of a risk it is—and you can show me the reward."

Author's Note

Many of the characters in this book are real—Lucky Baldwin, Wyatt Earp, Little Egypt, Lillian Russell, Ambrose Bierce, Martin Beck, and of course, Jack London, who knew them all.

Almost all the saloons, music halls and bars described were real too while the Barbary Coast was ten times as wicked and depraved as I could ever make it.

A few fictitious characters flit across the pages but I can't believe that any living persons—not even readers of this book—would see any resemblance to themselves.

The period in which the story is set is the end of the last century.

Lydia Adamson

An Alice Nestleton Mystery

A CAT NAMED BRAT   0-451-20664-9

In this brand-new mystery, New York actress and cat-sitting
sleuth Alice Nestleton sets out to solve the murder of a nightlife
journalist.

A CAT WITH NO CLUE   0-451-20501-4

When Alice Nestleton whips up an anniversary meal for her actor
friends, the happy couple just die—of food poisoning. The only
witnesses are the couple's two little kittens. Which means that
Alice is the prime suspect. And while the actor in Alice may love
the spotlight, this is not the kind of attention she needs...

A CAT WITH THE BLUES   0-451-20196-5

Alice is catsitting a beautiful Russian Blue at the center of a raging
custody battle. But when the doorman at the wealthy couple's
apartment building dies—and the contested cat disappears—she
must go on a nose-to-the-ground hunt for a catnapper...and
maybe...a killer.

A CAT OF ONE'S OWN   0-451-19769-0

When Amanda Avery decides to adopt a cat, she turns to Alice
Nestleton, who matches her up with an unusual looking feline
named Jake. But within days, Jake is catnapped...and though he
escapes with his life, his new caretaker doesn't. Alice must find
out why—by sniffing out Amanda's secrets before she's caught in a
lethal game of cat and mouse...

To order call: 1-800-788-6262